Kaia,

May you discover Y to

own unique abilities

make this world a better place.

Lisa A. Kramer

11/21/15

P.O.W.ER

LISA A. KRAMER

WORD HERMIT PRESS • USA
ISBN-978-0-9908593-9-0

Library of Congress Catalog number applied for.

*For Sarah: may you someday discover your own power
and use it to change the world.*

ONE

My stomach dropped as soon as Dad entered the kitchen scowling at a thick card embossed with the government seal. My hand started to shake so much that I had to put down my mug of tea. I knew this day was coming. After all, it was my seventeenth birthday, the first day of the last year of my life.

"That's the letter, isn't it?"

Dad looked at me with one of his half smiles, the one that never reached his eyes. I hadn't seen him smile with genuine happiness for years, not since Mother died. This smile made no effort to cover the sadness and defeat in his face. "Pour me some cocoa, please." He lowered himself into his customary chair next to me, "I'll do my civic duty and read this to you."

"I could always read it myself," I said. I waited for him to respond the way he always did. I hoped that provoking him a little would reawaken the Dad who let me believe I could do anything, while still protecting me from the cruelty of our society. That Dad had disappeared over recent years.

"Andra!" he said, "You know I don't like you to say that out loud. You never know if someone might be listening. If I could let you read everywhere, I would. We can't let your secret get out."

"I'm sorry." I handed Dad his cocoa and watched as he took several sips. For a moment he closed his eyes and his face relaxed. The secret to giving him those brief moments was in the cocoa. I make it just like Mother used to. She left us too soon to teach me all her cooking secrets, but she taught me a few. She was a woman who turned everything she touched into something beautiful, warm and comforting. She could make people calm even in the most terrifying circumstances. Mother and Dad both made me believe that my future wasn't set in the same stone used to build the giant walls that separated New North from the outside world. Mother believed that somehow they would find a way to return to some of the freedoms of the past and make a better future for all women. She never got the chance to do that. She died and Dad grew afraid.

"Ah, perfect as always. Now, to do my duty." Dad put his mug down and brought my attention back to the thick card, or the envelope of doom, as I thought of it. The government seal—the Eye of the Lord—gleamed with a hint of gold ink as it caught the light from the sun shining through the window. It sent a shiver down my spine, as if the eye was really watching me.

Dad once told me the story of how the Eye of the Lord became the symbol of New North. More than 25 years ago, New North had been part of a much larger nation that suffered the delusion that it was the greatest nation on earth. For complicated reasons that I never fully understood, the country tore itself apart as men clamored for more power and control over women, money, and resources. Finally, civil war broke out and the country split into smaller nations led by the men who had the most money and could control the most media. Rom Sandovar, who would become the Supreme Prime Minister of New North, not only had money but also something even more powerful— the power of persuasion. He convinced people that he had a direct connection with the Lord. He claimed to have a dream where the Lord spoke to him while looking down from the heavens through flaming eyes. According to him, the Lord gave him guidance on a daily basis. People began to call Sandovar the Lord's Eye on Earth. Sandovar commissioned artists to design images of that Eye to be hung throughout the newly formed nation of New North as a constant reminder that the new order was under the ever-present watch of the Lord. It flies over every meeting and can be seen in every building important to the government.

Rumors from the few people allowed to travel beyond New North's borders claim the Eye of the Lord is even carved onto the outside of the wall that separates New North from the other Nations that surround us. I wouldn't know because women are never allowed to leave. Actually, few men travel either. Since we have to rely mostly on renewable sources of energy, most of it is reserved for the basic necessities of life. Only the elite who can afford to own and pay for electrical vehicles or those who control commerce ever leave the safety of the walls.

I looked at the seal glinting wickedly over the announcement that my world was about to become even more confined. While I love art in all forms, thanks to Mother and her talents and love of beauty, I find the images of the Eye of the Lord an odd mixture of beauty and terror. I know so many girls who say they feel safe and protected under the watchful Eye and his representatives on earth. I've never understood how my peers could believe these things so completely. They practically worship the Supreme Prime Minister. I don't.

My parents told me that things may not be as they seem, especially when it comes to faith. Of course, in public they put on the façade of true believers. After all, with Dad serving as Head Scrivener, our entire lives would be destroyed if anyone at the Ministry suspected he wasn't a believer. That's why, whenever we were in the lower levels of the house, Dad wanted me to be obedient. He worried that someone might be outside, listening, trying to catch him doing something wrong. Even though I was capable of reading the letter myself, it was forbidden. Dad had his duty to perform. He opened the envelope and read.

"To Joseph Scrivener and his daughter Andra, we wish to send many happy returns on this momentous day, the day when Andra turns seventeen and achieves the full status of woman."

"Ugh!" I said

Dad gave me one of his strict looks. "I have to read this to you, please try to contain yourself. I know you're not happy."

"Sorry, Dad. Keep reading."

He winked at me so I knew he wasn't really angry. Then he cleared his throat and continued. "As you know, this is an important year for Andra. We hope that we will soon be able to celebrate her again in the coming year as she enters the sacred and important role of wife to one worthy of fathering a son to follow in the Scrivener's illustrious footsteps. Of course, according to the laws of New North, if she should not be blessed by such an event, on her next birthday she will be welcomed into one of our prestigious Women's Training Programs (WTP) where she will further develop her skills in proper feminine behavior and responsibilities. Again, many happy returns on this important day. We look forward to welcoming Andra into her womanly roles. Supreme Prime Minister, Rom Sandovar"

Dad folded the card. "Andra, are you going to eat that muffin or just destroy it?"

I looked down and saw the mess I had made of my cinnamon muffin without even knowing I did it. Crumbs stuck to my fingers and mounded on the table, evidence of my inner turmoil. I hate losing control in such an obvious way. It's too dangerous. Dad has enough to worry about without me revealing my inner thoughts through unconscious messes. I tried to brush all the sticky crumbs back onto the plate.

"I'm sorry," I said. "It's just that I wish I wasn't celebrating this birthday. Why celebrate the last year of life as I know it?" I pushed the plate away.

Dad reached across the table and grabbed my hand in his calm grasp. Callouses on his fingers, hardened by his years of writing with pen and ink, rubbed against my palms. Before the revolution he could have done work on something called a computer. He'd told me all about them but I've never seen one. Sandovar declared them tools of corruption, so people like my father had to perfect the art of writing things by hand.

My hand felt small in his. For a moment I became a young, scared child seeking strength from his touch. He'd always protected me. After Mother died, the government suggested I be sent away because his work was more important than his duties as a father to a girl. He stood up to the Ministry then and said, "I will raise my daughter. I've just lost my wife, nobody is taking my daughter." I remember clinging to him when he said it. I was so afraid they would take me from him, and that he would be punished for opposing the Supreme Prime Minister. But Dad stood, rock solid, eyes looking from face to face, not backing down. The Supreme Prime Minister relented, and I went home with my father.

That day I believed he could win every battle. The only problem is—over the years he stopped trying to fight for reasons he won't explain to me.

"We'll think of something, Andra," Dad said.

"What? You've been saying that for years and nothing has changed; it's the law. By the end of this year I'll have to leave you, give up my freedom, give up written words and become a slave to some man I don't even love. Or I can join a training program and be turned into a mindless drone."

"We don't know that happens, Andra."

"You weren't there the last time I saw Lauren. She didn't know who I was." I tried to shake away the memories of my older friend when I last saw her in a tiny room at the nearest, and largest, Women's Training Center. Gone was the idol of my youth, and in her place was a frail being—lost, alone, hopeless, and so terrified she could barely speak.

"Why does the world have to be like this, Dad? Why can't I stay with you and make my own choices?"

"I don't know. It wasn't always this way. I remember when . . . You know I would fix it if I could." He walked over to look out the window with his back toward me. "You also know the risks if I do anything."

I was tired of his vague answers and my frustration bubbled up inside. I had to get away from him. The chair fell as I jumped up to leave while throwing words at him intended to sting. "So you do nothing and support the injustice."

"Andra!" The agony in Dad's voice stopped me before I left the room. "I can't let you get hurt or disappear. I can't lose you too . . . We'll find an answer. You have to be patient." His face filled with sadness and a hint of fear. I couldn't bring him any more pain.

Guilt cooled my anger for the moment, but it lay inside me—a creature waiting to pounce. I used some of the techniques Dad tried to teach me to control my spontaneous bursts of emotion. Deep breaths into my diaphragm always helped center me, and filled me with the briefest sense of peace. I picked up my chair in silence.

Both of us jumped at a loud knock on the kitchen door. The silly scared look on Dad's face made me giggle. At least it broke the tension between us.

Dad peered out the window. "Ah," he said "That would be the inimitable Brian, who never misses a birthday or an opportunity to eat an entire basket of your delicious muffins. Who knows," he added with a wink, "perhaps he could be the solution to your problem. After all he's still single."

I couldn't believe he said that. I grabbed a muffin from the basket, intent on pegging him in the back. Food fights aren't exactly unknown in this kitchen, and sometimes they solved our biggest arguments. It's hard to disagree when you're laughing and wiping blueberry pie off your face. He stepped out of the way. My muffin missile hit Brian right between his deep brown eyes.

"Ow! I was about to wish you a Happy Birthday. Now I'm not sure I want to. What's with the pastry attack?"

"Sorry, Brian. That was meant for my meddling father who doesn't know what he's talking about."

Dad chuckled. "I was merely saying that Brian practically lives here anyway, so it would be a simple solution to our problem."

"What problem?" Brian helped himself to the basket of muffins.

"This." I pushed the formal letter over to him. I couldn't wait to see his reaction. Even though I thought Dad was being ridiculous, I never gave up an opportunity to make Brian blush. He was so fun to tease.

He didn't disappoint. His face turned about five different shades of red. "Are you saying that Andra and I should get married? That's ridicu—that's impossible."

"Like I said, Dad doesn't know what he's talking about. You're the big brother I never really wanted."

With a shy smile, Brian reached over and messed up my curly mop in a familiar gesture intended to annoy. I swatted his hand away.

"Cocoa?" Dad placed Brian's favorite mug filled to the rim with rich chocolate in front of his spot on the table. "How's your mother doing?"

My friend's face screamed frustration, although he didn't allow it to show up in his voice as he answered. "She's better. She still clings to the dream that father will be back, though. I wish she would accept reality."

"We don't know for sure," Dad said.

"The government has made it pretty clear that he's unwelcome and 'a threat,'" Brian said. "We also know that few people who disappear ever return. It's happened all over New North. Besides, it's been four years."

"True, however we still don't know what really happened to your father. I'm sure I would know if he had been imprisoned or killed. Maybe he left New North to protect you both, and will come back someday." Dad gave each of us that serious look which warned me that he would tolerate no objection to whatever he said next. "We all must be cautious now, especially you, Andra. These are dangerous times to be a woman, and you are now officially a woman."

"Now you'll have to start dressing like a lady, and pin your curls up like a proper woman," Brian tugged one of my thick reddish-brown curls to full length. He released it and laughed as it sprang back. He knew that would make me angry. Past experience taught him to duck away quickly or experience the wrath of my fists.

"Cut it out or I'll throw you out. I may be a woman but I can still take you."

"If you throw me out, you'll miss your present," Brian reached into his well-worn leather pack and grabbed a scroll tied with a ribbon, which he dangled over my head. He loved to taunt me with his height, since I am so short, but this time I refused to play. I glared at him until he relented. "Happy Birthday to my best friend." He handed me the scroll.

My cheeks warmed a little at his words. Even though he'd always been like a brother to me, I loved hearing him call me his best friend. He didn't need me in his life, as he had a huge group of friends and was popular with the girls. I tended toward spending time alone or with my father, or—in the past—with a few close friends although most of them were gone now, swallowed into the system. "You shouldn't have gotten me anything. I know money is tight without your father's income."

"I saw this and knew you had to have it. Go ahead, open it."

I opened the scroll to find an elaborate painting with images of birds and flowers in rich vibrant colors. My chest filled with its beauty. I could hardly breathe.

"This is spectacular." It was more than just beautiful. I followed the images carefully with my finger. "Did you know it has a hidden message in the secret language?"

"You know I can only read a few symbols of the women's language," Brian said, "especially since you refuse to teach me." He winked at Dad who chuckled.

I stuck my tongue out, and then realized I should probably stop doing things like that. After all, I was considered a woman. Heat rose in my face as both Dad and Brian laughed at me.

I gave them each one of my best glares and focused back on the scroll. "It's called a secret language for a reason. You aren't even supposed to know it exists. Besides, women need some way to communicate when we're stuck in our homes."

"I know. You don't have to preach to me," Brian said. "Look at the scroll. Don't you recognize who painted it?"

I searched for the special image that would tell me which woman created this message masterpiece. I found it and tears sprang into my eyes. I dropped the scroll as a tingle shot through my fingers and into my heart.

"What's wrong?" Dad asked. He picked it up and his eyes filled as well.

"This was painted by your mother." He sat down, and I watched him try to cover the emotion. I grabbed his hand and squeezed to stop it from shaking and him from falling apart. He hated letting anyone see him lose control, even Brian who was practically family.

I tried to distract Dad by focusing back on the scroll itself. "Where did you find this? I thought we had everything of hers, or it had all been destroyed."

"You can find anything if you look hard enough," Brian said. "I was looking in an art shop owned by an old friend of my father's, Mr. Mastak."

Dad gave Brian a sharp look that I didn't understand. "What's wrong?" I asked.

"Nothing," Dad said. "It's just . . . I was friends with Mr. Mastak too. We haven't seen each other since just after your mother died. I'm surprised he kept this from me."

"Was it wrong for me to buy this from him?" Brian asked.

"Of course not," Dad said. "Finish your story."

"It's not that interesting. I wanted to find Andra something painted by a woman. When I told Mr. Mastak what I wanted and who it was for, he said 'I have the perfect thing' and handed me this. He didn't even charge me what I'm sure it's worth. Actually, he wanted to give it to me, but I insisted on paying something."

"It's beautiful. Thank you." I smoothed the scroll down with care. I could see the love and thought placed in each line and color.

"I'd give anything to know what it says." Brian's quiet voice brought my focus back to the hidden words—words written by my mother for other women to see.

I followed the delicate lines and bright colors with one finger. I could almost sense Mother sitting next to me, guiding me to find the message hidden in the elaborate design. I breathed in and could smell a lingering scent that emanated from the scroll—the light lilac of Mother's perfume. Another tear slid down my cheek and I wasn't sure I'd be able to stop the deluge.

Dad handed me a napkin to wipe the tears away. His gentle voice broke into thoughts I could barely express, "Are you going to read this to us?"

I took a deep breath and read, "Women have powers that men fear. I hope my daughter uses hers to change the world."

We all fell into silence. I didn't understand what the words meant, and yearned to hear Mother explain them to me. Since I couldn't have that, all I wanted to do was cry, but I refused to give into the temptation—at least not in front of Brian. The sadness on Dad's face, as he wandered into the land of memory, gave me the strength to hold back the flood. If I fell apart completely, he would never be able to keep himself together. I had to be strong for him.

Brian grabbed another muffin, and stared at it as if it held the secrets of the world. He knew us both so well. I was grateful that he gave us a moment to regain control without asking questions.

"What power does she think I have?" I said once I had control of my voice. "What does this mean?"

Dad took my hand, "You have the power of words, Andra. Nobody taught you to read, you just absorbed words like water."

"It was inevitable that I learn to read. I was always watching you work."

"I never taught you. Your mother never taught you. We wanted to protect you. You learned anyway, without our help. Perhaps that's the power your mother meant."

"Well, it's a useless power if all I can do is get married or join the WTP." The anger started building inside me again. I picked up the government card and attempted to rip through the thick paper, but it defeated me. I threw it on the floor and stamped on it a few times. My temper tantrums were famous.

This one was mild. "I hate this birthday." I said.

"Well, hate it you may, but we still have to put on our party faces and celebrate." Dad grimaced in a false smile that made me laugh. "Don't forget Minister Rogerson's daughter is throwing you a party this evening."

"Cindy just wants a chance to dress up and flirt with potential suitors. Why did you agree to let them throw this party?"

"It wasn't a request."

I had no choice. Dad's position at the Ministry was always precarious, so I had to play along when the Rogersons were involved. Cindy was a few years younger than I. We used to play together before she became all-consumed by doing her womanly duty in the eyes of the Lord or the Supreme Prime Minister. I suppose with a father like Minister Rogerson, she had no choice about what to believe, but it pushed a wedge between us because I could never understand her faith and willingness to be controlled. We drifted apart, but remnants of the old days when we celebrated things like birthdays together still remained. Hence the upcoming party to celebrate my day of doom.

"Well, at least this is another chance to spend time with girls I don't like and pretend that I'm just like them," I said. "What a wonderful birthday. You'll be there, won't you Brian?"

"I wouldn't miss the opportunity to flirt with that bevy of beauties," Brian said with a laugh. He was asking to be walloped by another muffin, which I threw before I stormed out of the room. I smiled a little as I heard the thud and moan which indicated my aim was precise, and then slammed the door to be sure they got my message.

TWO

The elaborate party room twinkled with feminine energy, like a flock of colorful birds chirping in competition for the attention of eligible bachelors. Young men puffed out their chests and strutted around showing off their own fine feathers while pretending to ignore the noisy chatter and girlish giggles. I never liked these kinds of parties. The fact that this one was to celebrate my birthday made it worse. As soon as I could escape the birthday greetings and false warmth, I carried my drawing materials away from the crowd and found a place where I could sketch in peace. Nobody would really notice, as this was my customary role whenever Dad forced me into dutiful daughter duty. I attended gatherings to support him in his role as Head Scrivener, but that didn't mean I had to be social. People saw me as shy and reclusive at these functions. I counteracted the criticism by creating elegant drawings to give as gifts to the hosts and commemorate special occasions. I was grateful that my mother had taught me a skill which allowed me a little freedom.

"Andra, come join us. Don't hide in the corner on your birthday." Cindy's operatic voice carried across the crowd. I could sense everyone's eyes searching for me, the recalcitrant birthday girl. My skin crawled from the attention.

"I know, Cindy. I want to commemorate this evening with a drawing," I said. "Everyone looks so lovely, especially you. I thought I'd make you something special as a thank you."

"Well, then, we'll leave you to it. Just be sure to do justice to my new dress and all the handsome men here." Cindy sashayed over toward Brian and his friends.

Brian sent me a look that said, "Help me!" I winked, laughed, and ignored his unspoken plea. There was nothing I could do to save him without leaving the safety of my private world. Besides, I was pretty sure that deep down he relished all the attention.

I sat in the comfort of a cushioned window seat and pretended to draw the party. I let my pencil wander in doodles across the page. I admit this wasn't the smartest thing to do in a crowded room. My doodling had the tendency to turn into writing even though that was dangerous. I often had to hide my work from any eyes that came too near. I've mastered the art of distracting people away from my law-breaking tendencies. In my secure nest, where nobody could approach without my knowledge, I didn't worry too much.

I don't know what came over me, but I had the sudden urge to play with writing. When words demanded my attention, I could do nothing but obey. The impending loss of written words at the end of the year would crush me completely for that reason. Whether I married or joined the WTP, I would never again have easy access to books and writing.

Across the room, Cindy performed louder and sillier antics. It inspired my mischievous side—the side that could get me into trouble if I got caught. I picked up my pencil and wrote:

Cindy noticed an annoying tickle under her nose, which caused her to start sneezing. She peered around the room in search of a cause and blamed it on the innocent flowers that adorned the mantel. After a brief moment out of sight to fix herself up, she returned to her concerned admirers. "Whatever caused it, I can breathe again," she said. She breathed deeply to show off her endowments.

It was pure silliness, and wishful thinking. I hid the illegal paper away and then switched to a blank page to start a drawing of Cindy surrounded by the flowers on the mantel. I planned on hiding the evidence of my criminal act in the safety of my home retreat where I had a collection of words gathering under the floorboards of the attic. I kept them in the hopes that someday the voice and thoughts of women would be allowed into the world again.

As often happened, I lost myself in the delicacy of my drawing. I love falling into the trance of lines becoming images, colors forming patterns, and something appearing out of nothing. I inherited my mother's love of art, and every time I draw or paint it brings me closer to her spirit, even when the subject annoys me as much as Cindy could sometimes. At least Cindy's beauty gave me a challenge.

"Achoo!"

A booming sneeze startled me out of my artistic reverie.

"Achoo! Achoo! Achoo!"

Across the room Cindy's face turned bright red as cyclonic sneezes propelled her backwards. Madame Rogerson rushed forward with a handkerchief, which Cindy took before making a hasty exit.

The room filled with chuckles and a few malicious laughs. I went back to my drawing, but kept one eye on the scene.

Cindy returned a few minutes later, the picture of perfection. Her closest friends gathered around her, "Are you Ok?" "Do you have a cold?"

"I don't know what happened," Cindy made sure to regain the focus of everyone in the room. "Something tickled my nose, and I simply couldn't stop sneezing. Perhaps it's the flowers on the mantel, although they've never bothered me before." Cindy glided over to sniff a flower, handkerchief held in elegant preparation for another dramatic sneeze. Nothing happened. "Well, whatever caused it, I can breathe again." Cindy took a deep breath as she extended her ample bosom toward the young men who honored her with glinting eyes and smiles.

I got a chill down my spine. I pulled out the paper I had tucked away and reread the words I wrote. It was a ridiculous thought, but—

A hyena-like laugh from across the room brought my attention back to the gathering. This time, Cindy's best friend Lori danced through a group of young men with tempting looks and flirtatious touches.

I had to test my theory. I turned back to the page of writing and scribbled:

Lori didn't notice the loose carpet and tripped, falling toward Thomas. They both tumbled down in a clumsy pile.

My idea was crazy. My words couldn't have made Cindy sneeze, but I wanted to try again. I began to sketch a cartoon of my vision of Lori and Thomas as I waited to see if anything would happen. I was being ridiculous and laughed at myself. Cindy's sneeze had to have been a coincidence.

Crash! Across the room Lori and Thomas lay in a tangled mess on the floor; the famous flowers that caused chaos for Cindy covered them in a wet and colorful heap.

Alarm bells began to ring in my brain. Two times in a row, it appeared that something I imagined came to life before my eyes within a few minutes of me writing the idea on paper. As impossible as that was, something told me I wasn't imagining it. My words brought about events. I searched the room to find Brian; he was the only person at the party I trusted besides my father. He was helping clean up the mess caused by Lori's fall. I ran over and touched his sleeve. "I need to talk to you. NOW!"

"Andra, it's the middle of your party. We can't just leave."

"I know. This is important."

He shrugged in agreement knowing he'd never convince me to wait. "I'll meet you at the gazebo in ten minutes." Brian turned to offer Lori his jacket while she dried off.

It took me longer than ten minutes to get to the gazebo. People stopped to wish me happy birthday or ask me pointed questions about my plans for the coming year. I didn't want to discuss my future with anyone from the Ministry, and focused on all of my calming tricks to keep my temper under control. I attempted to be pleasant and answer each question, but my heart beat a frantic pattern as I searched for a means of escape. Finally I found my father near the patio doors talking to Minister Rogerson. I headed in their direction.

"Andra," Minister Rogerson put his arm around my shoulders. I never liked it when he touched me. My skin rebelled against his touch—heavy with condescension and wrongness. I wanted desperately to escape.

"This is a big birthday," he said. "Do you have any special man in mind to take you under his protection in the coming year?"

I shouldn't have been surprised that he asked me that question, but my anger flared and my tongue readied for a sharp response before I could control it. Dad placed his hand on my arm, a warning and a reminder that I had to be polite. I put on my fakest and sweetest smile, wishing I could step away from the heaviness of the minister's arm draped over my shoulders.

"Not at the moment, Minister Rogerson," I said. "I haven't really had time to meet anyone yet."

"She's been too busy taking care of her old father," Dad said. "I'll be sad to lose her."

"It's the struggle of every father." The minister cast a fond glance in his daughter's direction. "We've already begun negotiations for my sweet Cindy, even though she's only fifteen. It's her duty of course, as it is for every woman. I'll miss her when she leaves, she's my special girl." He sighed and then gave Dad a sharp look. "It's your duty as a father to find Andra an appropriate husband."

Dad tightened his grip on my arm to stop me from making a regrettable reply—a gesture of warning I've become all too familiar with. "Of course, Minister," he said. "Andra, you look thirsty, why don't you get a drink while the minister and I discuss possible appropriate matches for you."

My jaw hurt from clenching my teeth in a fake smile. "Thank you, Dad. I might step outside. It's a little hot in here. By your leave, Minister?"

"Of course, you're the birthday girl. Don't stay out too long. I'd love to see you dance with my son, Peter."

"I'd be delighted," I said. My stomach tightened at the thought. Peter was several years older than me, and I'll admit he is one of the more handsome men around. However, the thought of dancing with someone raised by Minister Rogerson made me nauseous. "First, though, I need fresh air."

I made my escape out into the garden, my mind whirling with the words I'd written as well as the tension between my father and Minister Rogerson. My seventeenth year had barely started, and I was just beginning to realize how dangerous it would be if I wasn't careful. Minister Rogerson and other ministry officials were determined to place me under their control through marriage, and I wasn't sure Dad could do anything to stop them. If I made any missteps, my father could be the one to suffer. If I was going to solve the problem, I had to do it myself. Maybe this little fluke with words could be the answer. I made my way to the gazebo where Brian waited.

"What's so urgent that we had to leave the party?" Brian asked as soon as I approached.

"I made Cindy sneeze and Lori fall."

"What are you talking about? You were across the room."

"I wrote that those things happened."

"Have you been sneaking some punch? You know women are only allowed to drink under supervision."

"Here, I'll show you. Just stand there and be quiet." Brian only believed things he could see for himself, so I pulled out a piece of paper and started writing. Brian watched with a panicked look on his face.

"You shouldn't be writing here. If anyone catches us . . ."

"Shh! I'll be done in a minute. Be on lookout."

Brian stood and watched the house to be sure nobody approached. I finished scribbling, put my pencil down, and looked up at him.

"I'm done."

"What's supposed to happen?" Brian asked, and sat down on the bench opposite me. He immediately jumped up, "Ouch! I think I just got a splinter."

I started laughing.

"What's so funny?" Brian asked. "Did you put something on the seat? Is this one of your practical jokes?"

"Listen to what I wrote." I read: "Brian stood impatiently while Andra wrote; worried that someone would witness them breaking the law. He tried to warn Andra, but she shushed him. Finally she finished. 'What's supposed to happen?' He asked. He sat down only to jump up suddenly, twisting around to look at his bottom. 'Ouch! I think I just got a splinter,' he said."

I waited for Brian to be impressed. The confusion on his face made me laugh out loud. For a smart guy, he was sometimes a little slow.

"Don't you get it? I wrote what happened to you!"

"That's impossible," Brian said.

"Impossible, perhaps, but it's happened three times now. See." I pulled out the page with my earlier writing.

"Are you crazy?!" Brian said without reading. "This is so dangerous."

"I know, I know," I brushed away the familiar scolding. The dangers of the ludicrous law had never stopped me from writing whenever I had the urge. Or at least nothing had stopped me yet. The imminent threat of marriage or the WTP might. "That's not what's important. Read what I wrote! I wrote things and made them happen."

Brian stared at my words then looked up with concern in his eyes. "Andra, promise me you won't tell anyone about this, not even your father."

"Why not? This might be the power my mother wrote about."

"That's what worries me. Don't tell your father. It could put him in danger. You don't want him to disappear like my father and all those other people deemed dangerous by the government, do you?"

"Of course not," I nibbled on my lower lip as I thought about his words. "I want to understand what's happening."

"Look, I'll try to find out something. Don't do anything until I get back to you."

"I have to find out what I can do, don't I? I mean, this could be important. Maybe I can make the world better . . . change New North somehow. At the very least, maybe I can get out of marriage this year. I have to have this power for a reason."

"Maybe . . . that's what scares me. Who knows what will happen if you try to rewrite the world. Or, worse, if you do something in a fit of temper as you're so apt to do."

He was right. My temper had gotten me into trouble too many times to count. But I couldn't just ignore this bizarre thing that had happened.

"Help me, then," I said. "I dare you." Brian never ignored a dare from me. He sighed in defeat.

"Please, don't try anything big until I do some digging." He moved over to the bench next to me and forced me to look into his eyes. "I'm serious about this."

I pulled away from his intense stare. Looking into the depths of his eyes I saw things I didn't want to see; they told me of feelings he had that ran deeper than friendship. I pulled away. I didn't want to face those feelings or see his eyes filled with pain and concern, so I stood up and began to pace. The energy inside me had to come out somehow. "How are you going to find out any information? You're not your father. Besides, who could possibly know anything?"

"I think I know what to do. Promise me you'll be careful or I'll tell your father—."

"You don't want him to know about this."

"He'll be upset enough if I tell him you've been writing in a public place."

"I promise," I lied—a little white lie. He knew I would never completely be able to abstain from trying. "I won't wait forever."

"I know you won't. When have you ever been patient when you want something? I'm holding you to the promise. Now, you better get back inside or you'll be missed. It must be time for cake by now. I'll wait a bit so nobody sees us come back together."

"Afraid that people will be matchmaking?" As I intended, he blushed. After Dad had suggested marriage earlier, Brian would be way too easy to tease.

"I doubt they think I'm worthy of siring the next Scrivener. They'd be concerned that I might follow in my father's footsteps." For a brief moment Brian's shoulders sagged with sadness. I hated bringing up memories that he still didn't like to discuss. He shook it off, straightened his shoulders, and put out his hand. "Leave the paper with me." I handed it to him. "Now, get inside. You don't want to miss your cake. And don't forget you owe Cindy a drawing." Brian tucked the writing into the hidden pocket in his vest.

"I won't forget. Thank you." I headed inside to face the rest of the evening, even though my words and their possibilities filled my mind to distraction.

THREE

Despite my promise to Brian, I couldn't resist sneaking up to my attic haven and testing my abilities. I avoided temptation for a short time, since Dad was home for a holiday and I always try to spend time with him on the rare occasions when the Ministry wasn't working him too hard. However, as soon as Dad returned to work, I headed upstairs and grabbed pencils and paper. I curled into my faded, overstuffed chair by the window, and tried different things. I encouraged a butterfly to flitter into the open window and land on my arm, and then laughed out loud at the surprising tickle on my skin. When the sky darkened, threatening a downpour that would keep everyone inside, I wrote about a sudden shift in the winds which swept the storm away to be replaced by a cerulean sky framed with a double rainbow. I couldn't believe it worked.

After the scent of a neighbor's fresh baked bread wafted through the window, I realized I was hungry. I didn't want to stop practicing so I wrote:

A plate of bread, fruit, and cheese appeared at my side, allowing me to focus on what was important.

Nothing happened. I guess it was too much to think I could create something out of nothing.

I wrote non-stop, my hand cramping with the exercise. Some things worked, some things failed. I tried to understand the rules that guided my power, and got lost in the complexity: I could do nothing that had a direct effect on myself, and had to word things with clear images in mind. After the first failed attempt at conjuring food, I sustained myself with leftovers. I only stopped long enough to cook for Dad. As soon as I could, when Dad was focused on his own pursuits, I flew back up to the attic to try something else.

This lasted for almost a week, with no word from Brian. I assumed he was keeping his promise and pursuing something that would help me understand what was happening.

In truth, though, I barely noticed his absence until Dad commented on it.

"Brian hasn't been around much this week," he said. "I hope everything's okay."

"I'm sure he's just busy." I spoke with care to ensure I didn't sound concerned. Inside, though, I wondered if I had sent Brian on a dangerous mission.

I wrote late into the night with the attic shutters closed so nobody would see my candle flickering in the window. I didn't dare use electric lights after curfew as that would cause other problems if anyone noticed. My writing grew messy and I neared exhaustion. I still wasn't willing to stop, so I thought I'd try to write myself a solution. I wrote:

I stood and stretched. The simple act of stretching gave me energy as if I had gotten a full night's sleep.

I stood, stretched, and . . . the walls started spinning. My stomach churned and I guess I blacked out. I'm not sure how long I was lying there, but the next thing I remember I was on the floor staring at the ceiling.

I had found one of the limits. I couldn't write my way into health and rest. I also couldn't write so long that my health suffered—my first lesson in caution. I pulled myself up into the chair and took some deep breathes to control the nausea before I stumbled down to the comfort of my bed. I sank into the welcoming softness and fell asleep almost as soon as I lay down. I was surprised by my exhaustion. Writing didn't seem like that much work, but perhaps I was using other energy as I wrote the world different.

The next day, I watched Dad leave for work with lines of stress engrained into his face. Even though there were other scriveners, the Ministry put too much pressure on him because he had the neatest hand and was Head Scrivener. In my opinion, Dad needed some time off, so I rushed to my writing perch and wrote:

In a surprise move, Supreme Prime Minister Sandovar gave all govern-

ment workers a half-day vacation to celebrate the success of one of his secret plans. While most of his employees had no idea why they were given this special treat, they took immediate advantage and left to spend time with their families or in solo pursuits.

I put the paper aside and continued to explore the limits of my ability. I lost track of time, so literally threw my pen across the room when Dad's voice startled me after what must have been hours of focused work. "Andra, I've come home for the afternoon! Where are you?!" I hid my experiments underneath loose boards and rushed down to greet him before he decided to come up and find me. He usually left me alone in my haven, but I wasn't going to take any chances.

"Dad, you surprised me. I don't even have anything ready for lunch." I kissed him on the cheek and grabbed some of the heavy load of scrolls and packages he carried. I tried to avoid his eyes by placing them neatly on his desk. He always knew when I lied.

"Weren't you going to eat?" Dad asked. "I expected that you would be outside on this gorgeous day."

"I guess I was distracted. Let me get something for us both and we can have a picnic."

I bustled around gathering bread, fruit, cheese, slices of meat and some leftover apple pie given to us by Brian's mother. I used extra care while packing the basket, intent on making it beautiful. My neck prickled with the intensity of Dad's eyes watching me, with a questioning look.

"What are you doing home?" I asked, attempting to sound innocent.

"The Supreme Prime Minister decided to give us all a half holiday, so I came home to spend it with my favorite girl -- I mean, young woman."

"That's a surprise!" I smiled, and hoped he thought the smile came from the pleasure of his coming home. "He's not usually that kind."

"I'm not sure he was being kind." Dad frowned, "He's celebrating another round of restrictions."

"What is it this time? Is he going to forbid women from going to the bathroom together?"

"Don't joke, Andra. He recently had me draft a recommendation that limits the number of women who are allowed to gather together without the supervision of men."

"Does he want to prevent us from socializing with each other at all?! That's ridiculous!" If women could not socialize, I thought, I might as well join the WTP as there would be nothing left for me. At least there I would be in the company of other women.

"It may be ridiculous, but it's exactly what he and others want. Or at least they want to control how women socialize." Dad sat at his desk, and followed the routine he always did as he prepared to write. He opened up the velvet cloth that held his pens and nibs, and started searching through his bottles of ink.

"What are you doing? I thought you had the rest of the day off. The picnic is ready."

Dad peered with weary eyes through the thick gleam of his glasses. "After we eat I'll have to get back to work. You know as well as I do that all the ministers will still expect my work to be finished on time tomorrow. I have several copies of religious mandates that need to be finished, so a day off simply means I'll have to work from home."

"I wish I could help you. You know I have neat writing."

Dad grabbed my hand and kissed it. "If anyone were to discover that your hand even touched these documents, you would lose it immediately. You know that. Besides, Minister Rogerson has been asking me how the drawing of Cindy at the party is coming. He's anxious to see it."

I couldn't believe that, in the thrill of exploring my newfound power, I had forgotten my promise to Cindy. I'd have to be more careful if I didn't want to get caught. "I'll finish it tonight."

"Are you sure?" Dad's eyes pierced me for a moment—looking for answers that I wouldn't share. I could tell he suspected something. "What have you been doing up in the attic?"

"It's a surprise. I promise I'll get Cindy's picture done right away."

"Good. I want you to deliver it in person tomorrow."

"Do I have to?"

"Yes. Minister Rogerson requested that I bring you in to discuss something with him."

"What does he have to discuss with me?"

"Your guess is as good as mine. It's a request we can't refuse."

Rather than start an argument I would never win, I said, "I understand. Shall we go outside for our picnic now?"

"It would be my pleasure." Dad grabbed the picnic blanket and held the door open for me.

I carried the overflowing basket towards our favorite spot under the weeping willow that my parents had planted when I was born. I appreciated the fact that Dad didn't try to carry on a conversation as we lay out the goodies, as the upcoming meeting with Minister Rogerson filled my brain. What could he possibly want with me? Visits to the Ministry always made me nervous, but to be called in by someone like Minister Rogerson terrified me. If I could have thought of words to write to fix it, I would have rushed up to the attic, but since I had no idea what the minister wanted I couldn't think of a single word.

Dad's serious tone interrupted my thoughts. "Andra, I'm glad we have time to talk this afternoon. I know you're doing something in the attic. I'm not going to push you to explain, but I'm worried. When you work on Cindy's picture, don't add any hidden messages. It's too dangerous."

"The women's language would be wasted on Cindy. And what would I write? 'This is a portrait of a spoiled princess, be warned!'"

Dad's laugh was contagious. It had been a long time since I heard him laugh in that free and abandoned way. For a moment I saw a reflection of the man I remembered from before Mother had died.

His laughter didn't last long.

"Please don't write anything." The intensity in his eyes made me uncomfortable. I shifted my gaze to my hands.

"I promise." I said. "No hidden messages."

Dad gave me a brief hug, "I'm very proud of you, Andra. Your mother would be as well."

"I hope so. I truly hope so." I intended to make him proud with a wonderful portrait of Cindy, even if it meant taking a break from my words.

* * *

The opulent mansion that housed the Ministry overwhelmed most visitors, and I was no exception. The curvaceous turrets, arched entries, and exquisite attention to detail reflected times long gone, when money and technological advances allowed people to build dream homes and visit cultures across the ocean accessible now only to the wealthiest and most powerful citizens. The government attempted to conserve the home's past grandeur with gleaming floors and colorful frescoes painted on the ceiling. Here and there, however, symbols of the current regime replaced the elegance of the past.

I particularly hated the painting that greeted visitors in the massive entry hall—strict men in formal attire standing in front of women who kneeled in supplication under the watchful Eye of the Lord. I avoided looking at it whenever I had to go through the lengthy process of gaining entry into the Ministry. My father had to provide proof of my identification as well as sign a statement that I would be under his control at all times.

The appearance of Minister Rogerson made the process go more quickly. "Andra is here at my request," he told the clerk. "Please let her through immediately."

"Of course, Minister. Anything you say." The slight man paled and stamped my paperwork several times while waving us in. I had to stifle a giggle. Dad's mouth twitched as he held in his own chuckle. Once we got home we would share a belly-laugh over the man's buffoonish behavior.

We followed Rogerson up the curved staircase which led to his office. I'd never been in it before. I believe it had once been a bedroom when the mansion was a home. A massive carved mahogany desk dominated the space. Sunlight shining through the arched windows glinted off brass and crystal decorations that filled the room. I moved toward the windows and appreciated the gorgeous view of the grounds, with exquisitely maintained gardens. I preferred that view to the room stifled by oppressive antique furniture.

"Andra, don't you look lovely." Minister Rogerson gave me a sloppy kiss in greeting as his hand migrated down the length of my hair in a caress that nobody could call fatherly. "I hope you're enjoying your entry into womanhood. Seventeen is such an important year."

"Yes, sir," I struggled to put a pleasant smile on my face. I pretended to be drawn to a painting on the wall, which allowed me to step away from his roaming hand. I hoped he didn't notice as I wiped at the kiss.

"This painting is lovely," I said. "Do you know who the artist was?"

"No, but I can find out. That's unimportant at the moment. I brought you here to discuss possible matches for you. I'm concerned that you haven't indicated a preference yet. Unless you think your friend Brian is a match?" His eyes glinted in a look that made me uncomfortable.

I wasn't sure what to say, so I shook my head and said nothing.

"Good. Brian would be unacceptable as you know. His father is not welcome in New North."

"I understand, sir," I said. I wanted to punch the man in defense of Brian's dad.

"Do you? I'm not sure you do. If you really understood, I think you would have been married by now. You know we encourage young women to marry soon after they have achieved fertility. It seems to be the best for their fragile minds, as well as for the replenishment of the population."

Dad jumped in before I could speak. "In my selfishness and grief, I couldn't bear to lose her after my wife died."

"Your wife's death was unavoidable, and all the more reason why Andra needs to display proper behavior. I suppose I can understand your need to keep her home, although we could have found you a suitable replacement wife from the WTP to take over the household responsibilities."

Dad said nothing while I fumed. How dare Minister Rogerson suggest that someone could ever replace Mother? I glanced over at my father. Lines of pain and anger etched themselves on his forehead and around his eyes. He surprised me by staring his superior down, in a look that reminded me of the day he had fought for the right to keep me and raise me as his own. That was the man who had disappeared for so long—the Dad I missed.

The air grew thick. I held my breath unsure how Rogerson would respond to this subtle display of Dad's strength.

Minister Rogerson moved behind his desk to straighten out an already neat pile of papers before continuing. "Yes . . . well . . . I suppose that explains why your daughter remains in your home. However," he somehow found the authority in his voice again, "Andra, I'm sure there's no need to remind you that the law requires you marry before you turn eighteen. I find the girls who marry earlier are much happier than the ones who try to remain single, but I realize that point is moot. You have always been a little rebellious, haven't you?"

I glanced over at Dad, who looked as if he might explode with worry. I opted for silence, rather than saying something that would get us both in trouble.

"Andra is loyal and obedient," Dad said.

"Of course, of course. I'm sure she learned from her mother's mistakes."

I clenched my hands but said nothing.

"Anyway, Andra," Minister Rogerson continued without noticing my tension. "I would be happy to recommend some acceptable marriage candidates and arrange meetings. My son Peter seems enthralled by your charms." He walked back around the desk and slapped my father on the back. Dad's eye twitched, but he said nothing. "It's about time she made you a male heir. She could do worse than marrying into my family, couldn't she, Scrivener?"

Dad smiled and winked at me. "I prefer to let Andra decide when and whom to marry."

Relief put a smile on my lips.

"We can't leave decisions like that up to the women or we'll have a society of dullards. I would hate to see Andra's talent wasted." He winked at me but I didn't respond. "Of course the Women's Training Program does wonders, but involuntary participants often seem to lose some *joie de vivre* for some reason. Andra always looks so lovely when she smiles; so full of life. It would be a shame to see her lose that charm." The Minister laughed, nudging my father in the ribs. I couldn't interpret Dad's smile.

I clasped my hands together more tightly and took several deep breaths. Dad told me to do that whenever the desire to speak first and think later became overwhelming.

Dad must have seen my distress, as he said something to change the subject. "Minister Rogerson, I believe you had some material you wanted me to look over?"

"Oh, yes, time to get down to business. Andra, I look forward to seeing the picture of my daughter. As usual we menfolk have to deal with business before pleasure. We can discuss your options another time. The year will pass quickly, and we must see you settled. I'd hate to see your father lose his position because of your choices."

I met Dad's eye. He sent me a calming hand signal, but I wasn't sure I'd remain calm. The threat in the words scared me.

"I'm not sure how long this will take," Minister Rogerson continued, unaware of the silent interplay between Dad and myself. "I have plenty of drawing materials in the corner, or perhaps you prefer to do some needlework? There's also a selection of freshly baked sweets, but I wouldn't eat too many. You want to keep your figure until we make that match." He ushered Dad toward the door, "Your father and I will be down the hall. We don't want to harm sensitive ears and we need to consult with another minister. When we return, you can show me the drawing."

"I look forward to it," I said in my sweetest, most sarcastic, voice. I headed toward the art supplies and pretended to examine pencils.

Dad sent a look of concern and appeal in my direction as they left the room.

As soon as the door closed, I threw a pencil at it. The thud didn't do enough to alleviate my frustration. I wished I could scratch the pompous smirk off the Minister's face, or do something even more violent. I fought the urge to scream. Instead, I paced the limited floor space and talked to myself, doing an imitation of Rogerson "Time to get you married, Andra. Aren't you a pretty little thing?" If Dad had heard my imitation he would have laughed before admonishing me to be careful. "If your father weren't here I'd show you what a man is," I continued, still with a mocking voice and a cautious glance at the door.

As I passed Minister Rogerson's huge desk, the pile of paper he left beckoned. It held the official seal of Supreme Prime Minister Rom Sandovar—the Eye of the Lord. I could never resist a pile of papers left out for my consumption. They called to me, begging to be read. I grabbed the first sheet, ears alert to any sounds outside. The first lines I read made me collapse into the leather chair in shock.

> *This is to warn all ministers that there has been a breach in security. We fear that sources outside the walls of New North have leaked scientific studies on the hidden strengths and powers of the female brain. It is crucial that this information never reach the public. We have our team of experts focusing on stronger support for our cause, as is detailed below. In the coming months, we intend to initiate further sanctions . . .*

I read through the pages of the document, and then flipped back to re-read some passages before falling into the chair and scattering the pages on the desk. My life had changed from reading that memo. The memo revealed that the government of New North had been built on lies intended to do one thing, keep power in the hands of men—and only particular men at that. My chest tightened. Did Dad know about this? The hand that wrote these lines used thicker, less elegant strokes. Some other scrivener had copied these memos. That realization allowed me to breathe more easily.

I heard movement in the hall and Dad's voice raised just enough to give warning. I hastened to gather the papers together and reposition the document exactly where I'd found it. Even though I had developed this skill over years of sneaking around reading forbidden words, my shaking hands made it more difficult this time. I rushed to the chair by the window and began sketching flowers on the blank page, just as the door opened to admit Minister Rogerson and my father, followed by the tall figure of Peter Rogerson. I jumped up and knocked my drawing materials on the floor in surprise.

"Look who dropped by to join us for a bite to eat," Minister Rogerson's over-jolly tone revealed that he had planned this meeting all along. "Peter, you know lovely Andra don't you?"

"Of course, Father." Peter bent down to help me gather the spilled materials. "I'm sorry if we startled you." He avoided making eye contact with me.

"It was entirely my fault. I was so focused on drawing I didn't hear anyone coming." I hoped Peter wouldn't mention the scarcity of marks on the pages he picked up.

"Andra," his father interrupted our awkward exchange. "Please show me the drawing of Cindy."

Relieved that I had something to show him, I pulled my finished creation out of its protective portfolio, and tried to ignore the young man standing nearby. After the Minister's words about marriage, Peter's towering presence filled the room and suffocated me.

"You've captured the beauty of my daughter perfectly!" Rogerson's loud voice broke the strained atmosphere. "She'll love this. I knew you had many talents, Andra. Peter, come and look at what this young lady can do."

"Of course, father." As Peter leaned over the picture, I stepped toward my father.

"I'm not feeling well, Dad."

"You look pale. What's wrong?"

"I think something I ate must have disagreed with me."

The Minister looked up, "I warned you about eating too many sweets. You don't look well at all. Women are so sensitive, Peter. We have to take special care of them. Perhaps we should put lunch off for another day. Scrivener, take your daughter home. I expect you back here in an hour to work on those papers."

"Thank you, Sir." I gave a brief curtsy, thankful that he had fallen for my lie. "I'm sorry about lunch. I hope Cindy enjoys the picture."

"I'm sure she will. Now take yourself home and we'll discuss your future very soon."

Not if I can help it, I thought as I followed Dad out the door.

FOUR

Brian hadn't intended to leave Andra to her own devices for so long. He knew her well enough to realize she wouldn't be able to stick to her promise. Yet, despite his confidence on the night of the party, he found it difficult to reach the people who could give him the answers he needed.

It was his own fault, he supposed, he'd cut off the connection years before.

He began his search in the warehouse district, wandering through the same area where he had discovered possible answers four years earlier. As he made his way through the maze of buildings and alleys he became lost and confused. Nothing was familiar, as fragile structures built to shelter hungry families cut off passageways and changed routes. The smell brought him back to that period after his father's mysterious disappearance, when his sixteen-year-old-self set out determined to find the truth.

* * *

In the early days, Brian's mother clung to him. "I can't survive alone," she said. "Don't leave me until he comes back."

"I don't think he's coming home," Brian said. At sixteen he had already learned a lot about the dangers of New North. "Once people disappear, they're gone for good. You know that, Mom. Either the government took him or he's gone outside the wall."

"Never say that." Her intensity frightened him. "I'm not sure what your father was doing, but I know he was always careful, and he would never leave us behind. If he left New North, he would bring us with him. He'll come back. Just stay with me until he does."

"I'll take care of you, Mom," he said. His promise didn't stop him from trying to find out the truth whenever he could slip away, which wasn't often. The more time that passed, the more his mother fell into a state of utter despair. Some days she wouldn't even get out of bed. Brian had to feed her like an infant in order to get her to take tepid tea and toast.

About three months after the disappearance, Marion BetScrivener, his mother's best friend and Andra's mother, came to his house leading a group of women carrying baked goods and flowers. "Your mother just needs some girl talk and support," she said. "We'll get her back on track and she'll be fine. Besides, you need time off once in a while. Go do something fun." She patted him on the cheek in a familiar fond caress and pushed him out the door.

Brian didn't waste time making his escape, determined that he would find some answers about his father that day.

He wandered through the warehouse district following a surprising lead that his father was often seen in that area—an area where a woodcraftsman had no reason to be. Brian had no clue where to go, so he walked from warehouse to warehouse, through alleys filled with the detritus of unwanted goods and unwanted people. He saw nothing to explain why his father would be there. The few people he met scurried off before he could say anything. Most of them shot fearful looks in his direction. Nobody spoke to him. He was about to give up in frustration when a deep voice echoed out of a dark doorway.

"This is a dangerous place to be walking alone, Brian Woodson."

Brian turned, startled to hear his name. "Do I know you, Sir?" he asked, peering into the gloom.

A large man with graying sideburns and a hardened face stepped from the shadow of the doorway. "You don't know me, although you've seen me before. I've been hoping to meet you. I was a friend of your father's. You can call me Johnson."

"Mr. Johnson, you knew my father?"

"Just Johnson. Yes, your father and I knew each other well."

"Can you tell me where he is? What happened to him?"

"I can give you some information, but not here. It's not safe. Will you come with me?" Without waiting for an answer, Johnson turned to enter the darkness behind him. The rifle slung across the man's large muscled back made Brian hesitate, as weapons of any kind were all under the control of the government as far as he knew.

"How do I know it's safe?" Brian asked.

The older man chuckled. "You don't," he said. "If you want information though, you'll come."

Brian followed.

Johnson led him to the back of the warehouse and through a door hidden behind a pallet of heavy crates. The older man grabbed two torches tucked away in a small cabinet and handed one of them to Brian after lighting them both. They entered a tunnel that led to labyrinthine passages below the warehouse district. The flickering torches emphasized the shadows and creepiness of moist, dank tunnels that echoed with the sounds of unseen creatures. Brian tried to keep track of the numerous twists and turns. He soon lost all sense of direction as they passed through hidden doorways and tunnels so low both had to duck. Each step deeper into the unknown caused his stomach to knot with nerves and doubt. Time grew meaningless. They could have been walking for an hour or mere minutes when they approached a door which didn't belong in a place made of stone and metal and filth. Brian, who had been trained well by his father, recognized the expensive teak and reached out a hand to caress the elaborate carvings on this piece of art. Johnson's torch revealed an image of a rose in the center.

"That's my father's mark!" Brian said, tracing the intricate carving. "What's it doing in this dismal place? Why is this door here?"

"This room was his special meeting place," Johnson said. "He built it and everything in it."

He opened the door and the torchlight filled a room covered in wood paneling, with comfortable chairs and tables also carved out of wood. Brian recognized his father's artistry.   "Wait here and I'll get us something to help our talk," Johnson placed his torch in a holder and headed to another door perfectly hidden in the paneling. Brian caught a glimpse of crates and supplies stacked on heavy wooden shelves. He moved across the room toward another torch bracket. Johnson returned carrying two mugs filled with cider.

"I don't understand," Brian said. "Where are we?"

The torchlight reflected on a carving in the wall—wings floating over the head of a woman holding a feather quill and a scroll with a man at her side. The flickering flame made it seem as if the figures moved. "Why did my father have this place? It's marked with the symbol of the rebels."

"You know the mark of the Freedom Readers?" Johnson asked.

"Of course I do," Brian said. "Everyone does. Still, I don't know what it has to do with my father." He turned to look at the strange man. "Who are you?"

"I told you, my name is Johnson. I worked with your father. He was a Freedom Reader. He was a rebel."

"No, he wasn't," Brian said. "He was an artisan . . . a woodcraftsman."

"The two aren't mutually exclusive," Johnson said. "I make a living as a handyman. Your father was a fine woodcraftsman. The proof of that is all over this room."

Brian placed his hand on the table and caressed his father's artistry. He had always loved the silkiness of the fine lines and smooth grain that came from hours of careful carving and sanding. Even the smell of the wood, more powerful than the remnant odors of the sewers, reminded him of his father.

"I still don't understand," Brian said as he collapsed into one of the intricately carved but comfortable chairs.

"Have a drink and I'll explain."

At that meeting, Brian learned that his father had been working for years to undermine the government he didn't believe in.

"Did he ever tell you about the rebellions that led to Sandovar's rule?" Johnson asked.

Brian shook his head.

"I'm sure he wanted to protect you. Your father fought against the dissolution of the old nation. Perhaps it was inevitable, but he believed there was a better solution than dividing a once powerful country into smaller nations. He was terrified of what would happen if people like Rom Sandovar came into power—people who had created a religious system to support their belief in the supremacy of people like themselves. Your father wasn't one of the leaders of the rebellion, but he worked in a quiet and steady way against Sandovar. You know what happened. Sandovar manipulated his way into power, using his version of religious belief, along with the distortion of scientific knowledge, control of technology, and his access to tremendous amounts of money. He took control and built the wall that keeps us separate from the rest of the world. Your father was a master of hiding his tracks, which saved him from disappearing like so many others who opposed Sandovar. That's why, when the Freedom Readers formed, he became one of the leaders. His luck ran out on his last venture, when he was trying to find evidence about some of Sandovar's lies. Someone caught him where he shouldn't have been. We can't be sure what happened to him. We know he never revealed our secrets, otherwise many more people would disappear." Sadness filled Johnson's face as he took a long drink of cider.

"Have you tried to find out what happened?" Brian asked.

"Of course we have. I have at least. Your father was my friend and a good man. If there is a chance we can save him, we will. We have people working on it, but we need more help. That's where you come in."

"What do you mean, where I come in? What can I do?"

"While our group of rebels is growing, many of us have been fighting for a long time, and we have a long way to go," Johnson said. The torchlight emphasized and deepened the weary lines on his face. "We need more people to join our cause and carry it on if we want to make permanent change to society. Sandovar and his allies have managed to convince many that their version of God is the only truth, and that their rules are the word of the Lord. They created the symbol of the Eye of the Lord to make sure that people always knew he was watching. There are those who haven't fallen prey to these beliefs, but they have become silenced and have kept their opinions hidden for the sake of survival. We need to bring them together. We need more young people, and more people we can trust. We need the sons and daughters of our best agents. We need you, Brian."

For the rest of that visit, Brian listened to all the arguments for his joining the Freedom Readers. He heard the stories of his father's bravery and passion. They talked for hours, as the desire grew in him to fight for change and make his father proud.

"How do I join?" he asked.

Johnson smiled. "I thought you would want to. You are your father's son.

But, you have to be sure. Your father wouldn't want me to pressure you into this. I'm not sure he'd even want you involved because of the danger and your youth."

"I'm not that young," Brian said. "I'm taking care of everything now that Dad's gone. Besides, he must have been about my age when he started all this."

Johnson laughed. "I know. I believe you have the right to make your own decision. Think it over for a few days. If you're sure, meet me by the Unknown Rebel's Tomb in the Commoner's Cemetery in three days. Do you know the place?"

Brian nodded.

"If you decide not to join us, and you tell anyone about this meeting, then I can't be responsible for what happens. Some Readers believe in destroying people they consider traitors to the cause. I don't think like that. I'll do my best to protect you because I loved your father, however, my protection may not be enough."

"I understand," Brian said. "I'll be joining you in three days."

Upon returning home that day, Brian discovered the doctor's wagon parked outside his cottage, and tense women trying to keep themselves quiet and busy in the kitchen.

"What happened?" Brian asked.

"Your mother was fine at first," Marion BetScrivener said, putting her arm around his shoulders. "As the day passed she became convinced that you were gone too. She thought you had disappeared and wouldn't return. She collapsed a few hours ago and we sent for the doctor. I didn't know where to find you."

Brian ran to his mother's side.

Three days later, he managed to leave her sleeping under the careful watch of Andra's mother and made his way to the Commoner's Cemetery.

"You came," Johnson said. He offered his hands for the rebel's two-handed handshake.

"I came, but I can't join you," Brian said. "I want to. I believe in your cause and promise to protect your secret and honor my father's work. I just can't join you, at least not yet. It's too risky and if something were to happen to me it would destroy my mother."

"Are you sure?" Johnson asked.

"I have no choice," Brian said.

Johnson adjusted a bag slung across his shoulder. "Well then, you won't hear from us again," he said, "Unless, of course, you reveal our secrets. Then you'll wish we had never met. I won't be able to protect you." With that he turned and disappeared behind the crypt.

Brian never told anyone about that meeting. He never tried to seek out the Freedom Readers again, even after his mother showed signs of improvement. Eventually, she could function without him. Some days, however, she fell back into the darkness and despair. Brian couldn't take any chances.

* * *

Andra's secret made him reconsider. He recognized immediately what her ability could do for the cause he believed in. He also realized the danger to Andra and her father if the government learned about her unusual power with words. He had to protect them at all cost. The bond between the two families had always been strong. To protect them all, Brian knew he needed information and help.

The day after Andra's birthday party, he set out to find the Freedom Readers.

His search of the warehouse district proved futile. He couldn't recall the exact warehouse where he had met Johnson, as so many of them were giant gray boxes without any distinguishable features. Four years had changed the landscape just enough to make everything seem different and confusing.

Day after day for nearly a week he travelled across the capital of New North from dreary location to dangerous dive in the hopes he would find someone who would help him. He dropped hints in sketchy bars and wandered by the homes of people suspected of rebel activity. He searched every place he could think of to find someone who would lead him to the Rebels.

Nothing worked.

Brian had given up. He had nowhere else to look—no new ideas. He made his way to the hidden refuge in the woods outside of town where he and Andra went whenever they needed a break from the world around them. That was his only place to think.

He thought back to the day they had discovered this hideaway. They were spending the day together while their parents were off doing something "not appropriate for children." Brian suggested a game of explorers.

"Let's do it!" Andra cried, always up for adventures that most girls shied away from.

They made their way into the woods beyond the town escaping tigers and mysterious invisible creatures until they pushed their way through dense underbrush to discover a small, rectangular clearing. Trees and brush that only determined explorers could make their way through protected two sides of the clearing. A cliff with a large cave opened on the third side and provided shelter in inclement weather. The rush of a branch of the river protected the fourth side.

"This is our secret haven!" Brian said.

"Yes!" Andra said. "And we shall call it Briandra's Haven."

He laughed at the combination of their names and her dramatic, formal tone. Briandra's Haven became their hideaway where they could share raucous games or the most intense secrets, or simply be alone to think.

After his frustrating week, it was the only place he could find comfort.

"You're easy to follow. You've been leaving a dangerous trail."

Brian jumped at the deep voice he would never forget. He turned to see Johnson flanked by two men with hunting rifles pointed in his direction. Brian put his hands up and wondered again how they had gotten weapons.

"Why have you been blazing a trail in our direction, Woodson?" Johnson asked.

"I didn't intend any harm," Brian said. "I swear. I need your help, and I think I'm ready to join the fight."

"What's changed?" Johnson asked, waving to the other men to lower their weapons.

"My mother's much better and I have some information for you. First, though, I want to make sure you won't take advantage of it."

"I don't know that you're in a position to make demands."

"I know. But this information could change everything, I think. I can't share it with you if I don't have answers first. I have to protect my family."

Johnson stared at him for a moment with thoughtful eyes and then lowered himself onto a nearby rock, wearily running his hand through short cropped hair. "I won't give you information that will harm our cause or reveal our secrets. If I answer your questions, there's no turning back this time."

"I know," Brian said. "I promise I don't want your secrets. I just have a few questions."

The two men stared at each other in silence. Brian wouldn't move until he got what he wanted. Finally, Johnson grunted and said, "Sit down." He turned to the men standing alert nearby. "Stand watch while Woodson and I talk."

The two men disappeared into the woods.

"What do you want to know? I'll answer if I can."

FIVE

Brian wasn't home after our Ministry visit, so I left a message with his mother asking him to come and see me first thing the following morning. I kept an eye out for him before the sun even made an appearance. I think I scared him to death when I opened the door and pulled him in before he could knock. The look on his face was priceless as I tugged him into the room.

"What's going on, Andra?" Brian rubbed his arm as if I'd hurt him.

"Shh! I have to talk to you before Dad comes down for breakfast. Where have you been? I thought you were going to help me. I have so much to tell you."

"I'm sorry," Brian said. "Getting information took longer than I thought. We have a lot to talk about."

Just then Dad walked into the kitchen, a smile on his face. "Brian, I thought you'd run away. It's unusual for us not to see you for a week."

"I'm sorry, sir," Brian said. "I had a special project to work on this week."

"You and Andra and your special projects," Dad said with a smile that didn't quite reach his eyes. "Is your mother all right?"

"She's doing much better. She sends her love and asked me to invite you over for tea today."

"I can't imagine a lovelier way to spend part of my rest day. Your mother always makes the most delicious scones."

"I was wondering if I could take Andra on an art adventure for the day," Brian said. "I found a new location that I'm sure she would love to paint."

"That's an interesting request, with a complicated answer," Dad said. "I've been meaning to talk to both of you about something. But this discussion requires sustenance. Andra, would you please get the hot chocolate? Brian, sit down and have some oatmeal."

"What's wrong?" I asked. I had no clue what was bothering him. Brian and I had often gone on art adventures together, although I was pretty sure that was just an excuse this time. We had more important things to discuss.

"Let's get settled and then we'll talk," Dad said.

Whenever he wanted to settle in first, he had something serious on his mind. I served the hot chocolate while Dad scooped out oatmeal. We sat at our much loved kitchen table, a gift to my newlywed parents from Brian's father. For a moment, the sound of spoons scraping bowls filled the room, while I grew jittery. My father took his time, relishing every bite, clearly in no hurry to speak. Brian was always content as long as he had food in front of him. I was impatient.

"Dad, what's the problem?" I asked when I couldn't wait anymore. "Why won't you answer Brian's question? There's nothing complicated about it. We've gone on adventures together for years."

Dad sighed and a look of weariness filled his face. "You're seventeen now, Andra. That's the problem. Everything has changed. If I continue to allow you and Brian to wander off alone together, people will talk. We can't risk your reputation."

I couldn't stop the angry retort that lashed out like a whip. "That's absurd and you know it. Why should we care what other people say? Brian's like my big brother! And besides . . . he's old."

"I'm only twenty," Brian said. "That's not a huge difference, you know that. Most people marry with ten years between them."

"I'm not most people. I don't want to get married, unless it's for love."

"We know that," my father said with exasperation. "We still have to protect both of your reputations."

Brian turned to Dad with a serious look. "I understand what you're saying, sir, but I think my reputation is solid. I'm often sought out as an escort when one is needed—a safe one who won't try to marry the girl. I know I'm not considered a worthy match, but most people think I'm harmless for that reason."

"I realize that, son. Things have changed." He glanced over at me. "You heard Minister Rogerson yesterday."

"What did he say?" Brian asked.

I hesitated before I answered, not wanting to prod old wounds. "He warned that a marriage to you would be dangerous, because of your father."

Brian stood and paced the floor. I sensed the turmoil inside of him, but I had no idea what to say to make things better. Sometimes he just needed time to process, and if I said the wrong thing he'd either lash out at me or disappear for a while. So I waited in silence. Dad waited as well; we had learned how to help Brian together. After a few minutes, Brian stopped pacing, gripped the back of his chair and spoke.

"I understand your concerns, Scrivener," he said. "You know me better than Minister Rogerson. Have I ever given you reason to mistrust me? Would I ever put Andra or you in danger?"

Brian's left thumb twitched against the chair. Whenever he tried to lie, that twitch gave him away, at least to me. I wondered what he wasn't telling my father, and what danger we might face.

Dad took a large sip from his mug. I could practically see his brain working to organize his thoughts. His face revealed a dramatic struggle as parental concern warred with fairness. "You're right, Brian," he said. "I can't let Minister Rogerson or anyone else dictate who I let Andra spend time with. You two may have your art adventure together. Please, be cautious. Don't do anything improper."

"Thank you, Dad!" I planted a large kiss on his cheek which caused him to spill some of his cocoa. "Oops . . . sorry. We'll be careful."

Dad laughed as he mopped at the spill. "Well, I'm sure Brian will be careful, at least." He tweaked my nose in a familiar gesture.

"Thank you, sir," Brian held out his hand to shake. "You know I'll take care of your little girl."

I grabbed the wet cloth and threw it at Brian in response to those words, while both Dad and Brian laughed.

*   *   *

"Where are we really going?" I shifted my pack filled with art supplies to make it more comfortable. "If I'm lugging this for nothing, you'll be sorry."

"I need to introduce you to some people," Brian said.

"Who?"

"We're going to meet the Freedom Readers."

I stopped and grabbed his arm. "We're going to meet the rebels?! How do you know them?"

Brian gave me a quick explanation of his meetings with Johnson as we started walking again. "I haven't told them your secret," he said, "just that you had something you needed to share."

"More than you know."

"What do you mean?"

I told him about the memo in Minister Rogerson's office. He listened but said nothing. We walked in silence for a moment.

"Don't you have anything to say about what I just told you?" I asked when I couldn't take the silence any more.

"I'm thinking. I need time to absorb."

"What's there to absorb? That memo proves that the government has been lying about women and using God as an excuse. If they lie about women, imagine what other lies they've fed us."

"I get that. I'm just worried. Let me think for a minute."

"Ok. You always were a little slow . . . ," I said.

Brian smacked me on the shoulder without much force which made me laugh. I walloped him back and he winced. For a moment we were back on childhood adventures, but then it hit me that we were about to enter a world that I had been warned against by countless Ministry officials—the world of the rebels known as the Freedom Readers.

"Let's go," I said trying not to let my voice shake.

We continued on the gravel path that led toward the Commoner's Cemetery.

"Where are we going, Brian?"

"We're going to meet up with a guide. . . Andra, before we meet these people, promise me you'll be cautious."

"I thought you trusted them. Aren't we meeting them to share my secret?"

"Yes . . . but . . . I don't know. We have to be careful."

I could tell that something bothered him. He never revealed much, but I always knew when his thoughts were running deep. "What are you worried about?" I asked.

"I have some doubts. Johnson wouldn't give me any specifics about my father's disappearance yesterday, no matter how many questions I asked. And then, there was the thing about your mother."

"What thing about my mother? What does she have to do with this?"

"It was just something Johnson said yesterday. He told me the evidence my father was looking for was crucial to the cause. Then he added, almost like he was thinking out loud, 'If he could have found it, then Marion BetScrivener wouldn't have died.'"

"What does that mean? What does my mother's death have to do with the Freedom Readers?"

"I don't know," Brian said. "I asked what he meant. He avoided the question and didn't mention her name again. He wouldn't tell me everything." He stepped in front of me and grabbed my shoulders. His grip hurt. He'd never hurt me before so I knew his feelings were intense. He forced me to look into his eyes. "Please be careful with what you say."

I wanted to tell Brian that he wasn't in charge, but his look of genuine concern made me censor myself. "I'll be cautious," I said.

"Promise?"

"Promise," I reached out for our super-secret handshake.

Brian smiled and completed the pattern. "Let's go find our guide," he said.

* * *

The journey toward wherever we were headed took forever. It didn't help that all of the bugs in the universe honed in on the scent of my sweat, and avoided Brian and the guide. I kept slapping them away, while the two men acted oblivious to their presence.

We'd been walking for over an hour since meeting a thin quiet man behind the crypt in the Commoner's Cemetery. He never introduced himself or said much, just told us to follow him and led us through a hidden tunnel that I believe took us under the river that marked the Northern boundary of the capital. After we left the tunnel, a group of mountains grew in front of us. Here and there mansions perched high above us with what must have been amazing views. As far as I could tell, we were headed in the direction of the largest one. These mountains separated us from the Outside world almost as completely as the giant man-made stone wall that started at their base.

"Are we heading to that mansion?" I asked. "Who lives there?"

"You'll find out soon enough," our guide said. I wished I could get him to talk, but he avoided all of my questions.

"Welcome, Woodson." A man's deep voice startled me as he appeared out of nowhere. He grasped Brian's arm in a special two-handed handshake and drew him into a back-pounding hug. He turned to me with a polite smile. For a moment I thought I had seen him somewhere before, but I couldn't place him.

"Miss BetScrivener, I'm Johnson. Welcome."

"Please, call me Andra."

He nodded in acknowledgment before he dismissed the nameless guide and led us on a hidden path toward the immense cliffs.

"Where are we going?" I whispered to Brian.

"I don't know," Brian said.

We scrambled through dense brush to reach the cliff walls. Johnson led us toward the right on a crooked path hidden by huge stones. He ducked into a stand of trees that blocked the view ahead and I couldn't see him anymore. The cliff swallowed him. I envisioned the worst. After all, we had put our trust in these people and we knew nothing about them. What if they were kidnapping us as some plot to discredit my father? What if they were really behind Brian's father's disappearance? My chest began to tighten. I glanced back at Brian who gave me a thumbs-up signal and gestured for me to continue. When I entered the trees, I saw a crevice that appeared too small for any human to squeeze through, especially one the size of Johnson.

"Come on." Johnson stuck his head out of the opening, making me jump with a slight scream. He chuckled. "I didn't mean to startle you. Come inside, it's bigger than it looks."

I turned sideways, my worst nightmares flashing into my brain. I have a terrible fear of being stuck in tiny spaces and not able to get out. Before I could panic, however, the entry widened into a tunnel lit by a series of flickering torches at random intervals. Johnson held two torches in his hands, one of which he handed to Brian, who followed me in.

"Follow me," Johnson said, and led the way into a damp, dark tunnel that extended into an unknown distance.

My toes hurt after several stumbles over protrusions. I hadn't walked that far for a long time, and my legs resented me. "Are you taking me to the center of the earth?" I asked.

My answer came just around the next bend. The tunnel widened out into a cavern that reflected the light of surrounding torches in a rainbow-colored cascade of hidden gems, and looming shadows cast by unusual rock formations. For a moment, I wished I could stop and paint the scene, but I knew I'd never capture the complex beauty. At the far side of the cavern, two carved wooden doors blocked the entrance into an unknown location beyond. Wooden doors in an underground cavern made no sense to me. I walked over to examine the carvings. When I touched the doors the wood gave off a sense of warmth. The central carving showed the symbol of the Freedom Readers. Other smaller images filled the area around the central symbol, including— to my surprise—images from the hidden language of women, actual written words, and a special rose.

Brian touched the rose. "My father carved this."

"Yes, he did," Johnson said. "He was a very talented man."

Johnson knocked an elaborate pattern on the door.

We waited a moment before the doors swung open. At first, I didn't notice who opened them, distracted by the sight of a bright and colorful room carved into the depths of the mountain. Comfortable looking chairs and couches surrounded small tables. The room was lit by a combination of flickering candles, firelight, and cozy electric lamps with stained-glass shades. Wooden bookshelves lined the stone walls, each filled with books and scrolls of all shapes and sizes. Soft carpets covered sections of polished hardwood floor. A large table in the center held a full setting for tea; china with a delicate pattern, a plate of fruit and cheese pastries alongside a bowl of strawberries and another bowl filled with cream.

"Welcome, friends." A dark-haired older woman stepped forward to greet us with a smile that made her eyes crinkle with laugh lines. She gave me the welcoming hug and two cheek kiss of the upper class. "Andra BetScrivener," she said, "it's been too long. Welcome to my humble hideaway."

For the first time ever, I lost my words. I recognized this woman. Madame Emily DuFarge was the widow of a former high-ranking minister.

"I'm sorry, Madame DuFarge," I found my voice and fell into an uncomfortable curtsy. I always hated the trappings of formality and fumbled through them. "I never expected to see you here. You can't possibly be a . . ." I couldn't finish the thought.

"What? A Freedom Reader? You have a lot to learn."

I glanced over at Brian who shrugged and then nodded in encouragement.

"Please sit down and have some tea." Emily turned to Brian. "It's a pleasure to meet you, Brian Woodson. We miss your father very much."

Brian blushed and bowed.

"Please don't be so formal." Madame DuFarge pulled Brian into a hug and a kiss which made him turn a darker shade of crimson. "Would you like tea as well or would you prefer cider like your father did?"

"Cider would be great," Brian said.

"Make yourself comfortable." Madame DuFarge gestured to one of the overstuffed love seats. Brian tried to look confident as he lowered himself in. I knew the truth signified by the tense twitch of his thumb; he felt as nervous and unsure as I did.

"Andra, please join me over here so we can talk." She seated herself at one of the chairs near the tea set and nodded to the one to her left.

"Johnson, are you having anything?"

"Already have it," Johnson said. He took a deep gulp out of a glass of ale and sat in a large chair in the corner. "Ah! Refreshing."

Madame DuFarge laughed.

"Is tea acceptable, Andra? Would you prefer something else?"

"Tea is fine, please, Madame DuFarge."

"Enough formality! You both must call me Emily. After all, we now belong to the same secret club."

"Okay . . . Emily." My mouth stumbled as it tried to form her name. The rules of formality, established by Sandovar and his government, were strict and unyielding. It was unacceptable to call someone from a higher class by their first name. He'd even brought in more formal sounding modes of address borrowed from times long past, when distinctions between social classes were well defined. You would never refer to a woman of Madame DuFarge. . . Emily's . . . stature as Mrs. DuFarge.

"I still don't understand how you can be a Freedom Reader." My voice sounded strangely insecure, even to my own ears.

Emily laughed as she got me set up with a cup of tea and some pastries. "Who better to help bring down a corrupt system than someone who saw that system from the inside out?" She filled a plate for herself. "What other women ever had the opportunity to learn what I've learned?"

"I guess that makes sense," I said, although my brain still couldn't catch up with the reality in front of me.

Emily patted my hand. "We have so much to discuss. I haven't seen you since you were a little girl, just before my husband's death."

"I'm sorry. I don't remember meeting you."

"Not surprising. It was at a garden party and you were much more interested in climbing trees than talking to a distant relative."

Brian laughed at this, "That's Andra; always a tomboy."

I shot him a look to silence him. "Relative? I'm related to you?'

"Yes, of course. Almost everybody who has any connection with the government of New North is related in one way or another, even those who are considered lesser functionaries like your father." I winced at the label. The fact that the society of New North divided itself based on family connections and position had always disturbed me. My parents had never adhered to that. Officially, Mother had higher status in society, but they had truly married for love. "Your mother and I were distant cousins," Emily continued, "although when we were younger some people said we looked like sisters."

I peered at Emily's face searching for a connection with Mother. To my horror, I couldn't bring a clear image of Mother into focus in my memory's eye. How could her image fade when I loved her so much? I removed a locket that I always wore and opened it in order to compare the living face with the delicate painting of my mother.

"I think you have the same eyes," I said.

"May I see that?"

I tightened my grip. I rarely removed the locket from my neck, let alone allowed anyone to touch it.

"I'll give it right back," Emily said.

I relented under the intensity of eyes that resembled my mother's.

I wiped away a few tears that snuck down my cheeks in the hopes of stopping the deluge that might follow. Emily's eyes filled as well, which eased my embarrassment. "She was such a lovely, talented woman," Emily said. "She would have helped us achieve our goals so much faster. Her death was a blow to the family and the cause."

Emily handed the locket back to me, and then wiped her eyes with a lacy handkerchief.

"What do you mean . . . the cause?" I asked.

"I thought you would have figured it out by now. Your mother was a Freedom Reader."

"That can't be true." I would have known, wouldn't I?

"The Scrivener worked with us as well—"

"He . . . what?"

"He was very active. He still is a believer in the cause but your mother's death dealt a crushing blow. He decided he couldn't risk your life as well and withdrew."

"My father . . . my mother's death?! I don't understand."

"What do you remember about your mother's death?" Emily asked.

"I . . . I hate to think about that day," I said. I had never shared my memories of it with anyone, not even Brian. "We were at some event at the Ministry. I often went along, even when I was very young, because the Ministry Officials liked my drawings. I sat and sketched in the corner, and handed the sketches out as gifts."

"I remember. I have one of your drawings right here." Emily took a framed picture off of one of the bookshelves and handed it to me. The sketch portrayed a youthful Emily and her husband, done in a childish hand and signed with my mark.

"I really met you."

"Of course. Why would I lie about that? Please continue your story."

"Back then I didn't mind going to the parties because I hated being separated from my parents. Now I hate it, but I have no choice. I have to support Dad. That day I wanted to go. I was happy. I loved watching my mother and the other women dressed in finery. I never wanted to be away from her. She was so vibrant and beautiful. I listened to her laugh, talk, and charm everyone around her . . . but then . . ." I found it difficult to continue around the lump surrounding my heart and filling my chest.

"Then what?" Brian moved to the chair next to me. He put a hand on my shoulder which gave me the strength to breathe.

"The discussion turned heated. Mother was never silent about her belief that women are as capable as men."

"Sounds familiar," Brian said. I made a face but appreciated the humor, it made telling the story easier.

"Please continue," Emily said.

"Mother was talking to several government officials and their wives. I can't remember who, except that Supreme Prime Minister Sandovar wandered over. I was afraid of him. He was big and powerful and . . . terrifying."

"He manages to make us believe that, at least. He's really a little man with lifts in his shoes," Emily said.

Brian and Johnson laughed, although I didn't think it was that funny. The Supreme Prime Minister still inspired terror in me whenever I saw him.

"Sorry, Andra," Emily said. "Please continue."

"One of the ministers made a comment about how much better off women are since they had been protected by the laws against reading and writing. 'I disagree,' Mother said. 'We've been cut off from so much.' 'For your own good,' the Supreme Prime Minister said. 'You know how harmful reading is to women's brains.'"

I took a few sips of tea before I could continue.

"Mother grew before my eyes. Her face was strong, her eyes flashed. She looked like a goddess. Dad put his hand on her arm in a gesture I'd seen before. He's used it on me since. This time his silent warning went unheeded. Nothing could stop Mother when she wanted to speak her mind. 'Supreme Prime Minister,' she said, 'I'd like to remind you that I learned to read long before these laws came into being. My brain has not been harmed in any way.'"

"Sandovar's face became hard; his silver-gray eyes glinted in anger. I was terrified of those eyes; they make him look like some kind of rabid animal." I shuddered as a cold chill moved through my body. I wrapped my arms around myself, but it didn't seem to help. Emily poured me more tea and I grasped the cup, seeking warmth. Everyone waited in silence until I found the strength to say more. "His voice sounded menacing when he answered my mother. 'Of course your brain hasn't been harmed, because you've been obedient to the law and stopped reading, haven't you?'

"The tension lasted forever as neither one backed down. Finally, someone broke in. 'What are we talking about? This is a celebration. Madame BetScrivener, allow me to get you some punch.' The group broke up. Supreme Prime Minister Sandovar wandered away, but I saw his face and it was dark and craggy with unhappiness. He glanced over in my direction and his eyes were cold. I wanted to find a place to hide. I gathered my things together as if I hadn't heard the conversation."

I stopped talking and took a sip of tea, hoping I could end the story there. I didn't want to tell the rest. I focused on my cup and avoided looking at anyone. The silence grew.

"What happened next?" Emily asked.

I hesitated. Brian gave my shoulder a squeeze of encouragement.

"A short time later Mother came over to Dad and me." My voice sounded stilted as I avoided the emotions welling up inside of me. "'I have a headache,' she said. 'I think it's time to take our leave.' Dad agreed and went to get our coats. He was gone only a moment when Mother collapsed on the floor. People rushed over. Dad ran back, whisked her up and took her to another room, calling for a doctor. Someone held me back. I tried to pull away. I wanted to stay with her but they stopped me." At that point I could no longer hold back the tears.

"I'm so sorry," Emily said. She handed me a monogrammed handkerchief. "If you can't finish—"

"No. I'll tell you. I've just never told this story before." I took a deep breath and several sips of the spicy tea before I could continue. "I'm not sure how much time passed before Dad came out of the room, his face pale and tears sliding down his cheeks. He came and hugged me without saying a word. The doctor followed him out, 'Madame BetScrivener has passed,' the doctor said. 'Without an autopsy I can't be sure but in all appearances she had a brain aneurism brought on, of course, by her inappropriate access to education and materials forbidden by our esteemed leader and the Lord.' I screamed and collapsed into Dad's arms. I don't know what happened next." I wiped more tears into the elegant cloth.

"Was your father ever given the results of the autopsy?" Emily asked.

"Yes. Dad said that the findings agreed with the doctor's initial assessment. I'm not sure he ever believed that fully, but he has never discussed it with me."

"I'm sorry to make you relive that, Andra," Emily said. "I think I need to show you something." She glanced over at Johnson who gave a subtle nod. She walked to a wall and moved a picture aside to reveal a small vault. She opened it, and returned with several documents that she placed on the table in front of me.

"You can read, Andra, can't you?"

"I'm my parents' daughter."

"Of course," Emily's smile reached her eyes. "It's time you read this."

SIX

I opened the folder to find a document marked with the official seal of Supreme Prime Minister Sandovar and dated two months after Mother's death. I read out loud so Brian could hear:

"Report on the Ramifications of the Death of Marion BetScrivener and the Freedom Readers

From: The Committee over the Control of Women

To: Supreme Prime Minister Sandovar

On this, the 20th anniversary of your illustrious reign over New North, we have uncovered a threat to the rulings laid out for us all by our Lord and handed down to us through your divine wisdom. As you are aware, the death of Marion BetScrivener (at a celebratory dinner in your honor) has led to questions and whispers throughout the community, fed by the rumor-mongering rebel group known as the Freedom Readers, who have claimed her death was not from natural causes.

To combat the rumors, we have circulated the following report to be communicated throughout the Territories of New North by all town leaders, scriveners and town criers as a reminder to citizens of the science and religion behind the laws:

> *Given the smaller size and structure of women's brains, as well as the electrical activity marked when certain forms of information enter the brain, we wish to remind citizens that the input of knowledge through the process of reading causes a massive surge of*

electricity in the brains of women that we fear has an adverse effect on their ability to function normally in the world. Continuous exposure can lead to death. This effect is less noticeable when women are engaged in creating art, playing music, nurturing children and other feminine arts. For the sake of our future, women must be protected from absorbing dangerous information through reading, writing, and mathematics. The Lord did not intend women to read, write, or do anything beyond basic addition and subtraction."

"Why am I reading this?" I asked. "I've heard all this before."

"Keep reading, Andra." Emily said. "It's important." I turned back to the document:

"In addition, we have taken the following measures to deflect the rumors and strengthen our cause:

• The family of Marion BetScrivener has been informed that her death was indeed caused by a brain aneurism and given an incomplete version of the autopsy report.

• We have strengthened the law requiring all women to marry by age eighteen or be placed in the Women's Training Program. Through this we hope to be able to gain early control of any woman who shows signs of superior mental ability.

• We have expanded our hunt for those scientists intent on refuting our findings with their own misguided opinions regarding women's ability to access a higher percentage of their brain functions. We are concerned that some of them have infiltrated from Outside and are feeding this false information to members of the rebel group. Any person disseminating this information will be immediately brought in for questioning, retraining and imprisonment or execution if they are not citizens of New North."

Rage bubbled up inside of me. I threw the document down. "Why haven't you shared this with everyone? How did you get this?"

"Let's just say a friend in the Ministry got us a copy," Emily said. "Someone whose identity we need to protect. We haven't shared this for many reasons. Soon after this was written, many of our allies from Outside the walls disappeared, and several of our own supporters were rehabilitated. We had to move with caution. We also have never been able to get a copy of your mother's complete autopsy, which we assume holds some valuable information. Besides, do you think that anyone would believe us even if we shared this?"

She paused to look at me and Brian. I knew she was right. We both shook our heads.

"So you see the problem," Emily said. "Too many people have been drawn into the belief in the Eye of the Lord and in Sandovar's claim as the Lord's representative. They've accepted that the restrictions on women are for our own good. Younger women can't read at all, so we wouldn't even be able to prove that these words are on this page. This document isn't enough. We need further proof that women have the ability to access and use a greater portion of their brains."

I caught Brian's eye. He shrugged.

"Brian told me that you have information to share with us." Johnson's deep voice startled me as I had nearly forgotten he was there. "Is it related to this?"

"I . . . well, I . . ." I couldn't find words with both Johnson and Emily staring at me.

"Before we tell you," Brian said. "You have to promise you'll protect Andra."

"Woodson, I warned you there's no turning back." Johnson's voice resonated with danger.

Brian rose and turned to Johnson. "I'm in. I'm not turning back. Andra and her father still need protection, especially after reading this." He grabbed the official document and reread some of it with disgust.

"We'll protect Andra and the Scrivener as much as we're able." Emily's soothing voice broke the tension between the men. "However, you must realize that none of us are safe. At any point, someone in our group could be uncovered. Too often we find that husbands have been spying on their wives, and people we trust have turned traitor. It makes it difficult to know who to protect."

"Husbands turn on wives? What do you mean?" I asked.

"In recent years," Emily said, "more and more of the marriages forced on our young women have been for the cause of the government. The government hand-picks men to keep an eye on women who they suspect might be a threat to their power. The men, then, either control their women completely or turn them in for retraining."

A ridiculous realization caused me to burst out in laughter releasing built up pressure after the tense and emotional discussion. My laughter built until I was nearly hysterical. The other three in the room watched me as if I had lost my mind, although I could see Brian holding in his own laughter even though he had no idea what had set me off.

"Sorry," I said as I wiped joyous tears away, "that explains Minister Rogerson's plan,"

"What plan?" Brian asked. "You didn't tell me about any plan."

I explained about Rogerson's interest in throwing Peter and me together. "Although Peter seems very different from his father, so maybe I'm wrong."

"You can't marry Peter Rogerson!" Brian said.

"Maybe not," Emily said. "But . . . maybe she should cultivate the relationship."

"You can't ask her to do that," Brian said.

"That should be Andra's decision," Emily said. "Shouldn't it?"

Brian's hand began to twitch but he remained silent.

"Why would you want me to do that?" I asked.

"I think you're right. They want to keep close tabs on you and are trying to match you with a person who will do that for them."

"Peter Rogerson . . ." Brian's face reflected the disgust in his voice.

Emily smiled. "It's actually a high compliment. Someone's worried that you might take after your mother, and perhaps with reason. By getting closer to Peter, you might learn something useful."

"Can I think about it?" I asked. "I'm not sure I could use anyone that way." Even though my parents seemed to have been involved in this rebel group, I wasn't sure I wanted to take the leap into spying for them.

"We often have to make choices that make us uncomfortable, Andra," Emily said. "However, we'll discuss this more later. For now, I'd like to hear about the information you brought us. Or was that it?"

I glanced over at Brian. He nodded.

"You already know I can read. What you don't know is that nobody ever taught me to read. I simply woke up one day able to make sense of written words."

"How old were you when you started reading?" Johnson asked.

"About four years old."

"Interesting," Emily said. "However, I'm not sure it's important or helpful, given your close relationship to the Head Scrivener."

"It didn't seem important, until I made another discovery." I told them about my birthday party, as well as my experiments over the past week. Emily's and Johnson's eyes glowed with excitement.

"I asked you not to do anything until I got back to you," Brian's hand twitched even more.

"You knew I wouldn't listen," I said. "Besides, you were taking too long."

"Work that out later," Emily said. "How far does this skill go?"

"I'm not sure . . . I know that I get sick if I try certain things. I can't create something out of nothing. It doesn't happen with everything I write, either. Sometimes it takes time, and won't happen for hours. I can't seem to control it . . . yet. It helps if I'm able to create a clear picture of what I want to happen with lots of specific details. If I'm able to draw the scene, really envision it, then somehow I manifest it into reality."

"Do you have to draw a scene as well as write the words?" Johnson asked.

"I don't think so; I just have to have a clear image in my mind."

Emily jumped up and went over to a roll-top desk against one of the cavern walls. She dug into a drawer and came back with some blank sheets of paper and a fountain pen.

"Show us," She said.

I took the materials, my mind blank. "I don't know what to write."

"Give us a small sample—something that we can see soon."

"I'll try. It may take a few minutes."

"Brian," Emily said. "Why don't we show you how we access my house from here so Andra has some quiet?"

"I don't want to leave Andra alone. I'm here to protect her."

He should have known that would annoy me. "Brian, I'm fine. I don't need your protection and I never have. Besides, what could happen to me here? Go."

"How much time do you need?" Emily asked.

"At least a half an hour, I think."

The three left through a door toward the back of the room that I hadn't noticed earlier. As soon as they left, I tried to write, but soon scratched out my words. I had no idea what to say. How could I prove to them this power worked? I began to wander around the room, looking at the books and scrolls that filled the shelves. I traced my finger along the delicate wood carvings found on every surface—elegant work created by a man I had loved almost as much as my own father. A man, who, it turns out, held many secrets along with my parents. Aha! I knew exactly what to do. I would give a gift to Brian from his father. I ran over to the desk and wrote.

A little over thirty minutes had passed when I heard the others return. I had long since finished writing, and was absorbed in reading a book called *The Training of Women* that I had found tucked away in the bookshelves. Written by Sandovar himself; it was filled with his egotistical reflections on his relationship with the Lord, and his beliefs in the inferiority of women. I had a difficult time keeping my anger from exploding out of me—I had the sudden urge to write a painful accident that would hurt the Supreme Prime Minister. I tried to control the anger with a few deep breaths before I turned to the trio as they entered the room. The sight of the large, goofy smile on Brian's face made me calm down more than any breathing exercises. He carried something covered in a soft blue cloth.

"Andra, you have to see what I found."

He sounded like a little boy who had discovered pirate's treasure. The youthful joy in his voice made me smile, along with my knowledge of the role I played in putting it there. "Show me."

Brian placed the wrapped object on the large table. He opened the soft coverings to reveal a box made out of beautiful purple wood. Carved into the top was an image of a weeping willow that looked like a younger version of my favorite tree. A small rose garnished the corner.

"Dad made this. It's your tree. Isn't it beautiful? Are you sure I can keep this?" He offered the box back to Emily. The wistful look in Brian's eyes made me send a silent wish that she would be kind.

"It belongs with you and your mother." Emily said. "We have many things here to remind us of your father." She turned to me. "Did you finish?"

I walked over to retrieve the paper, trying to hide my glee. "Yes, and it's already happened."

"What do you mean?" Emily grabbed the writing. She scanned it and started laughing enough for tears to form.

"What's so funny?" Johnson said. "Let me see."

"I'll read it," Emily said. "As Emily and Johnson took Brian on a tour, he asked question after question in an endless stream. He was only silenced when he came upon a special object carved by his father. 'This is beautiful,' he said. 'It's yours,' Emily said. 'You should have something of your father's that shows his commitment to the cause.' She wandered to a cupboard and grabbed a soft cloth. 'Wrap it in this for your journey home.'"

"That's exactly what happened," Johnson said.

Brian didn't say anything. He smiled and sent me a look of gratitude that brought a tear to my eye. I blinked it away before anyone noticed.

"Okay," Emily said. "I'm not sure how I feel about being manipulated like that—"

"I'm sorry," I said. I hadn't thought about the fact that what I write might affect people's freedom to choose behaviors. I would need to be much more cautious in the future, and think all the ramifications through before I wrote.

"It's okay. I asked for proof."

Brian wrapped the box again. "I'll give this back."

"Of course not," Emily said. "I'm thrilled to see the truth in Andra's words, and you deserve a reward for bringing her to us. Keep the box." She turned and gestured me toward a comfortable chair.

"Andra, how far reaching are the effects of your writing?" Johnson asked.

"I don't know. I've had no way to test that. I know that if I write something too big, it can make me weak. I . . . I passed out once."

"You what?!" Brian moved over and grabbed my shoulders. "You have to be more careful . . ."

"I know." Brian's intense gaze felt uncomfortable so I pulled away and turned toward Emily.

"Do you think . . . Are you willing to try something a little bit bigger?" Emily asked.

"As long as it's not going to hurt anyone, or make someone do something they wouldn't normally do."

"I promise you won't hurt anyone. I wouldn't ask that of you."

Emily's eyes reminded me so much of Mother. Their kindness wiped away my doubt. "Okay, what do you want me to write?"

"Did you ever meet Professor Albert?"

"Wasn't he the man who used to serve as head Doctor until some kind of scandal forced him out?" I asked.

"That's him. He now lives in the Pauper's Village and does what he can to make their lives better. In reality, someone high up in the Ministry arranged the scandal that brought him down because he was beginning to express his concerns about their so-called science. They silenced him as effectively as they could without throwing him in prison, because he had too much support from the common people. The government feared his imprisonment, death, or even disappearance would cause repercussions."

"I remember him. He was so kind to me when Mother. . . What does this have to do with my writing?"

"Professor Albert sometimes helps the Freedom Readers," Johnson said.

"I'd like to get Professor Albert's input on your ability," Emily said. "Do you think you could write a reason for him to come to us?"

"I . . . I can try. Does he ever come here on his own?"

"Yes, so you wouldn't be forcing him. I also promise to feed him when he gets here, which will make it worth his trip. Will that make it easier for you?"

"I guess so," I said, although the fear of manipulating people worried me. "I'll try. Remember, this may not have instantaneous results."

"I'm sure we still have many things to discuss while we wait," Emily said.

SEVEN

Professor Albert walked into the one-room hut and gagged on the smell of mold and sickness. He peered through the darkness, broken only by the sun sneaking through rips in tattered window hangings, until he could see the young woman kneeling beside the bed. Her head rested against the shoulder of an old woman whose eyes looked into oblivion—frozen in death.

"Lauren, I'm here to help you put your grandmother to rest."

"No!" Lauren cried. "She's all I have left."

"She's gone. It's time to let go."

"Go away," Lauren said.

Poor thing, I don't know how she'll survive. The Professor's thoughts always turned to worry in situations like this.

"Don't call me poor thing. I've survived more than this."

Did I say that out loud? Professor Albert watched Lauren caress her grandmother's face. He shook away his confusion and placed a hand on the disheveled young woman's shoulder. She flinched from his touch. "Let me help you, Lauren. You can't leave her body here. It's unhealthy. You know the villagers will be here soon to burn this place, and if we don't remove her she'll go up with the hut. She deserves to be treated with respect."

Lauren glanced up at the doctor, her bright green eyes filled with fear. "I don't know what to do."

"I'll help you," the Professor said. "Why don't you get some rest while I take care of your Grandmother?"

"Treat her well," Lauren said.

"I will, I promise," he said. *Then I'll help you,* he thought.

"There's nothing you can do to help me."

Surprised again, Professor Albert watched as the broken woman lowered herself into a fetal position on a pile of rags in the corner. She didn't close her eyes. Her feral stare bore into his back as he moved through the steps to prepare the old woman's body for burial. He infused every move with as much love and reverence as possible to avoid bringing a look of anger to Lauren's disturbing eyes. Finally, he wrapped the body in a ratty blanket and picked it up. To his surprise, he barely noted the weight of this revered older woman—it was like carrying a pillow full of feathers. The paleness of her skin glowed in contrast to the darkness of his. "Come," he said, "Let's give your grandmother a place to rest."

He and Lauren left the hovel. The Professor carried the frail remains to a pauper's grave in the cemetery at the edge of the village. The hole had already been dug by other members of the village, some who gathered to mourn the passing of the much beloved woman even though they feared both the disease that killed her and her peculiar granddaughter. They wouldn't touch the body themselves, but trusted the doctor to bring her for burial.

After the simple ceremony, the other villagers departed to dispose of the hut. Lauren remained alone by the grave, looking lost. The Professor watched her. She turned to him wrapping her arms around herself and staring at the ground.

"Now what?" she asked.

"That's up to you," he said. *I'd like to help you,* he thought.

"You can't help me. Go away."

"How do you do that?" he asked. "You keep responding to my thoughts."

Lauren glanced at him with fear in her eyes. "It . . . it's just . . . something I know how to do." Her voice shook as she spoke and the Professor noticed her whole body trembling.

"When did you last eat, Lauren?"

"I can't remember."

"Come with me. I'll get you some food and we can talk."

He brought her to his own home which reflected the poverty of the village but contained three rooms and remained clean. He offered her some bread and soup that he had made himself. She hesitated before taking anything, and then began to eat with the ravenous hunger of someone who had sacrificed all her food to keep her grandmother alive.

"Tell me about this thing you can do," Professor Albert said.

"I'm not allowed to tell. I'm not allowed to do it. They'll punish me."

"Who will punish you?"

"Them. The Trainers. You know they will."

"You mean the people from the Women's Training Program?"

Lauren didn't answer. Her eyes reflected wariness.

"You left that program about six months ago, didn't you?"

"They had no more need of me. They sent me away to die."

"That's not how the program is supposed to work." The Professor rubbed his temples to prevent the headache he knew would come. Whenever he thought about the reality of the Women's Training Programs, his head began to throb.

"That's how it works for women who they can't control," Lauren said. "They use us, destroy us and leave us to die."

"What do you mean?"

"You know. You were one of them."

She stopped talking, and nothing he did could entice her to speak.

"You know you won't be able to return to your grandmother's hut," the Professor said. "By now the villagers have destroyed it."

Lauren jumped up and headed to the door. She stopped before she opened it. She turned back to him, hesitant and pleading.

"You may stay here for as long as you like," he said. "I want to help you."

She nodded and returned to her food.

The Professor watched her for a while and then went to get the extra room ready for her. When she finished eating, he led her in. "Get some rest," he said. "We'll talk later."

He walked out of the room. He heard her bolt the door behind him.

Several days passed in near silence. Lauren wouldn't say anything beyond "Please," "Thank you" and a few other words. Whenever he broached or even thought of the subject of the "thing she could do" or the Women's Training Program she walked out of the room, either to lock herself in her bedroom or leave the house for some imagined errand.

He had run out of ideas. He was about to give up and allow Lauren to continue living in silence, when he got the sudden urge to make one last effort. *I need help*, he thought, attempting to make his thoughts as clear as possible in the hopes Lauren would hear. *THEY haven't contacted me in a while, I think now is the time for me to make a little visit.*

He began gathering some supplies for the journey, which would take several hours of walking. Gone were the days of public transportation, and only people who could afford them owned animals that could pull vehicles. Sandovar and his government believed that limiting people's ability to move around created a safer, more controllable society. Whenever Professor Albertson had to do something beyond the Pauper's Village he either had to hire someone to drive him in a cart, or rely on his own two feet. The place he intended to go wouldn't welcome outside eyes, so feet it would be.

Lauren watched his every move.

"Where are you going?" she asked. He hadn't heard her voice in so long that it startled him.

"I need some advice," he said. "I'm going to see some friends. You're welcome to come."

She didn't say anything.

Professor Albert finished gathering his supplies and opened the door. "I'll be back late, or perhaps tomorrow." He turned and walked away, not bothering to close the door.

After a few moments he heard the door close and Lauren's footsteps behind him. The professor smiled and waited for her to catch up.

"These friends are very private," he said. "I think they can help you."

"I know who they are. Lead on," she said. So he did.

* * *

Several hours passed as we waited to see if my writing would bring Professor Albert. During that time, we began to form some plans. We decided we needed to reach out to other women and girls to spread the word about the possibilities hidden in women's brains.

"How do we do that?" Johnson asked. "We can't be seen talking to large groups of women."

I hesitated to speak because I didn't know if Johnson knew about the secret women's language, but I took the chance because it was the perfect solution. I moved closer to Emily in case it should remain secret. "Why don't we use the women's language?" I asked.

Brian, who followed me around the room as if he could somehow protect me from attack, heard my question.

"You mean use the messages hidden in drawings?" he asked.

"How do you know about that?" Emily gave Brian a sharp look. "That's a secret we've kept from almost all our male members, except for a trusted few."

"Why don't I know about it?" Johnson asked.

"Now isn't the time, Johnson. I'll discuss it with you later."

"We certainly will discuss this," Johnson's face hardened.

I wanted to alleviate the tension. "It's my fault that Brian knows," I said. "Dad has always known, so I thought it was okay for Brian to know. He's my best friend and practically a brother. My parents never kept secrets from each other. It seems they only kept secrets from me."

"They did that to protect you," said Emily. "So your father can read the language?"

"No. Well a few symbols . . . not many."

Emily turned her glare back to Brian. "And you? Can you read the messages?"

"No. I've learned how to recognize the artist symbol and a few words . . . nothing important."

"Well, keep it that way." She turned back to Andra. "I understand your error. I should have known your mother had shared the language with your father. They shared everything. Your mother was one of the developers of our secret code. She was a brilliant artist and found ways to express meaning that surpassed all others."

"She helped create the language?!" My eyes started tearing for the millionth time that day. There was so much I didn't know about my mother—more than I ever expected. It made my loss seem even greater. But at the same time, I wondered if she would ever have shared these secrets with me. I was thirteen when she died. Thirteen was old enough to learn that my parents were fighting for justice, wasn't it? I tried to get control over my emotions. I didn't want Emily to think I would be a blubbering, useless mess. "I guess Mother taught me everything she could before . . . I'm not as talented as she is."

"Don't be silly, Andra," Brian said. "Your work equals or surpasses your mother's. I know I can't read it all, but I'm always amazed by your images."

"Andra," Emily gave me another kind look. "I think it's an excellent idea to reach out through the secret language. Are you willing to create drawings that will spread the word? It will be a lot of work and must be done with caution. I would help but I never mastered the art, and these will have to be precise."

"I want to help in any way I can."

"Even to the extent of getting closer to Peter Rogerson?" Brian asked.

Brian's teasing was beginning to annoy me. "I'm . . . I don't know. Peter seems decent," I said.

"Ha!" Brian said.

Emily intervened. "Let's see what happens and focus on what messages we want to send. They can't be too long, and they have to make women take notice . . . "

Our planning continued until a loud rumble from Brian's stomach reminded everyone of the time. "Excuse me," Brian made a face to hide his embarrassment.

Johnson laughed and slapped his hand on Brian's shoulder. "You're much like your father, Woodson. He too was controlled by his stomach."

"My apologies," Emily said. "I should have known tea and cake wouldn't sustain you. I'm sure we have something to fill more robust appetites while we wait. Are you hungry, Andra?"

I was starving, but I didn't want Emily to know that either. She sat in her chair with such an air of delicacy and refinement that I was sure her appetite was the same. I didn't want her to realize I could compete with Brian when it came to eating, and that I had learned my table manners from the boy next door. "I wouldn't mind a little something, if it isn't too much trouble," I said.

Brian started laughing and I kicked him under the table.

Emily went over to a contraption in the wall which must have linked to the kitchen above, and ordered a full meal to be sent down as soon as possible.

Actually, I didn't even think about that assignment. I wanted to do the right thing to help you. I hadn't decided anything about Peter. I'm not all that comfortable with the idea of being a spy and using Peter for information."

"I don't understand," Brian said. The confused look on his face was priceless. "What's going on?"

Dad and I burst into a fresh wave of laughter. Dad clutched his stomach as I tried to stop tears from ruining my makeup. It made me happy to laugh with him; he didn't do it often enough. Somehow the laughter made me realize everything would be all right.

When I could catch my breath, I finally answered Brian. "I'm 'dressed as a princess' as you so kindly pointed out because I'm about to go out to dinner with the Rogersons at my father's insistence."

"You're . . . you mean; you agreed to go out on a date? With Peter?!"

"She didn't have much choice in the matter, Brian," Dad said. "I insisted that she go. Now, it seems that the Readers want her to go as well, don't they?"

"Yes . . . but . . . but . . ."

"Brian, we'll talk about this more tomorrow." Dad ushered the befuddled young man toward the door. "The Rogersons will be here any moment, and it will only make them more suspicious about your relationship with Andra if they find you here."

Before Brian could say anything, my father closed the door on his face.

"Are you okay with this?" I asked.

"It is what it is," he said. "Let's just hope you don't have to marry him. I don't think I could stand spending any more time with Luke Rogerson than I already do."

With that we heard the approach of the carriage, and he opened the door in welcome.

* * *

A chestnut stallion and a dapple gray mare pulled the old-fashioned carriage that gleamed with fresh mahogany paint. Vehicles of any sort were reserved for only the wealthiest elite in New North. On rare occasions someone from the highest echelons of the government drove by in electric cars, avoiding potholes in streets that no longer get repaired on a regular basis. Those who could afford them owned carriages that could be pulled by horses; and some tradesmen owned carts pulled by various animals. When Sandovar decided to cut us off from the rest of the outside world, he pretty much forced New North to look back into history to solve problems that had been solved through the technology that he controlled. I had never even been in a horse drawn carriage, so when I saw the gorgeous animals, my excitement competed with the nerves that had been floating around my stomach.

"May I pet the horses, Minister Rogerson?" I asked.

"Of course," he said. "Leave it to the Scrivener's daughter not to be fearful of beasts that terrify other women. I told you she had spunk, Peter." He clapped his hand on Peter's shoulder.

Peter shrugged his father's hand away and went to hold the head of the chestnut. "This one is my favorite," he said in a quiet voice. "His name is Star. Be sure to approach him from the side."

I reached out to touch the magnificent animal's shoulder before I moved closer to his head. I love animals, and whenever I can I talk to them. I know they understand deep down inside. "Thank you for pulling me today," I whispered in the horse's ear, trying to keep my voice low enough not to be heard by Peter. "I hope we don't work you too hard." I would have continued communing with the animals, but sensed Peter's closeness with discomfort and noticed the amused smile on his father's face.

"Shall we go," the Minister said. "My wife is waiting in the carriage." He turned to my father who stood in the door watching the proceedings. "We'll be sure to have her home early, Scrivener. Unless, of course, I can't pull the two lovebirds apart; they may want to elope this evening." He laughed at his own joke while Peter turned vermilion and my stomach churned even more.

"I trust that you wouldn't deny me the right to give my daughter away in marriage to a man my daughter and I select, Minister." The coldness in Dad's voice both surprised and pleased me. He had been standing up for me a lot more lately, and I have to admit I loved it.

"I'm sure you realize that your daughter would do well to marry my son." The Minister's voice shook with contained anger.

"Father—" Peter sounded hesitant. I wasn't sure he would be able to prevent any hostilities, so I decided to step in.

"Dad, don't worry," I said. "I promised to bring you home dessert, didn't I?" I turned to Minister Rogerson and fluttered my eyes, while I bit the inside of my cheek to keep the nausea down. I despise flirting, but I couldn't think of another course of action. "I bet you didn't realize how much of a sweet tooth my father has," I said. "He's grumpy without something decadent and he hasn't had anything all day."

My father's laughter broke the tension.

Minister Rogerson followed with his own guffaw. "Peter, help your lovely date into the carriage," he said. He climbed aboard.

"I'm sorry about my father, Sir," Peter said to Dad. "This isn't what I wanted." He held his hand out to help me into the carriage. Aware of my promise to be on good behavior, I took it despite my desire to prove that a woman can manage without assistance.

"Andra," Madame Rogerson's high-pitched voice greeted me. "I'm so glad you agreed to join us for dinner. Come and sit next to me so we can get to know each other better. The men can face backwards. I hate riding backwards, it makes me nauseous."

So began a ride that I would have enjoyed more under different circumstances. We rode along streets built long ago to support other more complicated vehicles, so as long as the driver avoided potholes and cracks the ride was relatively smooth. I enjoyed the sound of the horse's hooves clopping over the pavement and wished I could simply relax into the sway of the carriage and watch the city pass in this unfamiliar way. However, Madame Rogerson insisted on chattering about current fashions, gossip, and the most recent parties, while Minister Rogerson inserted comments about Peter's value. Meanwhile, Peter avoided conversing with everyone by watching the scenery out the window with a stony expression on his face.

Finally, we reached the Wall. I had only visited the Wall once before. I had never been to the restaurant built on top, with a view that overlooked the Capital City of New North and then out into the neighboring nation that was forbidden to most. This was one of the few places in the entire country of New North that had a tram which would carry people from the base of the wall to the top where the restaurant gleamed like a magical castle. The view was stunning as we watched the sun set. As twilight deepened, I noticed a marvelous glow in the distance, clustered in one area of the horizon.

"What's that?" I asked.

"It's a city where they still use power into the night," Minister Rogerson said. "Wastefulness and sin! The wall keeps us safe from all that, but sometimes it is good to remember the dangers of what is out there"

Peter said nothing, but he had a look of annoyance on his face that surprised me. I wondered if he agreed with his father's interpretation of what was on the other side of the Wall.

"Now, I have arranged a surprise . . ." Minister Rogerson said as he led us into the restaurant.

"What did you do, Father?" Peter asked; the first words out of his mouth since we'd left my house.

"Ah! Minister Rogerson." The owner of the restaurant, dressed in a sharp tuxedo, welcomed us. "We've arranged things just as you asked." He led us to a cozy booth made for two, with a view of the Outside world beyond New North. The table held candles and a bouquet of fresh flowers.

"We can't all fit here," I said in confusion.

"I know you two don't really want to spend the evening with us old folks," the Minister said, "so we'll chaperone from a table across the room, where we can see you, of course. Don't do anything I wouldn't do, son." He laughed as he and his wife followed the owner to another elegantly decorated, but much less romantic table within sight of our more private booth.

Peter flushed as he tried to take over hosting duties. "Please have a seat, Andra."

I tried to avoid awkwardness as I slid into the booth. I didn't know where to look, or what to do with my hands. I focused on the view; the glow of the mysterious city in the distance fascinated me. The sky began to fill with bright stars. I wasn't often out at night so took a moment to appreciate the beauty. Neither of us said anything.

The interruption of a waiter bringing us sparkling water gave me something to do. I took a sip and watched the bubbles. I expected him to hand us a menu with hand-drawn images of the food available—images meant to enable women to pick since they couldn't read—but instead he brought an unfamiliar-looking appetizer. I stared at the dish of unrecognizable food, in some kind of rich, creamy sauce. "Don't we get to select our own food?" I asked.

"Father usually picks a set meal for the family when he takes us out," Peter said. "I'm sure I could ask for something else if you're unhappy."

"No, that's okay. I've just never had this before. We don't eat out much."

"Look, Andra . . . I'm really sorry about this." Peter gestured to the booth and indicated his parents who weren't hiding their fascination with watching us from across the room. "This wasn't my idea."

"Oh well, that's flattering. I thought you were interested in getting to know me better."

"No . . . I mean . . ." Peter blushed again. "I do want to get to know you, but I didn't mean for it to turn into this big romantic date thing. And marriage . . ."

I admit his blush amused me; his discomfort made me more comfortable. I also intended to be quite clear about where this might head, even if it meant taking a risk. "Look Peter, I know by law I'm supposed to get married this year, but. . . . I don't want to get married at all, and I'm definitely not ready to jump from a dinner date to an engagement, especially with someone I barely know."

"I know. I was going to say I'm not trying to marry you." He began playing with a piece of bread.

"So then why are we here?"

"Do you want the truth?"

"Of course."

"Okay. The truth is that I was trying to get my father off my back. I'm almost 25 and haven't expressed any desire to marry, which drives him crazy. He's been pressuring me to name a woman and parading eligible candidates in front of me since I turned 21. He truly believes that it's my duty to God and to the government to marry as soon as possible and produce lots of boy children."

"So, if he's been parading candidates in front of you, why am I here?" I asked.

"Well . . ." Peter began to tug at his shirt collar. I found his discomfort cute, but quickly pushed that thought aside. I didn't want to think about him in that way.

"Tell me."

"About two years ago, after a series of forced dates, I decided to try something to get him off my back once and for all. I told him I'd had a religious vision . . ."

Just then the waiter brought over the next course; a delicious-smelling butternut squash soup. Peter waited until the waiter departed and we both tasted the rich broth.

"What do you mean religious vision?" I asked. This sounded both important and interesting. I could never understand those people, like the Rogerson family, who could fall so easily into faith and believe in things like religious visions. I hoped to gain a little insight.

"You have to understand something about my father. He's a good man; a religious man. He trusts in the Lord to protect his family, and he believes in following signs. He loves us dearly, and tries to guide us into following his beliefs. He wouldn't work so hard to make sure these laws are followed if he didn't believe that it was the correct thing in the name of the Lord. He also believes that the scientific evidence behind the control of women supports the Lord's law."

"And you? What do you believe?"

"I'm not sure. I've been raised to believe in the power of the Lord, but . . . Did you know that this wall was modelled on something built on an entirely different continent in a place called . . . uh . . . China?"

I wasn't sure what that had to do with his beliefs but it sounded interesting. "No," I said.

"The Great Wall of China was built over a thousand years ago to protect China from invasion. It really has an interesting history. I learned about it from a book I got from my . . ." He glanced over to his parent's table to make sure they were eating and checked the area to see if anyone was listening before he leaned in and spoke in a quieter voice, " . . . from my mother."

It took me a minute to register the significance of his words.

"Your mother gave you a book? Your mother reads?"

"Sometimes, when Father is away, Mother sneaks into her private sitting room and reads. I've seen her."

"I'm sure she learned to read before the laws came into existence."

"I know that, but if it was against the will of the Lord and dangerous, then shouldn't she either have been punished or harmed by now? I mean, she's been doing this for years."

"Does your father know?" I realized this information could be valuable to the Readers. If one of the top minister's wives flaunted the laws and read without repercussions, why couldn't other women learn to read?

"I heard them fight about it once, long ago. She promised to stop, but she's just been more careful since. She doesn't give me books anymore."

"I never really believed reading would hurt women," I said.

"Don't you two look cozy?" Rogerson's loud voice, as he approached the table, startled us. We moved away from each other and I focused on my soup. "Are you getting along all right?" he asked. "Is the conversation moving? How's the food?"

"It's delicious, Minister Rogerson," I said. "I love this soup." I meant it. The flavors danced in my mouth.

"The brisket should be even better, it's a house specialty. And don't forget to leave room for dessert. It's great that you two are talking so . . . intimately . . . but please be aware of propriety."

Color rose in my cheeks again. I didn't realize what our intense conversation might look like to observers.

"Of course, Father." Peter said. "We were just having a serious discussion for a moment, nothing harmful."

"About what?"

"Um . . . about—"

"About growing up with father's who have such important jobs, sir." I was glad that I could think of a viable story.

Peter sent me a relieved smile.

"Continue on; but no kissing."

"Father!"

Minister Rogerson laughed.

Just then the waiter brought the brisket. "Ah, my favorite." The Minister returned to his wife and said something, which made her laugh and wave. I smiled and waved back before I focused on my food and tried to control my embarrassment.

We spent several moments in silence. The silence grew uncomfortable before I got the courage to speak again. I wanted to understand why I sat across from Peter Rogerson. "You started saying something about a vision . . ." I said.

Peter sighed. "Well, like I said, my father really believes things and he would never understand my doubts. So I told him that I had been praying for guidance, as I knew how much it meant to him for me to marry. I explained that, after praying I fell into a kind of trance and received a visit from an Angel."

"And he believed you?"

"He believes in signs of all sorts."

"What did this Angel tell you?"

"The Angel told me the name of the girl I should marry."

"And that name was mine? Why would you pick my name to trick your father? And why is your father only pursuing me now if you had this 'vision' two years ago?"

Peter smiled. "I picked you because I'd seen you at gatherings and found you interesting—you know, pretty, fun, talented and able to carry on a meaningful conversation."

My cheeks warmed again and I tried to hide my smile. I never realized that he had even noticed me. I didn't want him to see my emotions, but I couldn't stop them. Thankfully, Peter wasn't looking at me. He focused on his meat as he continued his explanation.

"The women my father had been bringing to me in a constant stream were vapid, silly, and uninteresting. You're a vast improvement over every single one of them." He glanced at me with a shy smile.

"Okay, um . . . thank you, I think. That still doesn't explain the gap of two years?"

"Your young age was an advantage. You know as well as I do that your father would never have considered allowing anyone to marry you before you turned seventeen."

"I see, so if your father believed my name had been given to you by an angel, he would lay off on the stream of women until he could legally pressure my father."

Peter smiled. "I knew you were intelligent."

"What now? I don't want to marry anyone at the moment, and it's clear that you're not in love with me." A flutter of something unknown moved in my chest when I said that, but I pushed it aside. I had no time for unfamiliar emotions.

"I really do admire you, please believe that."

"You admire me, but admiration isn't the same as love. And I still hardly know you."

"I was hoping to find some other answer over the two years. I also thought that maybe the fact that my father doesn't really like your father might dissuade him over time. He thinks your father lets you run wild and is dangerous."

"My father is harmless and . . . and innocent." Peter flinched at my tone of voice—as I moved into automatic defense of Dad. I attempted to sound more pleasant. "He doesn't let me do anything. He isn't exactly thrilled at the idea of me marrying into your family either."

Peter chuckled. "See, the perfect plan. With two families that dislike each other this much, I had hoped my father would become disillusioned with the idea. I'm not ready to get married and I don't really believe that it's necessary. There's a whole world out there where people live their lives so differently." He gestured toward the distant glow. "It's only in New North that marriage has become more important than relationships. In the past, people lived together before marriage, or never married at all, and the world kept turning."

"So, are you asking me to live in sin with you?" He left himself open for a little teasing.

"Of course not. I . . . uh . . . no . . . I . . ."

I laughed. "You're way too easy to tease. But seriously, what do you expect to happen now? Your father isn't going to lay off the pressure. He seems interested in a wedding." I nodded toward his parents' beaming faces caused, I assumed, by the smiles and laughter between us.

Peter pulled at his collar before he spoke.

"Maybe my mother wants this match to work, but I actually think Father's more interested in finding out information about you and your father. He wanted me to ask some pointed question."

"He did?" I wiped my mouth with my napkin in case my face revealed too much. "Like what?"

"Well, he wants to know if you and your father believe in the Lord and truly support the Supreme Prime Minister, or if your father has convinced you to rebel against the marriage law. Things like that."

"And I already told you that I don't want to get married." My nervous butterflies reappeared. What if I had said too much already? If I hurt my father I would never forgive myself. I fiddled with my utensils, as I awaited his response.

"Don't worry, Andra." Peter reached his hand across the table but fell short of taking mine. "I have no desire to act as a spy for my father. I'll be honest, I don't believe in all of the restrictions on women. I would be hypocritical if I turned you in for things I question myself."

"Thank you." I couldn't look Peter in the eye. The request from the Readers floated in my head. I took a sip of water before continuing. "Where does that leave us in this little game then?"

"I don't know. Do you think we could see each other a little? You know, keep my dad distracted and maybe get to know each other as friends?"

I took a few bites of the delicious brisket to give me time to think. If I accepted, I'd be playing the role of double agent, and I wasn't sure I could do that. Peter seemed like a decent person. Was the cause of the Freedom Readers worth spying on a new friend? Did I want to play along with his game of trying to fool his family? Would Dad be hurt if I agreed? Would spending time with him force me into a marriage I didn't believe in? I wanted to be cautious and clear.

"If we do this," I said, "we have to be careful. I need to trust that you won't get my father into trouble. I'll do my best to keep up the charade so your father keeps the pressure off, but I won't marry you at the end of the year. I know this law is wrong."

"Have you ever seen the Women's Training Program? It could be a much worse option."

"I know that. I don't know what I'll do, but you said yourself marriage isn't the only answer. Can I trust you to keep quiet about what I think?"

"Yes. Can I trust you not to tell my father about anything?"

"I won't get you in trouble with anyone," I said. I wouldn't share anything that would hurt him. I couldn't.

"Well then," Peter put his hand out to shake, "It looks like we're partners in crime. Friends?"

"Friends." I shook his hand and smiled, while my heart pounded in fear.

We spent the rest of the evening on more innocent topics of conversation.

Despite my reluctance to go, and my concerns about the tasks given to me by the Readers, I returned home that evening with a smile on my face and a slice of extra rich chocolate cake for my father.

ELEVEN

"By order of Supreme Prime Minister Rom Sandovar, the following message must be read in all households with members of the feminine sex. It has come to our attention that someone has been spreading false information regarding women's brains. The rumors suggest that women's brains are equal to or stronger than male brains. This is absolutely untrue. It is acknowledged by the leading scientists of our time that female brains are weaker and frailer than their male counterparts. Studies conducted by New North's premier scientists have shown the danger to women's brains if they are introduced to inappropriate knowledge. While we are unsure how this message is being conveyed, we assume that it was instigated by the dangerous group known as the Freedom Readers fed by false information from Outside. For the safety of the entire community, we have established the following procedures to take effect immediately:

1.   Females over the age of 12 may not gather in groups larger than three unless they are under the supervision of a responsible adult male.

2.   We suspect the spread of this message is somehow related to images recently found across New North, drawn by an unknown artist. Any suspicious or questionable drawings must be handed over to Ministry officials for examination. Anyone caught distributing these images will be brought in for questioning.

3.   Any female aged 12 or older who exhibits unusual skills that might indicate a malfunctioning or dangerous brain condition must be brought to the nearest Women's Training Center for testing, treatment, and supervision.

4. Please report any and all knowledge of movements by the Freedom Readers to your nearest Ministry Official. Anyone suspected of rebel behavior will be brought in for questioning.

These rules go into immediate effect on this day, during the 24th year of the leadership of Supreme Prime Minister Rom Sandovar under the guidance of the Lord."

* * *

As soon as the Crier left our house, I slumped into a chair. "I don't understand. How did they find out?"

"How did they found out what exactly?" Dad asked. "What message did you send in your drawings?"

"I can't . . ."

"Don't say 'you can't tell', or 'the less I know the better.' You've brought me into this again without my knowledge or desire. I deserve to know the truth."

Veins in his forehead began to pulse. It crushed me to realize that I had caused him that much distress. I didn't want to lie anymore. Just as I started to speak, Brian burst into the door without knocking.

"Andra, are you okay?"

"Of course, I'm just worried. How did they learn about the powers?"

"I don't know. Someone must have told them what the pictures said."

"WHAT POWERS?!" Dad jumped between us. I don't know that I'd ever heard him yell like that before. "Are you talking about the powers your mother mentioned in that painting? If someone doesn't explain every detail of what's going on, I'll turn the Readers in myself."

"You're right," I said. "You deserve to know. Let's go up to the attic and I'll tell you everything. It will be safer to talk there, and I have some things to show you. Brian, I think you should bring your mother over as well. She deserves to hear everything too."

Brian blanched and nodded. He turned without a word and returned a few minutes later, Mama Woodson in tow.

"Our little rebels are finally going to confess," she said. "What are we going to do about them, Ben?"

"Let's see what they have to tell us first," Dad said.

We all headed to the attic, where I kept the evidence of my power.

* * *

A few days later, Brian, Dad and I went to Freedom Reader headquarters for an emergency meeting. Dad had insisted on attending. Mama Woodson wanted to come too, and it took a lot of effort to convince her to stay behind.

"If I have to fight to protect you, I will," Mama Woodson said with a grim look as we prepared to leave.

"Andra's skill can protect us all," Brian said.

That scared me but I kept silent. I hadn't shared any of my doubts with Brian, doubts that came from my nearly harming his mother.

"I won't be safe if I'm looking out for you all the time," Brian said. "Please stay home."

"I'll watch over them both, Ruth," Dad said. "I promise I'll bring them home."

In the end, Mama Woodson agreed that her presence and anger would only make things worse. We left her behind cleaning up both homes.

I had expected to only meet with Emily and Johnson, but when we arrived at the hideaway, several people, men and women, filled seats throughout the room. Some looked vaguely familiar, but others wore travelling clothes with the emblems of towns far distant from the capital of New North. The dust on their clothing and their weary faces revealed the long journey they had taken to come to the meeting.

"I'm glad you're here." Emily came over to welcome us. "Your services are more important than ever. We have representatives from all across New North whom you should meet." She turned to my father to welcome him with her traditional embrace and kiss. "Scrivener, we've missed you. I should have known this emergency would bring you back."

"I'm not back, Emily. I'm here to protect Andra. You've brought her into a dangerous world and I want to see that she's safe."

"I didn't bring her in, Ben. She belongs here. She has something valuable that can help us achieve our goals—goals in which you once believed."

I wanted to interrupt, to claim responsibility for my own choices, but I remained silent. Dad was already on edge and I didn't want to push him too far.

"I still believe in them," Dad said. "But I won't allow you to use Andra or Brian in any way that brings them harm. Look what's already happened."

"That's what this meeting's about, of course." Johnson stepped forward with his hand out for Dad. "I've missed you, Ben."

To my surprise, the two men embraced and tears formed in Dad's eyes.

"I've missed you too, Jack. I'm sorry. It was too painful after Marion . . ."

"I know," Johnson said. "I hope you know I'll do everything in my power to protect Andra."

Just then Professor Albert and Lauren arrived. Lauren rushed over to me and pulled us to a cozy couch toward the back of the room, away from the others. "Andra, I'm worried."

"Me too, but for now let's just listen." I said.

"I'll be listening with more than my ears."

"Good, but be careful."

"I'm scared. I know what they did to women who exhibited too much intelligence or ability and rebellion at my Center, and now they want to bring in young girls. We can't let that happen to anyone else." Lauren pulled her legs up onto the couch, put her arms around them and started rocking.

I hugged Lauren hoping that would calm her. I'd seen her like this before, rocking in fear at the WTC. "I promise it's going to be okay." Although, deep inside, I wondered how I would ever keep that promise. I rubbed Lauren's back until the rocking stopped.

Lauren finally pulled her head away from her knees—her eyes red and puffy. "Would you hold my hand?" she asked.

"Of course." I gripped her hand just as Emily called the meeting to order.

"I can't emphasize how crucial it is that we continue to get our message out to women," she said. "The government's excessive reaction simply proves that we're on to something. We must continue the pressure and find those women who may be able to help us before the government can."

"What are these powers that the messages talk about?" The question came from an older woman I didn't know.

"It has come to our attention that some women exhibit unusual abilities that could help our cause," Emily said. "For the safety of those involved, we are unwilling at this moment to reveal any more information regarding those abilities, but it's crucial that we learn if any other women have experienced unusual talents. New North is a large place, and we rely on you to help get those women in contact with us."

"But how did the government learn of these abilities?" The same woman asked. "I thought the messages were only in the women's language."

"We must assume that some men connected with the government have the ability to read the secret language," Emily said. "There's no other explanation."

"Emily, no offense, but I believe your assumption is incorrect," Professor Albert said. "Although there are many of us who are aware of its existence, no man has ever been taught more than a few signs. I was never aware of anyone in the government who had more than a suspicion of the language's existence."

"You've been away from the Ministry for a long time, Professor," Emily said.

"But I haven't," Dad surprised me by speaking. "If anyone who fully supported the Ministry could read the language, greater restrictions would already be in place. Trust me; the Supreme Prime Minister has been out to place more controls on women for a long time. He would have no qualms preventing women from learning to draw or paint as well as read, and if he suspected the power and extent of your secret language he would have done just that. He's always been aware that some images convey messages, but he believes they are simple, meaningless and unimportant. He thinks they are limited to things like 'hello' and 'have a nice day.' He doesn't believe women have the intelligence or skill to create an entire visual language that can communicate complex messages."

"It seems he will always underestimate the power of women," Emily said.

Several chuckles came from around the room. I was fascinated by this eclectic group of people fighting for a cause that some would call hopeless. Sandovar's rule had lasted for so long, I wondered if we would ever defeat it, with or without special abilities.

"So if a man hasn't learned the language, how did the Ministry discover our message?" The older woman brought the conversation back to her burning question.

"The only other option is that a woman read the messages and passed them on to someone in the Ministry," Emily said. "We can't be sure that the wives of the ministers are all on our side."

"Or, there are traitors in our midst," Johnson said.

His comment stunned the room into silence. Lauren's grip on my hand tightened enough to make bones rub together.

"Ow!"

"Sorry," Lauren's eyes widened with fear. She moved closer to me so her whisper tickled my inner ear. I tried not to squirm away.

"Someone in this room is nervous and feeling guilty," Lauren said.

I took my time examining each person in the room, hoping to recognize a guilty look on someone's face, but all I saw was shock and concern. I didn't know most of the people in the room well enough to recognize duplicity.

Emily broke the silence. "That's why Johnson is one of our most trusted leaders. He's always the person who thinks the dark thoughts that keep us alert. His suggestion is one we must keep in mind. We must be vigilant about who we trust and how we share information. For that reason, Johnson and I will be meeting with you individually to discuss what your next move or contribution to the cause might be. Meanwhile, please help yourself to refreshments and become familiar with those in this room you don't know . . . but share no important information with each other, at this time. We'll meet in the adjoining sitting room, with the heads of units first." Emily and Johnson headed toward the door at the back, followed by the woman who had asked questions and several other people Andra didn't recognize.

Professor Albert aimed his intention toward the elaborate spread of delicacies laid out on the large table. "Lauren, join me. One thing you need to learn is that Emily is the perfect hostess and treats Freedom Readers well. We can't let the concerns of the day ruin our appetites."

"Andra, Brian . . . Professor Albert is a wise man," Dad said as he picked up a plate. "I must admit that one thing I did miss about these meetings was the food."

* * *

Johnson called me, Lauren, Brian and Professor Albert into the other room together. Dad followed without an invitation.

"Ben," Emily said as we entered the smaller room filled with a warm fire to combat the chill of the underground hideout. A collection of chairs covered in rich browns and reds clustered near the fireplace. "I don't believe we asked you to come in."

"Emily, I was once equal with you in this group. I worked hard for the cause until I lost the woman I loved because of it. You've brought two people whom I care about very much into this room. I'm not going to let you give my daughter orders behind my back."

"Emily, you know he's trustworthy," Johnson said.

"As you pointed out, Johnson, we don't know who we can trust."

"Are you accusing me of slipping this information to the Ministry?" I had heard that tone in my father's voice before, most recently when he insisted I go to dinner with the Rogersons. I knew better than to argue with him when he spoke like that. "I knew nothing about what the messages said until after the Ministry decree came out, when Andra finally revealed the truth and showed me her ability. I will not be accused of being a traitor to the cause. Nor will I let you use her ability in any dangerous way."

"Need I remind you that you stopped fighting for or with us a long time ago?" Emily's face took on an ugly cast.

I stepped forward to say something in defense of my father, but Johnson stopped me. "Your father's got this, Andra."

"I had no choice," Dad said. "The Ministry was coming too close to us, and Marion payed the price. If I had continued, they would have taken my daughter from me. Nothing will come between us. Nothing!"

He reached out for my hand and I grabbed it. His touch sent me a message of strength and conviction as he and Emily stared at each other for an interminable moment. I held my breath, unsure of what to expect.

"You're right." Emily finally broke the silence. "Marion's loss devastated us all. Your resignation from the Readers was understandable, and protected many secrets. Everyone, please have a seat so Johnson can explain our plan."

I could breathe again. We all found comfortable seats in the room. I sat next to Lauren on a small love seat. Dad leaned against the arm next to me and placed his hand on my shoulder—a reminder, I assumed, that he would protect me if he could. Brian sat in a leather armchair across from us. Professor Albert sat by the fire.

"Andra," Johnson said, "have you thought anymore about getting to know Peter Rogerson?"

I blushed. Dad laughed. Brian snorted. Everyone else looked confused.

"She had a date with him a few nights ago," Brian said.

"You did?" Emily sounded surprised. "Did you learn anything important? Did you hear anything about these new mandates?"

"No, I . . . the only interesting thing I learned was that Madame Rogerson reads in secret when her husband isn't around, although he caught her reading in the past. Minister Rogerson really believes that these mandates against women are the will of the Lord."

"Well, that's not surprising," Emily said. "Are you going to continue to cultivate this relationship?"

"She shouldn't have to do that," Brian said.

"Brian, calm down." I gave him my don't-mess-with-me glare. "It has nothing to do with you. Peter and I have decided to cultivate a mutually beneficial friendship."

"What does that mean?" Brian asked.

"It means that, by at least pretending to pursue me for marriage, Peter will be less harassed by his father with a string of annoying options, and I will be less harassed by everyone who seems to think my marital state is of crucial importance. Plus, I can perhaps aid the Readers, although I didn't tell Peter that. I don't know what information Peter can provide and I won't manipulate him for information."

"I respect your choice, Andra," Johnson said. "Let's move on. We have an idea of how you could help us with your power, if you're willing. You could both help us." His eyes shifted from me to Lauren who turned pale and grabbed my hand.

"I'll do what I can," I said, "But . . . I can't hurt anybody. I won't hurt anybody."

"We won't ask you to," Johnson said. "We'd like you to cause some kind of malfunction in the Ministry which will enable us to get workers, like Brian and myself, into secure areas to search out information that we need."

"What kind of information?" Dad asked. "I'm privy to a lot of classified things."

"We want to find the real autopsy report on your wife, for one thing," Emily said.

Dad colored but did not respond. His hand gripped my shoulder for a moment. I put my hand on his knee and his grip relaxed.

"Ben," Johnson said. "I'm sure you want to know the truth as much as we do, don't you?"

"Yes, of course," Dad said. "But I'm not sure why that information is still important. It was long ago."

"We think that it might carry some evidence regarding the true science behind the human brain," Emily said. "We also believe wherever we find that file we could find other valuable information, such as what happened to Brian's father."

Leather squeaked under Brian's twitching fingers. "The records are probably hidden away in the records room," he said. "Why would they keep them someplace secret?"

"Because the Scrivener has access to all the records in the records room," Emily said. "I'm sure they keep things like this far away from his prying eyes."

Brian turned toward my father for confirmation. Dad shook his head. "I've looked," his voice sounded husky. "They're hidden somewhere inaccessible to me."

The room filled with silence. Dad slumped down looking as if he might burst with emotion soon. Brian's fingers twitched faster and faster. I wanted to help them, to do something to lessen their pain.

"What kind of disturbance would I need to create?" I asked.

"We thought that you could make a wall collapse," Johnson said. "Not a retaining wall, but something small. If you made it look like a weakness in the building, nobody would question it. It's an old building, anything could happen. If the wall happens to be near the files . . . I will find a way to get to them while doing the repair work. Whatever accident happens, it needs to be sudden, so they don't have time to move anything, but nothing too damaging to the files themselves like fire or flood."

"That's too dangerous," I said. "People could get hurt."

"Not if you limit the area of destruction and we ensure that we do it when nobody is around," Johnson said. "That's where Lauren comes in."

"I don't understand. How can I help?" She looked over at Professor Albert as if seeking his protection.

"Don't worry, Lauren," the Professor said. "I'll be there for you."

"Let me explain," Johnson said, "We need you to get close to a Ministry official to find out where exactly these files might be stored. Unless, Ben, you can tell us?" Dad shook his head. "So our only option, which might take some time, is to get you close enough to discover the location through people's thoughts. Once we know that information, Andra can be very specific about what happens and nobody will get hurt."

"How's Lauren supposed to do that?" the Professor asked. "She has no access to the Ministry. I doubt very much anyone thinks about those files on a regular basis."

"That's why we have a long-term plan," Emily said. "We all know patience yields results eventually."

"Ah, I forgot," the Professor said. "The Readers have mastered the art of waiting and then rushing in blindly."

"What's that supposed to mean, Professor?" Emily asked.

"It means I joined this group long ago, but nothing has really been achieved except for people getting hurt because of ill thought out plans"

Emily glared at him.

"I don't mean to start an argument," the Professor said. "I apologize. What is this long-term plan you've developed?

"We thought Lauren could find some work as a maid there, or something," Emily said.

Lauren surprised everyone by laughing. She had a contagious laugh that I hadn't heard for a long time.

"What's so funny?" Emily asked.

"You're crazy if you think I'd go near the Ministry to seek employment. They set out to destroy me in Training. They know who I am or at least have records on me. They think they sent me out of the WTP to die. If anyone were to recognize me . . . I don't think they'll be happy to find out I'm alive. It will never work."

"She's right," Johnson said. "It's impossible. We need a different plan."

Dad started to laugh as well.

"Now you, Ben," Johnson said. "Why are you laughing?"

"It looks like I'm in whether I want to be or not," Dad said. "I think I can get Lauren into the Ministry. I don't think anyone will recognize you, Lauren. You've changed a lot from the young woman who went into the program. You've matured into a beautiful woman touched by darkness."

Lauren blushed and stared at her hands.

"Most government employees don't even notice the women who enter the Ministry—they treat them like wallpaper. However, to be safe we will need to come up with an identity for Lauren. I can get her in without forcing her to work there. We can go in as often as we need to until we find the information, although it might be like searching for evidence that aliens exist. Andra and Lauren, would you like to have lunch with me at the Ministry once or twice a week?"

Our eyes met. I smiled encouragement. She hesitated and then nodded.

And so our plans began to form.

TWELVE

Lauren hugged herself as she followed Andra and the Scrivener into the Ministry building. Deep down inside, she knew nobody would recognize her, but she couldn't control the fear that came from entering this building, where her journey into hell had begun just before she turned eighteen. Her parents turned her in to government officials when she continued to defy them and reject suitor after suitor. She hadn't seen them since. They moved to a different town in New North—out of shame, she was told. First, they brought her to the Ministry where they left her in the hands of the Committee over the Control of Women. After hours of questioning, a nameless minister moved her to the nearest training center for more analysis. She never left, or at least not until they had broken her. The terror of that time lived in Lauren's body.

She had entered the building with the BetScriveners several times over the past few weeks; each one another failed attempt at getting information. Yet her stomach clenched each time she entered, even with the Scrivener's assurances and explanations. Lauren still feared that someone would recognize her and she would be forced back into that nightmare, or even killed outright.

Several times during their planning sessions, when they worked out ways to give her access to more minds, Lauren had reconsidered. She doubted this would succeed, or that she would ever find the courage to help. So far their attempts had been useless; she hadn't gleaned any useful information from anyone's mind. The more they tried and failed, the more her doubts grew. Meanwhile, her fear upon entering the ministry building never diminished and seemed to be growing.

Just that morning, she expressed her concerns and doubts again, but the Scrivener said words that gave her strength to try one more time.

"Lauren," he said, "the people who evaluated you are busy going from training center to training center; or following up on law-breaking women. After the new mandates, they are even busier. I've heard they've already received numerous leads about young girls turned in for suspicious reasons all over New North."

She couldn't let other women get hurt, especially not young girls, even if it meant sacrificing herself. However, she found herself rocking back and forth in her chair as her fears built up inside her. Andra had tried to comfort her, but the Scrivener had the key.

"Lauren," the Scrivener said, "I promise I'll keep you safe, and away from anyone who might suspect who you are. Read my mind if that's the only way you can trust me in this."

Professor Albert had helped Lauren better control her power, so she could protect herself from the constant influx of other people's thoughts and emotions. In the time she'd spent with Andra and the Scrivener, she'd actually enjoyed maintaining brain silence, out of respect for the people around her as well as her own need for alone time. When she opened the connection with the Scrivener's mind, she heard only loving, concerned thoughts—almost those of a father. Unstoppable tears began to pour out of her.

"Dad will help you," Andra said, pulling Lauren into a powerful embrace. "And so will I."

"I know," Lauren blew her nose on the handkerchief the Scrivener gave her. "It's been a long time since I've felt this much love and support. Thank you." Her voice sounded strangled around the tears.

Their support gave her the strength to continue, so they headed back to the Ministry. As the Scrivener went through the long process of signing the two women into the building, her doubts grew again. Despite all the discussion and planning, none of them were sure how Lauren was ever going to gain access to the one or two minds that had the information they needed, let alone how exactly they were going to get the right people to think about records long hidden. The Scrivener had new ideas about how to motivate discussion and reach the appropriate people, but a lot of their plan depended on luck.

They picked an unlucky person for a plan based on luck, Lauren thought. She glanced back toward the door and wished she could turn around and leave.

A gentle touch on her shoulder made Lauren jump. "Are you okay?" Andra asked.

"This is crazy," Lauren made sure nobody was near. "We're risking everything in search of the impossible."

"We have to believe this is going to work."

"The chances of me hearing the right info—"

Careful. Andra had suggested Lauren stay connected with her mind while they were in the Ministry. Lauren was grateful for the connection for many reasons, especially at that moment. Andra's brief thought stopped her from speaking out loud when a group of lower-level ministry workers passed. One of them recognized the Scrivener's daughter and greeted her.

"Are you here to visit your father today?" The heavy man asked.

"Yes, sir, my father invited us to lunch again."

"I hope the dining hall cooks up something decent." The group of men around him laughed and began making jokes about the food as they walked away.

"See, Andra," Lauren said. "All they were thinking about was food and how they wished they could eat in the dining room reserved for ministers."

"I do too," Andra said. "The past few lunches have been awful. I finally understand why Dad is so skinny and yet eats so much at home."

Lauren surprised herself with a nervous giggle.

"Don't worry," Andra said. "Dad believes that we can get people thinking the way we need them to with a few simple questions."

"But what if our questions provoke suspicion? What if I get overwhelmed by all the thoughts? What if—"

"Ladies." The Scrivener walked toward them holding the paperwork that allowed them into the Ministry. "Shall we go in? We have some time before lunch and I thought I'd show Lauren the Atrium."

Andra grabbed Lauren's hand and whispered. "You've mastered your skill. I have faith." With that, she gave Lauren's hand a squeeze and caught up with the Scrivener to put her arm through his. "Dad, can we visit the library today?" she asked in a normal voice.

"My favorite place," the Scrivener said. He glanced back at Lauren, and a look of kind concern passed through his eyes. "But I think the Atrium is the best place to start."

Father and daughter headed down the hallway giving Lauren no choice but to follow in their wake.

* * *

I was glad Dad suggested a visit to the Atrium. I was worried about Lauren, whose confidence in herself and in the plan diminished each time we tried and failed. I admit I was frustrated as well, but I was more concerned that Lauren's thin grasp on health and sanity might slip under the pressure. The Atrium was one of the few places in the Ministry that I enjoyed. The domed glass skylight dripped light onto a collection of wonderful aromatic exotic plants interspersed with seating areas to encourage people to unwind and reflect. The Atrium remained free of any art displaying the Eye of the Lord symbol, which—in my opinion—made this the most peaceful, spiritual and relaxing space in the entire Ministry. Of course, in the reality of the Ministry where continuous production was the expectation and the norm, people rarely took the opportunity to come here, so whenever I visited it was empty. A stop in the Atrium would give us time to find courage again.

"There's nobody here, why are we here?" Lauren sounded surprised.

"It's a nice place to visit," Dad said. "I thought maybe we should take a minute to regroup before we begin today. Sit here for a moment." He indicated a seating arrangement toward a stone wall in the back, where we would have privacy while still able to see anyone approach.

"Lauren, are you okay?" He asked. "I'm worried about you. If you don't want to do this, you don't have to. We've tried and we haven't succeeded. There's no reason to keep trying. It's a crazy mission and I'm worried the pressure is harming you."

I started to say something encouraging to Lauren, but a look from Dad silenced me.

Lauren pulled herself into her traditional rocking position and then buried her face in her hands. "I . . . I don't see how this can work. How will I know who to listen to? What are the chances of us meeting with the person who has the information we seek? What if they realize what I'm doing?"

Dad sighed. "I can't promise you this will ever work. I already expressed my doubts to our friends. But," he pulled Lauren's hands away from her face and encouraged her to look into his eyes, "I'll say it again, you don't have to do this. Nobody can force you to do this. If you'd like, we will simply have a nice lunch, and I'll find some other way to get those records."

That idea terrified me. "No, Dad," I said. "That's too dangerous. If they catch you snooping—"

"Don't worry, Andra." Lauren's quiet voice interrupted the inexpressible thoughts in my brain. "You've both been so kind. I won't let anything happen to your father because I wasn't brave enough to do my part."

"Lauren." My chest tightened in worry for my friend. "You're the bravest woman I know. Dad's right. You don't have to do this. We can find some other way. I don't even know if I want to do this, anymore. We've failed too often, and each time I watch you fall into a deeper depression. I'm already scared that my words will hurt someone unintentionally, but now I'm afraid I'm hurting you by asking you to do this. Maybe these abilities are more bad than good."

"This isn't your fault," Lauren said. "I agreed to come." She reached out and grabbed my hand. "I wouldn't have survived without Grandma if you hadn't helped me, Andra. And . . . I don't think these abilities are either bad or good. They . . . they just are. We choose how to use them. I'm scared, but I have to use mine to stop other women from being hurt by the WTP."

I embraced Lauren who slowly hugged me back.

"There you are, Scrivener!" Minister Rogerson's booming voice announced his entry into the Atrium and made Lauren and I pull away from each other as he strode toward us. "I was informed that your lovely daughter was visiting for lunch today." He took my hand and kissed it. "How convenient; Peter will be coming for lunch with me. Why don't you all join me in the Minister's Lounge for an extra delicious meal?" He noticed Lauren who had jumped up from her seat and stood staring at the floor. "Who is this charming young lady?"

"Allow me to introduce you to my niece, Lauren." Dad used the backstory we had prepared before our first attempt. We hadn't had to use it yet, other than to check into the Ministry. "Her parents live in Upper North Town, and have been going through some challenges lately, so they asked if Lauren could stay with us for a while. She's been here for a couple of weeks and has enjoyed spending time with me at the Ministry."

"But shouldn't you be with your husband?" Minister Rogerson asked.

"If it pleases you, Minister," Lauren's quiet voice forced Rogerson to lean in, "I've only recently turned seventeen. I'm engaged to marry in several months."

"Oh, I would have thought you were older—my mistake." Minister Rogerson turned to me, "It's good to see your relatives setting proper examples. I hope you're paying attention."

"Of course, Sir." I forced myself to smile.

"So, will you all join Peter and me for lunch in the Minister's Lounge?"

"It would be our pleasure," Dad said.

I turned to Lauren with a smile and a wink, sending the thought *at least we are getting the good food today*. Lauren gave a weak smile as color drained from her face.

*   *   *

I was nervous as we entered the dining room. Each table contained expensive china and pristine table coverings which all gleamed in the light of an unusual chandelier built in the shape of an ancient sailing vessel. It wasn't just the fancy surroundings that bothered me, however. Peter Rogerson was close to Lauren's age and would have attended social gatherings with her. The chance of him recognizing her and blowing her cover worried me. He sat at the table fiddling with a fork as he waited for us. As I sat down, I tried to catch his eye with a meaningful look. He didn't seem to understand, so I gave a slight nod toward Lauren. He must have gotten the message, because he managed to blink back any evidence of surprise when my father introduced Lauren as my cousin.

We sat at a table toward the center of the room, which meant a steady stream of ministers and their guests came and went, often stopping by for a brief discussion with Minister Rogerson or my father. Dad answered succinctly, although once in a while he asked one of our trigger questions if he thought someone would have the information we needed. One minister came over to ask him about a historical reference in some files.

"I've never seen a reference of that," Dad said. "Perhaps there are files tucked away somewhere else that I need to search?"

I glanced over at Lauren, whose shoulders and forehead revealed her intense focus. She shook her head, a sad glint in her eyes.

Whenever someone stopped to chat with Minister Rogerson, he waxed on about the importance of the new measures and the wise decisions made by the Supreme Prime Minister to support the will of the Lord. This led to uncomfortable silences and stilted conversation between interruptions, as we all did not agree on these topics. I resorted to putting food in my mouth every time I wanted to say something argumentative. A couple of times, Dad placed his hand on my arm in warning.

This tense and unpleasant meal would never be touted as a successful social engagement, in anyone's opinion.

"This is awkward," I said when both men were called away for a moment to some kind of heated discussion at another table.

"Trust me; this is better than my usual lunch with him," Peter said. "At least I have someone to talk to while he conducts business. What's wrong with Lauren?"

Lauren's skin had become pale and her eyes appeared strained with dark hollows underneath. I wished I could help, but Lauren was trapped by the need to follow the conversation, respond when addressed, and focus on any relevant thoughts from the people around her. The invitation from Minister Rogerson had been a blessing in disguise for our plans, but it also meant juggling more minds than Lauren ever had in practice.

"Lauren, why don't you eat something?" I said. "You've barely touched your food. Here, try some of this." I leaned over with a fork full of fish while sending a thought toward Lauren in the hopes she would hear it. *Lauren, take a break. You don't look well. I won't let you harm yourself.*

Lauren blinked and took the proffered bite.

"Thanks, Andra." She pointed a fake smile toward Peter. "This is all so fascinating."

"Really?" Peter said. "I think it's all ridiculous."

"Peter, what's ridiculous about our work?" Minister Rogerson had returned to the table, followed by my father. "You'll never learn will you ... "

The Minister continued lecturing his son while Dad watched with an amused look on his face. Lauren took the distraction to eat a little more and regain control. I let my mind wander.

"Oh my!" The clatter of Lauren's dropped fork startled me back to attention. If possible, her face had become even paler with shock. I followed her gaze toward the entrance of the dining room, to see Supreme Prime Minister Sandovar enter with a woman on his arm.

"The Supreme Prime Minister is here," Rogerson said. "Peter, come with me and we'll greet him properly. Excuse us for a moment."

"Of course," Dad said.

I waited until they were far enough away. "What's Emily doing here with Supreme Prime Minister Sandovar?"

"*Madame DuFarge* has many responsibilities to the Ministry." Dad emphasized her name to remind us that in this location she was not Emily. "Since her husband died, she must perform certain duties in order to continue to have access to government support. Either that or she must marry someone of the Ministry's choosing. You know that. She was allowed to remain unfettered, but that means she has other responsibilities."

"What kind of duties?" I asked. I had known about these rules, but I never thought about what kind of duties women had to perform—women who were never allowed access to knowledge. I began to suspect what they might be.

"I'd prefer not to discuss that here."

"That's reprehensible!" The look on Lauren's face confirmed my suspicions.

"You mean she—"

"I told you, not here." Dad used the tone that tolerated no arguments. "And Lauren, please stay out of my mind. I don't have the information you seek."

Lauren blushed. "Sorry Scrivener, it's hard to keep control with so many thoughts around me."

I glanced around to make sure nobody was listening to our conversation and then asked in hushed tones. "Have you found anything important?"

"Possibly," Lauren said. "I've heard some interesting information, but I can't be sure any of it's useful. I'm sorry."

"No need to apologize. This plan relies too much on luck, and we knew that. What are we going to do?" I turned to Dad for advice.

"I suggest we eat a decadent dessert, courtesy of Minister Rogerson and then we hope for the best."

* * *

The interminable lunch eventually ended, but not without an awkward moment as we stopped at the Supreme Prime Minister's table on the way out. Emily couldn't completely hide her surprise and discomfort. She covered it by greeting us with her usual embrace.

"I didn't know you would be here," she whispered in my ear before pulling away to speak so all could hear. "It's so nice to see you with your father, Miss BetScrivener. It's been so long." She turned to Lauren with an uneasy smile. "I hope your visit with the BetScriveners doesn't contain any unpleasant surprises."

"I'm sure it won't, Madame DuFarge," Lauren said with a curtsy.

Emily now turned back to me. "You've grown into such a lovely woman. It must be nice having someone to gossip with." She encompassed Lauren and me with a sharp look, "Just remember some secrets are not meant to be shared."

"Of course, Madame DuFarge." I wondered if she was reminding us of our mission, or warning us against delving into her secrets. The fact that she had things to hide worried me. I wanted to believe that the Readers were guided by doing what was right at all times, but I guess that was a naïve wish.

"What's next on your agenda?" Emily asked.

"Um . . . Dad said he'd take us to the library."

"Scrivener, why would you bring your daughter and your niece to the library?" Until that moment, I thought Supreme Prime Minister Sandovar wasn't bothering to listen to our conversation. I was wrong. His voice sent shivers down my spine, as it always did.

Dad laughed. "It's my fault, of course, sir. Andra grew up surrounded by books she wasn't allowed to read."

"Of course." Sandovar nodded.

"She loved to touch them, and separate them into size and colors. Sometimes she even created sculptures that resembled animals or trees. She would rearrange them to draw or paint, like building blocks. So one day when she was little and had to come with me to work because her mother was doing something for you, I took her to the library here as a distraction."

"Yes," I caught up with the story. "I love going in there just for artistic inspiration. It amazes me that those little packages can convey so much meaning to . . . um . . . to men. I like to touch them and wish that my brain could be stronger."

Emily and Sandovar both laughed at this.

"Ah, the naïve dreams of the young," Emily said while she sneaked a look of approval toward me.

"Do you ever open the books?" Sandovar asked.

"Oh, no, Sir." I tried my best to look innocent. "Sometimes, if they are illustrated, Librarian Bookman would show me the pictures, but he always stayed with me. Or, as Dad said, they let me pile books for still life's and such, but I've never even thought about trying to read a word. Not that I would be able to even if I tried." I giggled to cover my lie.

Emily started coughing. "Excuse me." She covered her mouth with her napkin, an amused glint in her eyes.

"Is it acceptable for me to take them to the library, Sir?" Dad asked.

"I suppose it's harmless. However, I need to meet with you as soon as my meal with Madame DuFarge is over, Scrivener. They are not to be left alone near the books."

"Yes, Sir. I'll just take Andra and Lauren over to the library where I'm sure Bookman can keep them entertained until I can escort them home. "

"He never fails with the stories, does he?" Sandovar said. "Meet me in my office in an hour,"

With that we made our escape. We took our time getting to the library, pausing to have short conversations with possible sources. By the time we made it to the giant room filled with the remnants of history Sandovar allowed men access to, Lauren was glassy-eyed from concentration. My own frustration at our lack of success made me want to explode. I wished I could write some words to make this easier, but I didn't know what to write.

I loved the library almost as much as I loved the Atrium. It contained thousands of old books, some of which could only be accessed by a rolling ladder, others loading down a balcony that contained sculptures and masks and artifacts collected from a very different world than that of New North. It would have been my favorite place in the entire building, if I had ever been allowed to read the books. On the ceiling overhead, someone had painted a horrific image of the Eye of the Lord; an intimidating reminder of what I couldn't have.

Given our previous failures, Dad thought a visit to the library was crucial, because if anyone knew where documents might be hidden in the building it was the ancient librarian who loved to share his knowledge of the history of the place. It was also a key location for people to stop in, looking for answers throughout the day. If we could spend several hours in the library, Lauren would have entry to the minds of a lot of people in a harmless way; people who would already be thinking about accessing records.

"Welcome, Scrivener," Librarian Bookman said, "Andra, I haven't seen you since the last time I had to clean up a huge pile of books."

"Hello, Librarian Bookman," I greeted him with a hug. He was one of my favorite people in the Ministry. My instincts told me that he would give me books if I had been allowed. He shared stories whenever possible—stories from books I would never read. "I'd like you to meet my . . . um . . . cousin, Lauren. I hope you don't mind the visit. I was hoping you could tell us some stories about this place."

"Ah, you know my weakness, young Andra." He patted my head with an age-spotted hand. If anyone else had done that, I would have flinched away with a sharp word. Plenty of people had tried because they found my short stature cute—I always found the gesture demeaning. But Librarian Bookman was like a grandfather since I had never met my real ones; all my grandparents died in the early days of New North. Librarian Bookman's gesture always felt more like love and kindness.

"Have a seat, girls," the old man said, "and I will regale you with tales as long as we aren't interrupted."

We spent the rest of the afternoon listening to stories about the Ministry and about times long gone. He even told us stories that were dangerous to tell—stories from before the wall was built. Librarian Bookman spoke with caution, one eye on the door, so that he could talk about something more innocuous whenever someone came in looking for information, which happened often.

Lauren's appearance changed as people came in. Her face hardened in intensity and her eyes became unfocused. I hoped nobody noticed her bizarre demeanor. If Librarian Bookman did, he pretended not to. If I didn't know better, I might have thought he intentionally brought the focus of his visitors away from the two of us sitting at the table. But why would he do that, when he had no idea of our real purpose? He introduced us and then pulled the visitor elsewhere for discussion. After each person left, Lauren's face softened and she gave me a look that said no, she hadn't uncovered anything useful.

After several hours, a handsome, dark-haired man who I had never met before came in to discuss something with Librarian Bookman. The only thing that marred his features was the startled and disdainful look he aimed at Lauren and me.

"Librarian Bookman," he said. It sounded to me like he had a false elite accent—as if he wanted to sound smart. "I need to discuss something important with you. But I am appalled! What are these young women doing in the library?"

"Minister Achan, surely you've met Andra BetScrivener before? This is her cousin Lauren."

"Oh, the Scrivener's daughter . . ." Minister Achan gave us an awkward bow. "That doesn't explain what they're doing in the library!"

"You ministers are always so concerned with the rules. Andra loves to hear my stories. She doesn't come in here to read. You yourself once followed me around begging for stories about secret passages and other mysteries of this house."

"I don't think those stories are appropriate for feminine minds," Achan said as he turned toward the back stacks gesturing that the librarian should follow. "I need to talk with you, and I want this kept private." He glared back at us. "You women shouldn't be near books."

I couldn't resist. "Supreme Prime Minister Sandovar gave us his permission to come in here today, Minister Achan."

Achan blanched and then walked with more purpose toward the back of the stacks.

"Entertain yourselves, girls," the old librarian said with a wink. "Be sure not to open any books." He made a face toward Minister Achan's back and followed him into the depths of the library.

I turned to Lauren in excitement. "He doesn't have to worry about the books. Did you hear what Librarian Bookman said about secret passages?"

"Hush," Lauren said. "I'm concentrating. Minister Achan was really thrown by what Librarian Bookman said."

I could barely sit still as Lauren went silent. I got up and started browsing through books, glancing at titles with no recognition. Time crept by until I heard movement coming toward us from the back of the library. I rushed to my seat, away from the books.

"Girls," Librarian Bookman said. "I'm afraid story time must end for the day. Minister Achan has some business I must join him in. Can I trust you to wait here until your father comes?"

"Ahem," Achan gave the old man a pointed look.

"Nonsense, the Scrivener is just down the hall. They don't have time to look at a book."

"We promise," I said. "We won't even leave our seats."

"I'll just get the Scrivener, myself. You wait here, Bookman." Achan slammed the door on his way out.

"I remember the days when people respected knowledge." Bookman caressed some nearby volumes with loving hands. "Times have changed, but not for the better."

I wanted to wipe away the sadness in his eyes. "Thank you for sharing stories with us, Librarian Bookman. I love hearing them." I gave the man another hug.

"Yes, thank you, your stories are wonderful." Lauren hesitated before she too hugged the old librarian.

"Come back and visit soon," he said.

"Bookman!" Achan's voice echoed from the hall just as my father opened the door and came in.

"Thank you for entertaining Andra and Lauren," Dad said, "but it seems you're needed elsewhere."

As soon as the door closed behind the Librarian, I turned to Lauren whose complexion had faded into an even paler version of herself.

"Got it," she said with a weak smile.

THIRTEEN

My writing task should have been easy now that we knew roughly where in the Ministry we might find the documents the Readers wanted. Yet, as I sat down at my desk in the attic—a mug of tea by my side—my fears, doubts and questions made my hand shake and my thoughts shoot in a thousand directions.

When we had returned from the Ministry the day before, Lauren explained that Minister Achan's thoughts whirled as soon as Mr. Bookman mentioned the secret passages. "Achan's mind practically screamed 'That's privileged information.'" Lauren settled down onto my attic couch and pulled an afghan over herself. Her body shook from exhaustion.

"Are you okay?" I asked.

"I'm just a little chilled and tired. Today took a lot out of me."

"The librarian knows about secret passages?" asked Brian, who had been lurking outside the house waiting for our return and joined us in the attic for the discussion. "Did you know about them, Scrivener?"

"Brian, let Lauren talk," Dad said. "Of course I knew there was a rumor of their existence but I never learned their location. Continue, Lauren."

Lauren swallowed before she spoke again. "When they moved away from us, Achan scolded Mr. Bookman. 'You shouldn't be telling women about those passages, especially not the Scrivener's daughter.' 'Why not?' Librarian Bookman asked. 'Surely we have nothing to hide from the Scrivener?' 'You must not have high enough clearance to know,' Achan said. I could almost hear the smirk in his mental voice." Lauren shuddered. "He oozed self-satisfaction. I caught an image from his thoughts of a file cabinet marked with official seals."

"How could he be so rude to Librarian Bookman?" I asked. "Doesn't the librarian know everything about the Ministry?"

"Achan is an officious oaf," Dad said. "Ever since he joined the Ministry he's been oozing his way into the trust of the most powerful people, and loves to lord it over others with his connections and information. Whenever possible he uses his knowledge about other people to manipulate and control. Librarian Bookman is one of the greatest people in the Ministry, with the most knowledge of everything that came before, but he still has fond memories of the country that used to exist. He has friends and family on the Outside. He has never been fully trusted by the Supreme Prime Minister and his followers. Bookman was only brought into this position because he had the most knowledge about everything that could affect Sandovar's rule. There's an old saying about keeping your enemies close; I think Sandovar kept Bookman close for that reason. It's the same reason Sandovar's kept me close, I'm sure."

"Is he a Freedom Reader?" I asked.

"Not officially, but he's definitely an ally. So," Dad turned back to Lauren, "we know the files exist, did you see where?"

"Through one of the back library stacks," Lauren said.

"So if I want us to gain access," I said, "I'm going to have to damage part of the library?! I can't do that. It would be like destroying Librarian Bookman's family. Besides, he rarely leaves the library. I think he even sleeps in his office. There are always people in and out of there. How can I ensure that nobody is in there to get hurt even with Emily's help?"

I started to hyperventilate. Dad took my hand and helped me regain my breath. "Andra." His calm voice eased my worry a little. "Getting involved with the Freedom Reader's is always dangerous and complicated. I can't tell you what to do, but we at least need to pass this information on to the Readers and then you can decide."

"I'll take the information to Johnson," Brian said. "I believe in you, Andra. You'll think of something."

But so far I hadn't been able to write a word.

* * *

"Our plan hinges on Andra gaining you and Johnson access," Emily said to Brian a few days later when he went to discuss Andra's concerns and her inability to write. "What worries her? I've promised to hold a party and invite all of the major players in the Ministry, including Librarian Bookman. If Bookman is not in the library, nobody else will enter. If the Supreme Prime Minister insists, everyone will attend, and I assure you, he will insist."

"She knows that. We both do," Brian said. "But . . ." He stared into the mug of cider he was drinking as if he could find answers in the amber depths.

"But what, Brian?" Emily's sharp voice forced Brian to look at her. She began to pace in front of the fire.

"We've promised to keep your secrets, and we won't back out on that promise," Brian said. "But this is about Andra's power. She's the one taking a risk. I've seen how weak she becomes if she pushes too hard or does something against her conscience. The cause isn't worth her destruction. You already pushed Lauren too far too fast."

"What do you mean?" Johnson said from his seat in the corner of the room.

"After the day at the Ministry, Lauren collapsed. She's been recuperating in her room at Professor Albert's home ever since and will barely talk to anybody."

"Lauren was weak when she went in," Emily said.

"Emily . . ." Johnson had a note of warning in his voice.

"I'm sorry about Lauren." Emily sat down in the chair next to Brian and placed a hand on his arm. He fidgeted under her intense gaze. "We'll do whatever we can to help her recover. But, we're simply asking Andra to cause a minor malfunction at the Ministry, something that will gain us access to the secret passage in the library."

"I know, and I've told her that, but . . ."

"Go on, Brian," Emily said. "We have to trust each other and be honest."

"That's just it," Brian said. "Neither of us understand why a party thrown by you would clear out the Ministry. What connection do you still have with the Ministry, Emily? If you could explain that, I think I can get Andra to focus."

"That isn't information you need to know," Emily said.

"But you just said that we have to be honest and trust each other. It seems like that rule only goes one way." He got up and put on his heavy jacket. "I'll talk to Andra, but I can't promise anything. It seems to me you're not sharing everything, and I don't like it."

He slammed the door behind him and began the long walk through the tunnels. Only a few moments passed when he heard footsteps following him.

"Brian, wait."

Brian stopped and allowed Johnson to catch up.

"I'll tell you what I can, even though Emily thinks you don't need to know."

"If you don't share what you know, why should we trust you?"

"You're right. Let's go find Andra and I'll answer your questions."

*　*　*

"Lauren." Professor Albert knocked on Lauren's door. "I've brought you some tea." He waited for an answer, which didn't come. He turned back to put the tea on the rough wooden table in the middle of the room when he heard the lock slide and the door open.

"Good, you must be feeling better."

Lauren appeared even more fragile than she had when he had brought her from her grandmother's deathbed. She stood barefoot in a white nightgown that almost blended in with her skin, her streaming red hair forming again into a knotted mess. *A strong wind will blow her away,* the Professor thought.

"Well then you better not open the door." Lauren's weak voice startled the Professor as it had been so long since he'd heard it.

"Now I know you're better, if you're making jokes and spying on my thoughts."

"I'm sorry." Lauren's face rivaled her hair.

"It's okay. I'm just glad you're feeling well enough to use your power. Sit down. Have some tea and toast."

Lauren took small slow steps and smiled with relief when she reached the chair the Professor pulled out for her. She took a few sips of the hot tea and nibbled on the freshly buttered bread before speaking again. "Has . . ." She sipped again, her hand shaking. "Did Andra write the accident?"

"I don't think so," Professor Albert said. "The Readers haven't notified me, but then again, they may not. I'm not really part of that plan."

"I . . . I'm not sure she should."

"Why not?"

"After I used my power . . . with all those voices . . . I couldn't . . ." Lauren's hands started shaking again and the violence of the tremor caused her to drop her mug, which crashed onto the floor and broke. "I'm sorry!" Her eyes filled with tears.

"Don't worry about it, Lauren." The Professor leaned next to her chair and placed both hands on her shoulders. "Take a deep breath . . . again . . . again. There, better?"

She nodded, her shaking stopped.

"Now let me get you more tea and then I think we need to visit Andra. We have a lot more to learn and understand about these powers before we ask either of you to risk yourselves again."

"But what about the plan?"

"You girls are more important to me than anything the Freedom Readers have planned. They often rush ahead without thinking, and that's when people get hurt. I won't let that happen to you."

* * *

I put the finishing touches on my writing and let the ink dry before handing the paper over to Johnson. Brian watched over me with a protective eye. "How are you?" he asked.

"I'm fine, Brian. It won't work unless I envision it happening. I've just written the words, but I haven't done the hard part."

"Are you sure you want to do this?" Brian asked.

"Have you told us everything?" I asked Johnson who sat in the corner reading my work.

"What more do you need to know?" Johnson said. "I've explained that after her husband's death Emily has had to serve as a hostess of sorts, at the beck and call of Ministry officials. While she loves entertaining, she hasn't relished the task, except that it gives her an insider's perspective of what goes on in the Ministry, which has helped the Readers formulate plans for change. It has also allowed her to get close to the Supreme Prime Minister, who often turns to her when he needs to be entertained."

"I'm still not sure I understand why you haven't made any major moves since my father's disappearance and Andra's mother's death," Brian said.

"Because those two events were connected somehow, and indicated that the government was coming too close to the Readers. If they learned of Emily's role, or the Scrivener's, or of any other agents of ours that have access to high Ministry officials, do you think it would take them long to destroy us one after another? We haven't been sitting and doing nothing, however. We've slowly recruited other men and women connected to the Ministry to our cause. We've made subtle inroads and planned for what happens after we finally break the grip of the Ministry."

"Who are these other people?" I asked. "I recognized a few people at the meeting, but not many. I didn't see any Ministry workers."

"I'm sure you understand why I want to keep their names hidden. The fewer people who know the extent of our infiltration into the Ministry, the safer those people are."

"I guess I understand," I said.

"Okay, I'll give you that," Brian said. "But what happens if we do win? What are the plans?"

"We'll work toward creating a government of elected officials that represent the will of the people, with members of the Freedom Readers taking the lead, we hope."

"In other words, a return to a system similar to the former representative democracy?" I asked. "A return to a system that allowed the division of the country and led to Sandovar's creation of New North? How can we ensure that we don't run into the same problems?"

"I'd like to think we've learned from past mistakes," Johnson said. "The failures of that government began when the rulers allowed money and extremists to have more power and voice than everyday people. Of course, it won't be easy, but I have to believe we can create a better system. I wouldn't still be in the Freedom Readers if I didn't have hope." He held the paper out to me. "You're the key to that hope at the moment, Andra, but I can't force you to do this. It has to be your choice."

"Emily might think differently." Dad stood leaning against the attic doorway, bending his head to avoid the low doorframe. Nobody had noticed his entrance.

"Emily isn't here," Johnson said. "I know how much you've already sacrificed for this cause. Each one of you, even before you knew what your losses meant. I won't force Andra to do this."

"I appreciate that, my friend." Dad entered the small attic room and reached out to give Johnson the hand shake of the Readers.

Tense emotion filled the air between the two men. I locked eyes with Brian who shrugged his shoulders. I realized at that moment I had no choice.

"I have to do this for my mother and your father," I said. I curled up onto my favorite spot on my old couch and began to focus my intent on the words I had written.

"This isn't going to happen immediately, is it?" Johnson asked.

"I'm the one who insisted nobody get hurt," I said. "I've written this to happen when everyone is at Emily's party and when the guards will be away from the library, according to their routine scheduled rounds. Now I just have to envision my own words and focus on when I want them to happen. It helps if I have quiet."

The men watched in silence. Brian's hand twitched. Johnson's face hardened in intensity. Dad paced, his focus on me.

I sat and pictured every detail—a gathering at Emily's mansion, a library empty of people, a crack that develops in the wall, and a crash that brings down a tumble of wall, books, and artifacts revealing a hidden tunnel. My heart beat faster and my breathing grew heavy and then . . . everything went black.

*   *   *

I heard voices in heated discussion that beat to the time of the throbbing pain in my head. I couldn't raise my head or move my limbs that must have weighed a thousand tons. I kept my eyes closed and listened, hoping that the pain would subside and voices would quiet. I didn't want to see anyone, or to join in the debate. I wanted peace.

"How can you ask Andra to do this?" Dad's voice sounded full of concern. "She passed out and the act hasn't even happened. We don't know enough . . ."

"I know that, Ben," Johnson said. "But what choice do we have? She made her own decision to get involved."

"We have the choice to move slowly and not risk these young women." Professor Albert's voice surprised me. When did he arrive? "Lauren, can you hear anything in Andra's mind?"

"I . . . I didn't want to intrude." I could hardly hear Lauren's whispered response. "I don't think she'll mind," Brian said. I didn't mind. I didn't want to speak but needed the support of my friend. Brian's voice also comforted me. When he was around, I was safe. He would never let anyone hurt me. "She'll understand."

Someone took my hand and I recognized Lauren's frail touch.

Lauren, are you listening to me? Please make them go away. I can't stand the arguing. I won't open my eyes until they're gone.

I'll do my best.

Did Lauren just say that out loud? I wondered. I had heard her words, but inside my head.

What is Andra thinking? Lauren's voice spoke again, inside my head. *I didn't say anything.*

I HEARD your thought just then.

That's impossible. Even in her mind, Lauren's voice sounded panicked. *Does that mean you can read minds as well?*

No, maybe your power has shifted. I can't hear anyone else, just you. Make them leave. Lauren's hand shook in my own. She gave mine a subtle squeeze. *Tell them they can take their noisy selves out of this room and leave you here to watch me. Their arguing is making things worse.*

"I can hear her thoughts," Lauren said in a shaky voice. "She's thinking she wishes you would take your noisy selves out of the room because your arguing is making things worse."

Brian laughed. "That sounds like Andra."

"I'm not leaving until she opens her eyes," Dad said.

"I'll stay with her," Lauren said. "I think she just needs quiet."

"Come on, Ben," Johnson said. "Our arguing isn't going to solve the problem or help Andra. Let's leave Lauren with Andra and talk downstairs."

"You know how I feel."

Johnson sighed. "I do, Ben. I do. But this is bigger than both of us. Come on. If I know you, you have a delicious cider stored away somewhere. Let's have some and talk about the good old days. Woodson, Professor Albert, you too. Let's leave Lauren and Andra alone."

I waited for the sound of footsteps heading downstairs before I opened my eyes. I started to sit up, but that made my head spin.

"Let me help you." Lauren's unusual green eyes stood out big and worried in her pale face. She helped me into a sitting position. "What just happened?" she asked. "Did you really hear me?"

"I don't know," I said. "Let's try again. Don't speak, just think."

Lauren moved away from me to sit at the desk chair. She scrunched up her face as if she was thinking extra hard.

I laughed.

"What's so funny? The thought I just sent you was serious."

"You look like you're trying to lay an egg. But wait, you sent me a thought? I didn't hear it that time. Why not? I swear I heard you before."

We stared at each other in confusion for a few moments.

"Wait, you were holding my hand. Come sit next to me." I made room on the sofa. "Hold my hand and try again."

Lauren sat on the faded sofa and we joined hands.

I'm so scared. What if our powers are dangerous? What if they're hurting us? What if it hurts others? I heard the thoughts as if Lauren had spoken.

"It worked," I said.

"What was I thinking?" Lauren asked.

"You were thinking you're scared and concerned that the powers are dangerous. You wondered if they were hurting us or if we would hurt others."

Oh wow! Lauren thought.

This is good. I responded. *Are you okay? Is this draining you?*

"No, I'm all right. How about you?" Lauren said out loud.

"I feel better than I did when I was writing before."

Me too. I feel stronger than I have in days.

I wish we didn't have to be touching for this to work, though, I thought.

A sudden inspiration hit me. I dropped Lauren's hand and jumped up—

only to stumble with dizziness. "I have an idea!" I said as I regained my balance and moved with slow steps to my desk to grab a fresh sheet of paper and a pen.

"What are you doing?" Lauren asked.

"I'm going to make us stronger, I think."

"But that sounds like something really big, and you just collapsed writing an event that won't even happen for days."

"I think I can do this with your help. Lauren. We have to try. I feel better and stronger because of you. You feel better because of me. We have to see if this is going to work."

"What if you pass out again? Your father will kill me."

"Dad would never kill anyone, especially if you tell him I was being stubborn and stupid. He'll recognize that I'm to blame."

Lauren smiled, but I could see the worry in her eyes.

"Professor Albert is downstairs. He'll help if something goes wrong. I don't think anything will go wrong. I know deep inside that this is right, and I've learned to trust my feelings when it comes to writing things into reality. Do you want to try?"

Lauren stared out my window for a moment before answering. "I like the idea that you might be able to hear me too. It makes me less lonely." She turned back. "What do you need me to do?"

"Pull the rocking chair closer to my desk." I sat down.

Lauren lifted the chair, admiring the carved softness of the wood. "This is beautiful."

"It was my mother's," I said. "I think Brian's father made it. She used to tell me stories while rocking me in that chair. Dad let me bring it up here because it makes him too sad to look at it, but he knows it gives me comfort. Okay, now sit down and hold my left hand. Do not let go until I tell you to, even after I stop writing."

"What are you going to write?" Lauren asked.

"I'm going to strengthen our connection. You'll see."

I dipped my pen into the ink and started writing. It didn't take me long. I blotted the pen, put it down, and closed my eyes while I envisioned what I wanted to happen.

There, it's done, I thought to Lauren. *Drop my hand and go sit on the sofa.*

But you won't be able to hear me then.

I will if this worked. Try.

Lauren moved over and sank into the cushions.

Think of something, I urged in silence.

I don't know what to think. This is crazy.

I started laughing. *It may be crazy, but it worked. I "heard" you think that. How do you feel?*

Good! Strong!

I jumped up without even a touch of dizziness and pulled Lauren into a wild dance of joy. Lauren let out a surprised yelp of laughter. The sound of running footsteps pounded up the stairs followed by a knock and Dad's voice calling out, "What's going on? Is everything okay? Is Andra all right?"

Should we tell everyone? Lauren asked.

Not right away. I think this is something we should keep to ourselves for the moment. I opened the door.

FOURTEEN

On the day of the party, I developed a case of what Dad called "the clum-sies." Whenever I am nervous or excited about something, I drop anything put into my hands, walk into walls and trip on lint.

"It's amazing you're able to look gorgeous and not give yourself a black eye." Dad poked his head into my bedroom and watched me fumble with makeup. I dislike putting on makeup, and resent that now—as an "official" woman—I have to wear it for public events. But of course, it had to look natu-ral because proper women don't put too much color on their faces. A woman could be sent to the WTP for inappropriate makeup use.

I dropped the applicator with a clatter and stood, knocking my chair over. Dad laughed, picked up the chair, and gave me a kiss on the cheek. "You've been to Ministry events before. Why are you so nervous?" he asked.

"Everything's different this time." I took a deep breath and changed the subject. "You look handsome. I haven't seen you so dressed up in a long time."

"Is my tie straight?"

I reached over and fixed it for him. "There, now you're perfect."

"The carriage Emily sent is waiting outside." Dad offered his arm to me. "Shall I escort you downstairs so you don't break a leg before the festivities?"

"Ha ha! Very funny." I laughed at his over-exaggerated attempt to look gallant, and took his arm.

"There's my girl," he said. "I love to see you smile. You have your mother's smile."

We walked downstairs in silence, but as Dad helped me with my wrap the reality of what I had written for that day settled in. "Are we sure everyone is going to be at the party? Nobody has been left at the Ministry to get hurt?"

"We've been over this. The Supreme Prime Minister 'highly recommended' attendance at this gala honoring him, thrown by 'good friend of the Ministry, Madame Emily DuFarge.' Anyone who ignores that will become suspicious in his eyes. Plus everyone knows Emily's talent for entertaining. The only people left at the Ministry will be the two guards on duty and they were selected by drawing straws. They're grumpy about not going to the party, as occasions like this are one of the few perks of a thankless job. I explained their rounds to you. You wrote the event to happen when they both will be in other parts of the building."

"I know, but what if something goes wrong?"

Dad took both my shoulders in a grasp that almost hurt. I winced as he forced me to look into his eyes. He eased up on his grip, but his eyes remained serious.

"Andra, you've decided to join what amounts to a war. In war, people get hurt. I tried to protect you from this, but you're just like your mother." He blinked several times in a somewhat futile attempt at stopping tears. One dripped out and I reached a finger up to wipe it away as I listened to his words. "Anything can happen when you interfere with the Ministry and get involved with the Freedom Readers. Promise me you'll be cautious when they ask you to do something else."

"Emily said this would be the only thing they would ask for a while. Don't worry, Dad."

"Emily says a lot of things. I know these people. If they want more from you, they'll ask for more. The fight is more important than the individuals who do the work, at least to some of the Readers."

"Aren't you and Johnson good friends? Don't you trust him?"

"I trust him with my life, but there are many people involved in the Readers, and there are some who just want to come out on top no matter which side wins."

I hesitated before I admitted, "I'm scared."

"You should be. That will keep you alert. But meanwhile . . . ," he dropped my shoulders and offered me his arm again. "We have a party to attend."

* * *

I had never been to the DuFarge mansion, or at least not the living portion of it, only the secret portions hidden in the depths of the mountain upon which the mansion was built. As we walked in, I recognized Emily's exquisite taste down to the last detail. Fresh flowers adorned every table and shelf. The silver gleamed on a table almost hidden by pastries covered in chocolate and cakes with elaborate decorations, fruit plates with fresh whipped cream on the side, mini-quiches and meatballs each with its own silver toothpick, lavish cheeses from unknown origins. There was something for every taste and desire. In the corner, a trio made up of harp, piano, and flute played a delicate melody without overwhelming the general hum of conversation that filled the room.

Andra, thank goodness you're here. I hate this. I'm so nervous. What if someone recognizes me?

I peered through the crowd to pinpoint my friend across the room. *They all know you now as my cousin, and you look exquisite—nobody has seen you dressed like this*, I sent. *Nobody will recognize you. I promise it will be okay.* Emily had created a disguise for Lauren that involved a party gown more extravagant than anything she'd ever worn before. I could hardly recognize the elegant woman in an emerald green silk which made her skin look creamy, her red hair gleam, and her eyes sparkle. For a moment I felt my own pale green dress was too shabby for the occasion compared to hers, but I brushed that concern aside. I had more important things to worry about.

I buried my own concerns since Lauren's thoughts bordered on panic. I didn't want her to know that my fears made me want to run from the party and stop what was about to happen. "There's Lauren," I told my father. "I'm going to join her."

"Be cautious today," he said.

"You're the one who reminded me this is a party. What can happen to us here?"

Just then Emily approached, followed by a Ministry official I didn't recognize. "Scrivener, it's always so delightful to have you visit," she gave my father a formal greeting. "You've avoided my parties for years. Shame on you!"

"Madame DuFarge, the time was right. How could I not celebrate on this occasion?"

"Do you remember Minister Brown who manages *Upper North Town*?" Emily gave me a significant look and put a slight emphasis on the words. I had no idea what she wanted me to know.

"Of course, it's good to see you, Minister Brown." Dad smiled, but his cheeks held tension in them. What was wrong? Was this man a threat?

Lauren, something's wrong, listen in but don't come near. I sent a quick thought in her direction. She stopped making her way toward me and got a look of concentration on her face.

My attention turned back to Dad, who was introducing me to Minister Brown.

"Hello, Madame DuFarge, Minister Brown." I dropped into an appropriate curtsy. "Thank you so much for inviting me to your lovely home, Madame DuFarge."

"Welcome, Andra. It's so good to see you. You've always been like a daughter to me." Emily swooped me into a hug, and whispered in my ear, "Don't let Lauren come near Minister Brown."

I checked to see if Lauren had heard the message. She nodded acknowledgement and shifted direction toward one of the food tables.

I turned my attention back to Emily who had continued talking.

"—such an exciting occasion. Andra, I hope you find some of the other young women entertaining. I've arranged for a room in the back of the house for a little hen session, with the approval of the Supreme Prime Minister, of course."

"That will be lovely, Madame DuFarge. I hope you didn't go to too much trouble."

"Not at all, I love making my guests comfortable and I know how much young women hate being caught up in all the boring ministry talk."

"Are you having the women supervised?" Minister Brown asked.

"The Supreme Prime Minister has agreed that as long as my butler checks on them every once in a while, the girls will be perfectly safe alone."

"He knows what's best, thank the Lord," Minister Brown said.

"Of course he does." Emily took the Minister's arm. "Scrivener, I hope to have a chance to chat later. Andra, do enjoy the party and get to know some of the other young women here. You may find you have a lot in common." With another significant look, she steered Minister Brown toward another group.

"What was that all about?" I asked.

"Minister Brown knows I don't have a niece in Upper North Town."

"Oh, I forgot about that. Why do you think Emily wants me to talk to the other women? What does she think I'll have in common with them?"

"I'm sure she's hoping you will find those with power, today," Dad said. "Please, be careful. Even a woman with abilities might believe in the words of the Lord. Now go, mingle and don't forget to warn Lauren to avoid Minister Brown."

With that, Dad turned away to greet some other ministry workers. I made my way through the crowd, relieved that Lauren had already disappeared. I assumed she had gone to the safety of the separate women's room, as I couldn't connect with her mind. We had to be in the same room for the connection to work. My own passage across the party took a long time as I responded to greetings from ministry workers and other people I knew. Some of my tension released as I recognized numerous faces, especially when Librarian Book-man waved to me from the buffet as he treated himself to rich looking food. I smiled and waved back before escaping to the young women's room and the comfort of my friend.

Light filtered through gauzy curtains over floor to ceiling windows and made the pale coral walls glow with warmth. Emily had placed elegant but comfortable seating areas all around the room. One area held craft supplies for those who wanted to do needlework or paint. Across the room, sheet music sat on a grand piano, with other instruments standing by, ready for a musical extravaganza. A table held more beautifully crafted treats, including a chocolate fountain with a selection of fruit and bread for dipping.

"Andra! I'm so glad you came." Cindy Rogerson's operatic squeal greeted me as soon as I stepped through the door, followed by a smothering embrace. "I never got a chance to thank you for the wonderful picture of me. And I hear you're going to marry my brother. Did you see him? He's here today. I'm sure he wants to see you. It's wonderful! You'll be able to paint me any time I want a new one."

"Um . . . we're just getting to know each other. We're not engaged."

"Oh don't be modest. You know that will happen soon enough and then we'll be sisters. Won't that be wonderful?"

Help me! I sent an urgent thought in Lauren's direction.

What can I do? Lauren's reply contained laughter. *It looks like you get to be one of the popular girls now. Isn't that WONDERFUL?*

"Come sit by me," Cindy cut into the silent exchange. "Tell me everything about your date."

The next half hour was torture, as Cindy clung to me with a barnacle grip. Lauren sat across the room from us, sometimes talking with another guest, but mostly watching with an amused smile on her face. I couldn't figure out any way to escape Cindy on my own, but eventually her ever-present need to be the center of attention gave me the answer.

"I want to play the piano and sing. Come with me, Andra."

"You know I don't sing, Cindy. I think I'll sit and draw for a while."

"Will I be in the picture?"

"I wouldn't want to ruin the surprise."

I sat in a small loveseat near Lauren and picked up some drawing supplies. I settled in for a few moments while letting my hand wander on the page as I sought the comfort of my familiar escape into art. Lauren and I began to chat about unimportant things. A few other young women wandered away from the noise near the piano, and picked up various projects to work on.

"May I see what you're drawing?" A girl with long black hair leaned toward me in an attempt to peek at my work. At that moment, I realized the danger I might be in if anyone could recognize my style. My first instinct was to hide the drawing away, but my reputation for sharing my work preceded me. If I hid it, people might become suspicious.

"This is lovely," the girl said. Then she lowered her voice. "It looks a little bit like one of those drawings the government dislikes."

I dropped a charcoal pencil as Lauren's clear internal warning came through. *Be careful!*

"Have you seen one of those drawings?" I asked, trying my best to sound nonchalant.

"My friends and I have tried to collect them. My name is Heidi. This is Jenna and Beth." She gestured to each girl who nodded at their name, but didn't speak.

"I'm Andra, and this is my cousin Lauren."

Heidi settled next to me on the loveseat and spoke in a conspiratorial tone. "The drawings have messages you know—important messages."

"You know how to read the women's language?" Lauren asked.

"Of course, doesn't everybody?"

My heart pounded in my chest. I glanced over at Lauren's intense and concerned face. I wanted to keep these girls talking without revealing too much. *What do I do?* I asked in silence.

Don't admit to drawing them, Lauren thought. *Find out what they know.*

"Not everyone." I found my voice. "We both do. We've only seen one or two of the drawings. Why are the messages important?"

"Heidi, be careful what you say." Another woman approached with a sour look on her face. I recognized Alice, the daughter of a minister who wanted my father dismissed after Mother passed. We had been friends as children— close friends—but everything changed when Mother died. "That's the Scrivener's daughter."

I pushed aside remnants of hurt feelings and anger from those long gone days. I tried to calm myself before I spoke and said anything I'd regret. Heidi surprised me by coming to my defense.

"And you are a minister's daughter," she said with a toss of her black hair, "but we trust you."

I found my calm center, gave Heidi a grateful smile and put my hand out in the old pinkie-swear gesture Alice and I used as children. "I promise, I won't tell anyone, Alice," I said. "For old times' sake."

The corners of Alice's mouth competed against her sour pucker to form a small smile. Alice joined pinkies with me.

"I . . . the message I read was interesting but confusing," I said. ". . . Something about powers."

"Shh! Don't talk so loudly. What about her? She may turn us into the Ministry." Alice thrust her head in Lauren's direction.

"I have no love for the Ministry." Lauren's face hardened in remembered pain.

Tell them who I really am, Lauren thought.

Are you sure?

Yes.

"Lauren isn't really my cousin." I lowered my voice as much as I could and still be heard. "This is Lauren Freeman."

"Are you the one who fought as they carried you into the training center?" Heidi sounded excited. "You're practically a legend. I know many girls who wish they had the courage to do what you did."

I worried that Lauren would burst into flames from the color her face turned. I don't think she ever realized how many people she inspired by standing up for what she believed in. *I'm not the only one who knows you're a brave woman,* I thought.

Thank you. Even her inner voice sounded overwhelmed and surprised.

"Someone told me you caught a mysterious illness and died in the center," Heidi continued, oblivious to the silent interchange. "How come you're here? Did you get married? If you're married you're supposed to be out there." She gestured toward the door.

"I'm here as a guest of the Scrivener," Lauren said.

"Is she going to be your new mother?" Alice said with a cruel gleam in her eye.

"It's not like that." Lauren's cheeks flamed.

"Dad and I helped Lauren recover from an illness caused by her time in the WTP." I took Lauren's hand. "We have become good friends. She's like a sister to me."

Lauren gave me a quick, shy smile before her face reflected the seriousness of the conversation. "I have no love for the Ministry," she said. "I was sick because of them, not because of some mysterious illness. Someone told you I died because they assumed they had killed me. In a way that's good, because it means they aren't looking for me. They see what they expect to see, and I seem free to be where I want to be."

Lauren started to shake with emotion. I squeezed her hand to give her strength while I sent a silent message. *I've never heard you say so much about the WTP. I'm here. You're okay.*

We can't let anything happen to other women and young girls! Lauren's silent reply was an internal scream.

"I didn't know the WTP was that bad," Heidi said.

"It's bad for certain women," I said. "We were talking about the messages. What do you know?"

Heidi glanced over at Alice.

"Go ahead," Alice said. "If she turns us in, I'll deny everything. But be quiet and pick up something to do. We'd better look busy." She picked up some needlepoint and sat in another chair as she glanced across at the raucous crowd gathering around the piano. "We don't want to attract attention."

Heidi gestured for everyone to move in. The two girls who hadn't said anything yet pulled chairs closer into the circle and grabbed some busy work.

"Before the declaration from the Prime Minister," Heidi said, "I started looking for those images wherever I went. I kept as many as I could find and tucked them away where nobody else would find them."

Just then, the door from the hall opened to reveal Emily's butler, wearing his sharp black tails and carrying a heavy tray laden with more delicacies. The girls jumped and focused on the activities in their hands. It took me a moment to recognize Johnson; I had never seen him in anything but workman's clothes. His butler uniform made him look like a completely different man. I knew he'd planned to attend the party in disguise, as he would have no reason to be there otherwise, but I never expected this. I choked back a laugh and glanced at Lauren who hid a smile behind her needlepoint.

"Ladies, I've come to check on you," he said in an unfamiliar drawling voice. "Is everybody enjoying themselves? Do you need anything?"

"This is such a wonderful party." Cindy's voice carried over the music. "Please tell Madame DuFarge everything is perfect. I hope she'll come spend some time with us."

"I'll pass the message on to her," Johnson said. He turned to our group. "And you, ladies, what are you doing? Do you need anything?"

"We're just working on crafts and gossiping." Alice's hand shook as she raised her needlepoint toward Johnson for approval. I tried to hide my chuckle and noticed Lauren purse her lips in an attempt to hold her own laugh in. Alice sent a scathing look in our direction and then pulled herself up into full haughtiness. "We would like something to drink while we work."

"There are plenty of refreshments available." Johnson turned so that only I could see his wink. "Shall I serve you?"

"Yes. I'll have hot cider," Alice said.

As Johnson went about getting drinks for all the girls, Lauren and I held a private, silent conversation.

I'm glad it's Johnson, I thought. *Otherwise this conversation would be terrifying.*

I know, Lauren replied. *But it is fun watching Alice jump like a nervous chicken. Johnson wants me to convey a message to you when I have a private moment. He's thinking really loudly. He says that he'll let us both know as soon as they've gotten notice from the ministry. He also keeps thinking "Be careful! Be careful!"*

What's he worried about I wonder?

I don't know. He's buried his concerns too deep for me to read them without pushing.

Johnson served me last. "I hope your conversation is fruitful. If you ladies don't need anything else, I'll be back later. You can always ring the bell pull if you need me." He pointed at an elaborate rope hanging against one wall. "Don't get into any trouble while I'm gone." With that he left, closing the door behind him.

"That was too close," Alice said. "He was very impudent for a butler. At least he didn't hear anything. We shouldn't be talking about this here."

"As long as we pay attention, we'll be okay," Heidi said. "Just keep looking busy. Where was I?"

"You've hidden the drawings." I said. "Why? What's so important?"

"If you look at all of them . . . I don't know if I have all of them, but I have a lot. My parents even bought a framed one for me, and Mother can read them as well. 'This art is important,' she told me. They talk about women having powers—brain powers—that men don't have."

I remembered the woman in Mr. Mastak's shop. Heidi resembled her.

"And . . ." Heidi leaned in even closer, her voice sinking into the lowest whisper. "We think we have some of those powers."

My pulse raced in excitement. "What do you mean?"

"Show her, Jenna," Heidi said to the woman next to her who had been silent up to that point.

"Are you sure?" Jenna asked with a tremor in her voice.

"Do it. I think Andra's safe. Our mothers used to be friends. 'You can always trust the Scrivener family,' she says. "

"If your mother told you the moon was falling, you'd believe her," Alice said.

"You're just jealous because my mother actually talks to me," Heidi said. "Go on, Jenna, show her."

Jenna nodded. "Watch that candy dish," she indicated a small crystal dish that sat on the coffee table between us. As we watched, the dish moved across the table toward Heidi, who reached out and caught it before it fell onto the ground.

"Did you do that?" I asked. "How?"

"I'm not sure." I had to lean forward to hear Jenna's quiet voice. "I can make anything move, even heavy objects although that can sometimes drain me."

"What can you do?" Lauren turned to Heidi. I could hear the excitement in her voice, as it matched the energy coursing through my own body.

"Give me your hand." Heidi held her hand out to Lauren.

"Why?" Lauren sent a nervous look in my direction. "Can you read minds?"

"No, why would you think that?" Heidi said. "I can heal people, to some extent. Or at least make them feel better. I tap into people's emotions and enhance them or change them. Don't worry. I like to help people. Right ladies?"

Her friends all nodded. I sent Lauren a silent message. *We need to find out what they can do. Do it.*

"Okay." Lauren placed her hand into Heidi's.

"Now, close your eyes and relax. Right now I can sense that you are nervous, sad, scared, and holding onto a lot of pain and anger."

"She just told us that," Alice said. "You aren't proving anything."

"Be quiet, Alice," Heidi said. "This isn't easy." Her face clouded into an expression I had seen Lauren wear before. Heidi's voice softened and fell into a soothing sing-song directed toward Lauren. "What happened to you was truly horrible. I want to help you. This is a party, so let's make you happy. Think about something you loved to do as a child. Picture it in your mind. What does it look like? What does it smell like? What color is it? How does it feel? Take two deep breathes and fall into that moment."

The tense look on Lauren's face melted into a relaxed, peaceful state that I hadn't seen since before she was sent to Training.

"Keep your eyes closed," Heidi said. "And describe what you feel or see."

"It's like I'm being hugged by Grandma, the way she did when she took care of me as a child. Do you smell apple pie baking? It smells delicious. It's lovely."

"I thought that was what I smelled," Heidi said.

"I don't smell anything," I said.

"If you take both our hands you'll be able to smell it as well. You'll be able to sense what Lauren is feeling."

I grabbed both hands. As soon as I touched Lauren's, I got a sudden whiff of what smelled like apple pie and an overwhelming sense of peace tinged with a touch of sadness.

"That's amazing," I said.

"Now I'm going to send healing energy into Lauren," Heidi said. She dropped my hand and held onto both of Lauren's. It almost seemed like her hands glowed, and the glow spread into Lauren's body.

Heidi dropped Lauren's hands. "How do you feel now?" she asked.

Lauren blinked her eyes open as if coming out of a dream.

"Thank you." Her voice sounded muffled as silent tears dripped out of her eyes.

Heidi handed Lauren a handkerchief. "Tears heal. I hope I gave you a moment of comfort. You have a lot of pain inside you. I'd have to work with you many more times to make it stick, I think."

"Do all of you have abilities?" I asked.

"I can't show you mine here," Alice said. "I can start fires with my mind. Beth here claims she can communicate with animals, but I'm not sure that's true. She can barely communicate with humans."

"You've s-s-seen me do it," Beth said.

"I've suh-suh-suh-seen animals obey you, but that doesn't mean you're communicating with them, Beth," Alice said.

"Stop picking on her," Heidi said. "So what about you, Andra? Lauren? Have you noticed that you can do anything special?"

What should we do? I asked in silence, making eye contact with Lauren.

I think we need to tell them, Lauren thought.

Shouldn't we check with Emily first?

No! We need to let them decide for themselves whether or not to join the Freedom Readers. They should have a choice.

You're right.

"Ladies, could you stop staring into each other's eyes please," Alice said. "Why do I think you're talking without words?"

"Because . . ." Lauren took a deep breath. "I can read minds."

"Really?" Heidi clapped her hands together. "And you can too, Andra?"

"Well, not really. I mean, I've somehow learned to be able to read Lauren's mind, but I can't read anyone else's. That's not my talent."

"But you have one?" Heidi said. "I knew it."

"I created the art—the ones with the messages—"

"That's not a talent," Alice said. "I mean, you're a decent artist, but we all can create messages using the women's language.

"Let her finish, Alice," Heidi said. "Why did you create them? What's your talent?"

"I can't show you here," I said. "It's too dangerous, but . . . I can read and write and—"

"You can!" Alice said. "My father was right. He always suspected your father was disobeying the laws and teaching you to read."

"Dad didn't teach me! One day I just picked up something and knew how to read it and then . . ."

"What else can you do?" Heidi asked.

"On my birthday this year, I discovered that I have the ability to write some things into reality."

"What?" Alice said. "So you could make something out of nothing. Or you could write yourself beautiful?"

"Be quiet, Alice," Heidi said. "I'd kill for Andra's hair. So, can you write anything into reality?"

"Not exactly. I can't make something out of nothing and there are certain limitations. I can't really do things that affect me personally. And, sometimes—" A wave of weakness moved through my body.

"Andra, what's wrong?" Lauren asked. "You suddenly went pale."

"Beth, get her some water," Heidi said. "Here, put your feet up." She moved a footstool closer and took my hands. "Let me tap into you, I can help."

I gave a weak nod. My hand tingled as Heidi began to use her power.

"Should I ring for the butler?" Jenna asked.

"No, I'm just a little dizzy," I said. "It's already going away. Heidi's helping."

"Is this your way to distract us?" Alice asked. "You couldn't figure out how to flesh out your ridiculous power."

"Shut up, Alice!" This time four voices mingled together, which made me smile despite my dizziness and nausea. I wished I knew what was wrong; the last time I had gotten this sick, I had tried to write something beyond my abilities. Beth handed me water and a dampened linen napkin to wipe my face.

I took a few sips as Lauren wiped my brow and Heidi sent more healing through my hand. The dizziness passed. "I feel better already," I said.

"Are you sure you're okay?" Lauren asked. "What happened?"

"It was nothing," I said, although I couldn't be sure of that. I didn't want to tell them that my reaction only happened when my power went wrong. "Let's get back to our discussion. I'd be happy to show you that I'm not lying, but it's too dangerous here. We need to meet somehow. Somewhere safe."

"C-c-can we bring others?" Beth's voice surprised the group. "I know a f-few more people who th-th-think they have powers."

"You do?" Heidi said. "Why didn't you tell me? I think I might know others as well."

"This is all nice and everything," Alice said, "but you're forgetting that we aren't allowed to meet without male supervision. How are we going to do that?"

"I think I have an idea," I said.

We spent the next hour planning for a secret meeting until the door opened again to reveal Johnson followed by my father, whose face made me jump up in concern. The sound of distressed voices drifted in behind them.

I ran to my father. "What happened?" I asked.

"There's been an accident at the Ministry." Dad avoided looking at me as he tried to hide his pain and sorrow. "Somebody was killed."

My legs collapsed underneath me.

FIFTEEN

It didn't take long for the party to break up after the news. Dad was called to Sandovar's side, as some of the more important party guests gathered in a private salon in the mansion. Those not important enough to be part of the meeting headed home. At Dad's orders, Lauren stayed with me until I could walk again, then we made a show of preparing to leave. Johnson pretended to escort us out the front, but led us through a passage hidden in the pantry that would take us down to the Freedom Reader's meeting place. There we found Professor Albert and Brian waiting below, since neither was welcome at the party. Johnson changed into his normal clothes then left to offer his well-known skills as a handyman to the Ministry, Brian in tow as his assistant.

Time passed with infinite slowness as we waited for news. I didn't want to talk. I didn't know what to say. I paced as Professor Albert tried to distract us with stories of happier times. The stories just made me upset and I couldn't let him continue.

"I'm sorry, Professor," I said. "I'm too worried. Who died? Why was somebody there? Everyone promised me this wouldn't happen. I don't want to use my power to hurt people." I collapsed onto a small sofa and burst into tears. I couldn't stop the flood.

Lauren moved in to comfort me. "How could this happen, Professor?"

"No plan is fool-proof." Professor Albert leaned back in his chair with a weary sigh. "I don't know why someone was in the library when Bookman wasn't there. What confuses me, though, is that I read what you wrote, Andra. You specifically wrote, the words, 'nobody got hurt.' Up until now, everything you've tried to write has happened exactly the way you intended it, hasn't it?"

"N-not everything." I tried to get ahold of my emotions. "I mean, there are those things that wouldn't work. And there were those times when I've tried something too big. Sometimes part of that will happen, but not all of it. Often I envision something, but the details fill themselves in."

"In the past, what happened when you wrote something that didn't work right?" the Professor asked.

"I'd feel nauseous or dizzy."

"You passed out when you wrote this event," Professor Albert said.

"I did, but I thought that might be just because it was so far into the future, and I was so worried about writing it," I said.

"Andra," Lauren said. "You got dizzy today just around the time the accident must have happened."

"Hm, interesting." Professor Albert stood and began to pace the room in deep thought. "Obviously, if something unintended occurs in the changes you write, it causes you to have a physical response. Have you written anything else recently that made you sick?"

"No," I said. "I found a way to be stronger when I write."

"What do you mean?" the Professor asked just as Lauren's thought reached me. *Are you going to tell him?*

He's the only one who has any understanding of our powers, I thought. *We need his help.*

Lauren nodded her acquiescence.

"When Lauren tried to reach me with her mind after I passed out that time, we discovered—"

Emily entered from the door leading above. "I'm sorry it took so long for me to get down here," she said. "I had to stay with the Supreme Prime Minister until he dismissed me."

"Where's my father?" I asked.

"He was sent by carriage to check on what happened. He left about an hour ago. He should be able to return soon. As everyone else is headed there now, he shouldn't be needed anymore."

"What happened?" A switch inside me snapped into anger. Emily had broken her promise and my words had killed someone. I jumped up to confront her. "Who was killed? You promised me nobody would get hurt."

"Andra, calm down. Let me get you some tea." I gave into her soothing mother-like ministrations as she led me to a comfortable chair, handed me a warm drink, and cooed calming sounds.

The tightness I hadn't noticed in my chest began to ease.

"Emily, please . . . tell me what's happened?" I said.

"All I know at the moment is that someone was in the wrong place at the wrong time and got trapped under some bookshelves that collapsed, pulling a portion of the library wall down with them. They assume the damage was the result of termite activity that caused a support beam to fall." Emily smiled as she said this. "You wrote just the right thing, Andra."

"I did not!" The anger resurged, a red hot flame inside me. I threw my teacup against the wall where it broke into tiny fragments.

"Andra," Emily said. "I know you're upset, but there's no need for such a display of temper."

"If I had written the right thing, nobody would be dead now. I told you I wouldn't hurt anybody, and someone got killed. And you're sitting here, drinking tea and smiling at a job well done. Doesn't the death of an innocent man bother you?"

"Very few of the ministry officials are innocent." Emily placed her teacup down with precision, wiped the corners of her mouth with a cloth napkin and then crossed her hands on the table.

I watched these movements in confusion. How could she be so uncaring and complacent about a person's death—even a ministry official's?

"Now, listen to me." Emily's cultured voice commanded obedience. "We're fighting against evil men who want to keep all women subservient. In this fight, people will sometimes get hurt. Accidents happen, but you did nothing wrong."

I didn't know what to say. My thoughts traveled all over the place, and I couldn't find any logic in them. My emotions had complete control, and they were shooting off like fireworks. The sound of the secret knock made me jump. My father entered.

"Dad!" I rushed to be enfolded in arms that had comforted and protected me my whole life. My tears began again so that his shirt was soon soaked in hot liquid. He just held me, whispering the comforting words of fatherhood that had eased so many of my hurts and pains. I also heard echoing words of comfort and soothing from Lauren's thoughts.

"Scrivener," Emily said, "do you have news?"

"Not now, Emily! I'll deal with you after my daughter has calmed down."

I had never heard Dad speak so harshly to a woman. The severity of his voice brought me back to clarity. I took several deep breaths to gain control, while wishing I could stay in the comfort of my father's arms forever. However, I knew that I had to face what had happened. I chose to join the Readers. I chose to write the words. I had to face it like a woman. I began to regain control, and with one more exhalation pulled away to see everyone else in the room watching with various levels of concern reflected on their faces.

"I'm better now with you here. Tell me the news."

"The man who was killed was Minister Achan," Dad said.

Lauren yelped. The face of the handsome man who had scolded us in the library flashed into my mind's eye.

"Minister Achan . . ." I said. "But why? Why was he in the library?"

"That's what I'd like to know," Dad said. "Perhaps you can explain, Emily?"

Emily stood up and stepped toward my father. Despite the discrepancy of their two heights, with Dad towering over the petite woman, she stood strong and appeared to grow in stature, aided by the reflection of the room's lights on her elegant silken party gown covered with flowers stitched out of gold thread. "Are you accusing me of something, Ben?"

Professor Albert stood as if to intervene, but Dad waved him back. I held my breath, suddenly aware that something was going on that I didn't quite understand.

"Emily, everyone is aware of the history between you and Achan," Dad said.

"I'm not," I said. My anger flared up again at evidence of more information kept from me. "What are you talking about? I deserve to know."

"Hush, Andra," Dad placed his hand on my arm. I pulled away.

"Don't tell me to hush. Lauren and I deserve an explanation."

Dad sighed. "Do you have anything to say, Emily?"

"Achan and I have a history and I have no love lost for the man. I hated him, I don't deny it. But why would I know that he was the unfortunate victim of an accident, or that he was even in the library in the first place?"

"There was a note in his pocket, written by one of the delivery scribes," Dad said. "The note said that an informant from the Freedom Readers would provide him with information that would ensure his promotion to Vice Prime Minister if he met the person in the library. The time written was only moments before Andra had scheduled the accident. The note continued with instructions to destroy the evidence, but, knowing Achan, he decided to keep it in the hopes of being able to use it in the future for his own gain."

"Are you accusing me of sending this note?" Emily asked. "Was the note signed with my mark?"

"No."

"Then why would you assume I'm the traitor? There are plenty of people in the Freedom Readers who were aware of what we had scheduled for today, if not of all the details as to how it would be accomplished. Johnson, for one. He's killed before."

"Johnson would never do this," Dad said. "You know he's only killed in self-defense or to protect others. He has no reason to hate Achan, and he would never hurt Andra this way."

"Emily," Professor Albert startled me with the sternness in his voice as well. He had always spoken with kindness. "You're the only one who hated Achan enough to want him dead."

"We all had run-ins with him," Emily said. "Nobody will be sorry for his loss. But fine, I decided that it was time to get rid of the person who was the biggest immediate threat to our cause. Nobody else got hurt. Nobody will ever be blamed, and we are rid of a vile human being who knew too much."

"I don't understand," I said. "What are you talking about? Dad, what's going on?"

"Andra deserves an explanation, Emily. Will you explain or should I?"

An array of emotions played across Emily's features; from pride to fear to resignation. She took my hands and led me back to the couch, where she sat next to me. Her eyes softened and filled as if she might cry at any moment.

They were Mother's eyes.

"I'm sorry if my actions brought you pain, Andra," she said and I yearned to believe her. "I hope that once you hear my story, you'll understand this was necessary for the cause we all believe in. Everyone, make yourselves comfortable, this will take a while."

* * *

Emily had grown up knowing she was meant for important things. Both her parents played substantial roles in government and she was raised with the best education money could buy. All that changed when Rom Sandovar, aided by wealthy and powerful men, seceded from a failing country and created the nation of New North in the name of the Lord. They let nothing stop them and destroyed anyone who stood in their way. At first they started with subtle manipulations, planting stories in the media to destroy reputations or buying elections to place people who supported their cause into power. Soon, government officials who moved against Sandovar and his allies disappeared or died mysterious deaths.

Both her parents became victims of Sandovar's purging. Her mother ended up in a coma after a terrible accident and never recovered. Once Sandovar put restrictions on health sciences, her mother couldn't be maintained in the coma. She died.

When Emily's father was in deep mourning for his beloved wife, Sandovar's people approached him with the option to either join them in support of the new government and the new country, or his daughter would be the next to face an accident. Emily's father had no choice. He joined Sandovar but it destroyed him. Emily grew into her young adult years watching the shadow of her father drag himself to the newly formed Ministry on a daily basis. As Sandovar pushed through more and more of his agenda—including controlling access to technology and manipulating science and religion to support his cause of subordinating women—Emily's father began to return to his old self and fight against the restrictions. He tried to gather other powerful people who expressed discontent with the new regime to rise against Sandovar. As might have been predicted, the disappearances and deaths began again. Emily feared for her father's life, until an opportunity came for her to save him. She received a visit from Minister DuFarge, a man twenty-five years older than her. "Marry me; join the side of the Lord and the Government. I'll protect your father," he said.

Against her father's objections, Emily agreed. Her choice sheltered him from any retaliation by the government, but she lost him anyway. Within six months of her marriage to DuFarge, her father had stopped eating or taking care of himself. Emily could do nothing to help him. She was with him, holding his hand, on the day he lay in his bed and succumbed to the slow suicide he had chosen. "I'm going to join your mother," he said. "I hope you find joy in this life. Find a way to fight against the government. Fight for equality for all."

Sadness overwhelmed her after the loss of her father. She found no comfort in the cold arms of her husband. Her only joy lay in establishing her reputation as the best hostess in New North. It was at one of her own parties that she met Ronald Achan, who had just joined the Ministry as a lower level aide, but had aspirations of his own. Closer to her age, Achan was handsome and charming, and he made Emily believe that he was on her side. They fell into an affair. She confided in him her hopes of finding a way to defeat Sandovar. He convinced her that, once he had risen in the ranks of the Ministry, he would help bring about a more just society. But, he said, he needed her help to get there. So she helped him. She introduced him to her husband, and convinced Minister DuFarge to promote him to personal aide. From there, Achan made himself indispensable to her husband and the Ministry, all the time continuing the affair with his superior's wife. Meanwhile, Emily fell more in love with him, until she was desperate to find a way out of her loveless marriage.

"I'll think of something," Achan said. "Maybe if I become Junior Minister, I'd be able to find a way to annul the marriage so we can be together." She continued to help, and made sure he was recognized by the right people. Once he won the position of Junior Minister, she reminded him of his promise. "I'll take care of it," he said. A few months later her husband died of an apparent heart attack. His death, however, surprised Emily, as he was a healthy man who took good care of himself. She began to suspect the truth when Achan visited her in an official capacity to discuss what her responsibilities would be to the Ministry if she wished to be supported after her husband's death.

"Can't you find a way to allow us to marry?" she asked. "I know Sandovar will marry me off as a replacement wife for political gain, or he will allow me to remain single as long as I work as a servant to the Ministry in some way. Can't you ask for special dispensation to marry me?"

"Why would I do that?" Achan said. "Now that your husband is gone, I can move up in the ranks and become a full minister. Meanwhile, if you wish to retain the lifestyle you enjoy, you must do whatever the Supreme Prime Minister asks, and that includes acting as wife to anyone who requests it of you. Why would I want to take on the responsibility of supporting you, when the Ministry will do that while I get the fringe benefits?"

"What are you saying?" she asked. "I've already welcomed you into my bed. Don't you love me?"

"I loved what you could do for me. Now that I've gotten rid of your husband, my path is clear to become full minister and from there, I'm sure I can make my own way up in the ranks."

"You killed him?!"

"Of course, at the request of his wicked wife who seduced me into an illicit affair . . ."

"That's not true! You seduced me, and you murdered my husband."

"You know as well as I do that women will always be held responsible in the case of an affair. Women are the evil danger that must be controlled. You also know what happens to a woman who is caught having an affair. Are you willing to face that in order to see me punished for the death of a husband you didn't love?"

Emily realized that the only way to make up for her own mistakes was to agree to Achan's demands and find a subversive way to undermine the government. The seeds of her anger against Achan helped her initiate contact with the people who would eventually become the Freedom Readers. As the Freedom Readers' activities grew, however, Achan suspected she might have a connection with them and continued to blackmail her and others as he gained more and more power in the Ministry.

*　*　*

"We've all run into Achan and faced his manipulations and schemes. Even you, Professor," Emily turned to Professor Albert. "He was behind the plan to destroy your reputation and get you out of the Ministry. And you . . . Ben. He has been trying to undermine your position since before Marion died."

"That's true," Dad said. "But I would never have killed him for it. Nor does it justify you using Andra's power to cause his death without her knowledge."

As Emily told her story, I had been distracted from my own thoughts and emotions by the dark sense of Lauren's mind slipping into some kind of panic mode. She started hugging her legs, rocking back and forth, mumbling. *What's wrong, Lauren?* I thought, but she had blocked my connection to her mind.

I moved closer to Lauren and touched her on the shoulder. She shuddered and began to speak. "They brought them to the Training Center. Women who had affairs. Girls who fell in love and had intimate relations before marriage. Women who were raped. They brought them, and told the outside world that they would be rehabilitated and trained in proper feminine behavior. But they weren't. They brought them to the hidden places in the training center. An amphitheater shaped room. They forced us to come in and watch . . . to learn. The women . . . the girls . . . were stripped naked, and the Trainers—male and female—touched their bodies but without tenderness. They were tied to posts, spread eagle. Then the Trainers . . . they . . ."

"Lauren." The Professor attempted to calm the trembling woman. "You don't have to tell us this."

"I have to," she said, and pulled away from both of our touches. "They handed us rocks. If we didn't throw the rocks, we would be whipped or stoned ourselves. 'Throw them!' they yelled. 'Throw them and purge these creatures of the wickedness they carry. Stone them, and you will be purged of your own vile wickedness. You will become good women.' And so, women threw the stones. I aimed to miss, but that did no good. Others aimed to hit, to hurt, to maim, to kill. At first the bodies simply turned red, as the victims screamed. Then black and blue and green. Then skin ripped and blood dripped and the screams would stop as blood pooled on the floor. By the end, nobody would recognize the pulped victims when their binds were cut."

Lauren fell into silence. Nobody spoke. I hugged her. Lauren's hot tears began to flow.

"Emily," the Professor said. "What Lauren described is terrible, and I understand your desire for revenge. But that doesn't justify what you did. I'm aware of Achan's role in my departure, but I was disillusioned by the Ministry long before he pushed me out, because I knew things like that were happening. I knew the Training Program destroyed more lives than they saved. I did what I could to stop it. I continue to do what I can to help the women inside. I've always believed women deserve more. I chose to join the Freedom Readers because I believed that you were good people who would try to promote change through peaceful means. Instead, you've used both these young women to further your own cause of revenge."

"That wasn't my intent." Emily's voice sounded thick. "Lauren, I'm so sorry that you had to witness that atrocity. Please understand that's why Achan needed to go. He knew or suspected too much, and his attitude hurt women. Lauren's story is proof of that."

The pleading tone in Emily's voice disarmed me—a woman who had reminded me of Mother's strength and power, who wore Mother's eyes—now turned into a woman who had betrayed me in the most painful way possible, by corrupting my words.

"I had nothing against him," I said. "You used me."

"Yes, I used you," Emily said. "We're forgetting something important here. We've achieved our goal. Johnson and Brian are in there, aren't they Scrivener?"

"Yes, but—"

"And could you tell if they can get the information we seek?

"The hidden tunnel lay open with cabinets revealed along its sides. There were too many people around for anyone to gain access to those files without being noticed. The area was also unstable."

"So Johnson and Brian will be the first ones in as they work to stabilize the area?" Emily said.

"I hope so," Dad said, "or this whole attempt was useless. There will be guards watching at all times so I'm not sure how they will access the files. Besides, a successful mission doesn't negate what you've done, Emily."

Emily waved his complaint away, and regained her usual composure. "Johnson knows how to distract the guards. Meanwhile, we're close to finally having the information we've sought for so long. Is it so horrible that I also removed one of the greatest threats to the Freedom Readers while we achieved this goal?"

I waited for my father to respond, but could tell by the look on his face this was one of the rare occasions he was speechless. The Professor looked defeated.

Lauren sent a weak request, *Say something.*

I found the words. "Emily, I trusted you," I said. "I've never believed the ends justify the means. I made it clear to you that I wouldn't use my power to hurt anyone, and you manipulated me into killing someone. I'm not sure I trust you and the Readers anymore." I walked over to grab the wrap that I had draped over a chair when we came down into the hideaway. "I need time to think. Dad, can you take me home?"

"The carriage is waiting outside. Professor Albert, Lauren, can we give you a lift?"

The Professor helped Lauren stand and they gathered their belongings, only to be stopped by the hardened tone in Emily's voice.

"Don't be naïve, Andra. You know the risks every time you use your power. Whenever you write something that affects another person, you risk harming that person. You don't think it's harmful to remove someone's free will by encouraging them to do something they hadn't planned on doing? You're all foolish if you think we can win this war without hurting others. Lauren's story proves how vicious they are, and we need to be willing to be vicious as well. You'll see that Andra's powers, and Lauren's too, will have to be used in much darker ways if we want to get rid of Sandovar. Do you think he's just going to walk away from his own power? Because this is what this war is all about—power and who controls it. We have a secret weapon and I'm not afraid to use it, for the good of women."

I turned back. "You may be right, Emily, but I believe that a woman's ability should be her own to use or not, as she will. I thought you believed that as well, but perhaps we have different goals and understanding of what defines freedom." With that, I turned and walked through the door leading into the mansion, followed by the others.

SIXTEEN

During the carriage ride to Professor Albert's house, I finished explaining how Lauren and I had strengthened each other, and suggested I stay to help Lauren, who hadn't spoken a word since we left. Everyone objected, even Lauren. She soundlessly said *I just need to be alone in my head* before blocking access to her mind. Silence filled my head. I hadn't realized how much the mental connection had sustained me. I wanted desperately to help her, but wouldn't even be allowed to comfort her in person.

I spent the next day torturing myself with my thoughts. I wanted to visit Lauren at Professor Albert's and make sure she was all right. I worried about her, and focused on that in order to avoid my own guilt. I had failed to protect her from terrifying memories. I couldn't even think about my own horror, that I was an unintentional murderer. My guilt ate at me, only to be replaced at times by an overriding sadness or vicious, biting anger.

Dad wanted to stay home with me.

"You know you can't," I said. "Everyone will become suspicious if you take a day off when so much has happened. Besides, you need to keep an eye on Brian. Keep him safe. He doesn't know about Emily."

"Johnson will take care of him," Dad said.

"Johnson is one of them," I said. I had decided that all the Freedom Readers could not be trusted.

"He's a good man. You can't judge all the Readers by the actions of one."

"Go to work." I didn't want to argue. I didn't want to think. I didn't want to talk.

He gave me a look of sadness and concern, shook his head and left.

I couldn't settle into any activity. I burned muffins. Drawing or painting had no appeal. My thoughts ranged from anger to sadness to confusion and everything in between. I even thought about trying to write something that would remove my power completely, but realized that I couldn't leave Lauren alone with her ability. We supported each other. It wouldn't be fair or right to put all the responsibility of power on someone already fragile because of a broken system. I also couldn't desert the other women who had started coming forward. I had to live up to Mother's hopes.

By the late afternoon, I couldn't stand to be alone with my thoughts anymore. I yearned to discuss what I had learned about Emily with Brian. I went to see if he was home yet.

"Andra! What a nice surprise." Mama Woodson wore her usual apron covered with flour while delicious smells wafted out of the kitchen. "I was just pulling some fresh scones out of the oven, would you like one?"

"I was hoping to talk to Brian."

"I assumed you knew that he headed to the Ministry early this morning to help with the reconstruction. Wasn't that part of your plan? What an awful business that a man was where he shouldn't have been! I'm sorry. That must have been a terrible shock."

At the mention of the dead man, I burst into tears.

"Oh, honey!" Mama Woodson enveloped me in her arms. "Come inside. I'll fix you some tea and we'll talk."

I inhaled the scents that emanated from her like an unseen halo—the cozy comforts of cinnamon and chocolate. I missed being held like this, in the arms of a mother. Mama Woodson had been too lost in her own depression to fill in when Mother had died, so her comforting embraces only came on rare occasions. This hug made me wish I could speak to my own mother now. She would give me the strength to understand.

Mama Woodson pulled away from the embrace. "Let me get that tea," she said.

I followed her into the warm yellow kitchen, filled with the memories of my youth. I'd practically spent as much time in that kitchen as my own, until Brian's father disappeared and his home fell into chaos as Mama Woodson lost herself to depression. Now, the pots and pans gleamed and spices sat in neat, decorative rows. The sight helped calm me like tea could never do. "You seem so much better, Mama Woodson," I said. "Your kitchen reminds me of good times."

"I feel more like myself every day. In a way, your involvement with the rebels has brought me back to myself. I can't sit and wallow in the loss of my husband if it means that I'm not alert enough to protect my son. Now grab a scone, sit down, and we'll talk. Be careful, they're hot."

I grabbed a wooden plate out of the cabinet and sat at the sturdy kitchen table, built long ago by Brian's father. I breathed deeply of the platter of cinnamon scones before selecting one and taking a bite. It was the first food I'd eaten all day. "Delicious."

"I'm glad." Mama Woodson set a pot of tea, some mugs, and honey on the table. "Now tell me what's troubling you."

I made no attempt to stop the flood of words as I explained the events of the day before, and what I had learned about Emily. Mama Woodson didn't interrupt once, not even for clarification.

"I always knew there was something inappropriate about that woman," Mama Woodson said when I ran out of words. "Minister Achan was a wicked man. However, it sounds like Emily went into that relationship with eyes wide open. I've never fully trusted her, now I know why."

"You mean you didn't know her story? I thought you were involved with the Freedom Readers."

"I was, but that doesn't mean I knew everything. Patrick tried to keep me out of some of the darker situations, which is why I didn't know he was heading into a dangerous mission that would take him away from me." She grabbed a napkin and crumbled it in a ball as if fighting her emotions. "I mostly worked with your mother to develop the women's language, and helped find people who might be interested in supporting the cause."

"Do you know what exactly happened to your husband?"

"No, but I'm sure some Readers know more than they're telling me. For a long time, I blamed myself for his disappearance, because I never shared my doubts about the Readers with Patrick. I learned something important from that mistake. I want you to reflect on the lesson I learned." She took one of my hands in her own and squeezed. "You cannot take on the guilt for others' misdeeds."

My tears began to build again. "But my words caused the wall to collapse on that poor man. Whether he was a good person or not, my actions led to his death."

"That's not true, Andra." Mama Woodson released my hand and pointed at me with a determined finger. "It was Emily's actions that put him in the wrong place at the wrong time. Your words opened up the possibility of us finding some important truths. Your mother, who was my best friend, would never want you to blame yourself for this and I won't let you do it."

"Wouldn't my mother be upset that I killed a man? Wouldn't she want me to stop using my power?"

"You know the answer to that." The sound of Dad's voice startled us. "I'm sorry to just let myself in like this, Ruth. I came over here wondering if you knew where Andra was. When I realized you were talking, I didn't want to disturb you with a knock."

"You know you're welcome here anytime, Ben. In the past, our doors were always open for each other and we barely knocked. Have a seat and let me get you some tea." Mama Woodson busied herself preparing fresh tea for Dad.

"What do you mean I know the answer? Mother would never have wanted me to hurt anyone."

"True, your mother wouldn't even hurt a spider, unless it would somehow protect you. But that's not what I mean. Your mother would also never want you to give up your power. She already sent you a message on your birthday. Remember?"

"You mean the scroll that Brian gave me?"

"Yes," he said. "Do you remember what it said?"

"It said, 'Women have powers that men fear. I hope my daughter uses hers to change the world.' Well, I've certainly changed the world. I've killed a man."

"That's not want she meant and you know that," Dad said.

"Your mother would blame Emily too, just as I do." Mama Woodson rejoined us at the table. "Here's your tea Ben, just the way you like it."

He took a sip. "Delicious as usual, may I have one of these scones?"

"How could I stop you?" Mama Woodson laughed and pushed the scones closer to my father.

Their comfort with each other made me think of the past. I longed for those days, when life was filled with love and joy. But, I had made my choice to fight for justice and I had made mistakes. I wanted . . . no I needed to understand the meaning behind Mother's message.

"I still don't understand," I said. "Mother wouldn't want me to use these powers to hurt people."

"Of course she wouldn't," Dad said. "She would want you to use them to create something good, to change the bad for good."

"How can I do that if writing something into reality manipulates and hurts others?"

"You do it by writing to inspire," Dad said. "Use your words to bolster the abilities others already have, like you did for Lauren and yourself. Give them the strength to face their fears, and to follow their instincts. Don't write words that make people go against their natures. Just as it harms you to try to write against your own nature, you'll only harm others if you try to change them to achieve your own goals."

His words made a light spark in my brain. I knew what I had to do. I jumped up and kissed him, energy filling my body. "Has anyone ever told you that you're a brilliant man?"

His face beamed with an underused smile. "It's been a long time since I've received any compliments, but may I ask what was so brilliant about what I just said?"

"You've given me an idea. Mama Woodson, could you give a message to Brian when he gets home?"

"Will it get him more embroiled with the Freedom Readers?" Mama Woodson asked.

"No, as a matter of fact, this has nothing to do with the Freedom Readers and everything to do with strengthening the power of women."

"Then, of course I'll pass the message along."

"Tell him I need him to meet me at Briandra's Haven in two days. 10 am."

"I haven't heard that place mentioned in a while," Mama Woodson said. "What do you plan on doing there?"

"I plan to help women find their power."

* * *

The next day I rushed to the attic as soon as I finished breakfast and saw my father off to work. I wrote with the frenzy of the early days after I first discovered my power. I became so absorbed in my work that I didn't notice the passage of time. Dad's voice calling up the stairs startled me. I blinked, only then noticing how the shadows had moved across the wall with the waning day.

"Andra, I'm home. Could you please come down?"

"I'll be right there, Dad." I stretched. My spine crackled from being in the same position all day. My stomach rumbled its neglect. I shook my hands out and my weariness weighed on my limbs.

"I'm sorry I didn't make dinner," I called as I made my way down the stairs. "I hope you don't mind leftovers." I stepped into the kitchen only to stop short when I realized Dad wasn't alone. Johnson stood by the doorway, his hat in his hands.

"As long as there's enough for three," Dad said.

"What's he doing here?" I asked, trying to remain calm.

"I invited him to dinner," Dad said. "We need to talk."

He placed his hand on my arm in the familiar gesture. I shook with rage.

"He's a Freedom Reader. He's friends with Emily." I pulled my arm away. "I don't have anything to say to him."

"Please, Andra," Johnson said. "I had no idea what Emily had planned. All Readers are not like her. Please just listen to what I have to say, for your father's sake."

I glanced over at my father. He said nothing and gave no indication of what he was thinking. That left the decision up to me. I remembered the emotion shared between the two men, and relented.

"Come in, then," I said. "Let me scrounge up something to eat and we'll talk."

"Could I clean up?" Johnson brushed at his clothes, which were covered in sawdust. "I've been working in the library all day and didn't get a chance to clean up when your father found me."

"You found him?" I asked.

"Yes, Andra, I did." I recognized the no-arguing tone of his voice. "I'm sure you remember where to go, Jack."

Awkward silence filled the room as I set the table and placed an array of leftovers out for our meal. I didn't want to look at my father who had betrayed me by seeking out and inviting this man into my house. I didn't have the words to explain what I was feeling. I wasn't ready to hear anything Johnson had to say. When Johnson returned from the bathroom, the two men picked up on my mood and held only a mumbled conversation about the weather and other unimportant issues while they watched me bustle around the room. Finally, I joined them at the kitchen table, but nothing changed. We worked through the reheated meat and vegetables in near silence.

Unable to stand it any longer, I broke the tension, my voice louder than I had intended. "Okay, I'm here. We're eating. Dad, why would you invite a Freedom Reader to our table after what happened?"

"Jack has been a friend of this family for a long time. He deserves to be heard."

"Then why don't I remember him?" I dropped my fork onto my plate with a loud clatter. "Why hasn't he been here since Mother died? You two keep saying that you would do anything for each other and trust each other with your lives, but I don't know who this man is."

"That's my fault, Andra," Dad said. "Let me explain."

"I'm listening," I said.

"I'm actually surprised you don't remember Johnson from your childhood," Dad said. "He spent a lot of time here when you were little. As a matter of fact, he gave you your favorite toy—you know the rocking horse that you claimed took you on adventures to other worlds?"

"That was given to me by big smiling Uncle Jack, who had the loudest laugh I've ever heard, not . . ." I suddenly saw the big, graying man who sat across from me eating a piece of bread with new eyes. He put the bread down and smiled. The smile was unfamiliar on a face that I always saw as somber. When he smiled his eyes twinkled, and I realized that I had indeed seen him before.

"I guess I don't smile or laugh as much as I used to," Johnson said. "Less to laugh about. I remember how excited you would be to tell me the story of your latest adventures on the horse. You even drew pictures. Once you tried to show me a story you had written, but your mother took that one and made you promise never to show anybody else."

"So you knew I could read and write before Brian ever brought me to the Readers?"

"Yes. That alone should prove you can trust me. I never shared that secret with anybody."

"Okay, so you're an old family friend. Why haven't you been around since before Mother died?"

"For a while I was on a mission Outside, gathering information to help the Readers. I returned just before Woodson disappeared. If I had gotten back sooner, I would have talked him out of the insane mission that led to his disappearance. After Marion died, I wanted to help, but . . ."

"When she . . . when your mother . . ." Dad pushed his plate away, removed his glasses and rubbed his hand over his eyes and through his hair. He cleared his throat and tried again. "After your mother died, I kind of lost control for a while. I knew deep inside that your mother didn't die of any brain aneurysm, but that she had been murdered by someone at the Ministry."

"Dad—"

"Please don't interrupt or I'll never finish."

I nodded.

"I was determined to avenge your mother's death, even if I had no evidence of who might have done it, or how. I set out on a course to find the culprit or culprits, blindly seeking clues and pursuing any lead I could find. I was going to kill each and every one of them. I forgot the danger I was under, and the fact that the Ministry will destroy anyone whom it sees as a threat."

"Your father was reckless," Johnson said. "I was worried that he would be killed and you as well, so I stepped in to stop him. I met with the doctor who did the autopsy on your mother and paid him to send a copy of the autopsy report to your father, including all of the tests taken; a report the Ministry had held back for its own reasons up to that point. I knew the report probably lied, but at least it would be some sort of evidence to dispute your father's assumptions."

"I received the copy, and it confirmed your mother's death was caused by an aneurysm," Dad said. "It's the copy I showed you. Johnson was here when I read it. 'There, Ben,' he said. 'You should be able to put this to rest now, for the sake of Marion's memory and your daughter.' I exploded. 'This is a lie!' I yelled. 'You know that.' 'I do,' Johnson said, 'but if you continue on this path without any evidence, the only one you'll hurt is Andra.' I didn't want to hear that. I didn't want evidence that contradicted my belief. I wanted revenge and my best friend, someone who I had always seen as a brother, was trying to stop me from achieving it. I told him to leave our house and never come back."

"I didn't want to make things worse," Johnson said. "So I obeyed your father's wishes, even though it was one of the most difficult things I've ever done."

"I regretted my words almost as soon as I said them. I'm so ashamed, Jack. You were right. I had to go on without pursuing my vendetta. I wanted to apologize, but I didn't know how. I was still angry that I lost Marion because of our involvement with the Freedom Readers. But, you were right. I realized the risk when they tried to take Andra away from me. I couldn't let that happen. So I stopped. Everything."

"I understood, Ben. I really did."

The two men pushed away from the table and embraced, silent tears pouring down their cheeks.

I busied myself clearing the table in silence. I didn't want to embarrass them by paying too much attention to their display. I also didn't know what to say. My mind whirled.

The men pulled apart and helped me clear.

"Do you understand now, Andra?" Dad asked.

"I think so." I stood with my back to them, leaning against the sink. "You two were close. He was once part of the family." I turned toward Johnson. "But you're still part of the Freedom Readers, a group led by a woman who used me and my powers for her own form of vengeance. You carry weapons and you've killed people, I'm told. How can I trust you?"

"I understand your confusion," Johnson said. "Emily is an important part of the Freedom Readers, but she's not the only person in the group. She doesn't speak for everyone. I won't lie; there are others who think like her, who want to achieve victory by any means. But, there are many who truly believe that we need to find another approach. I'm one of them. I carry weapons to protect the people I care about. I've killed because I was forced to protect someone else, or to defend myself. I know you may not want to work with us again, Andra, but I'm hoping this will at least help you trust me." He walked over to a knapsack that sat on the bench by the door and pulled out a file. "Brian and I gained access to the secret files, with a little creative distraction. I haven't shown these to Emily nor any of the Readers. I want you to see them first." He handed me the files. "I'll leave you two alone now. Thank you for dinner. Promise me that you won't react to these files in anger, without a clear plan."

"What do they say?" I asked.

"Read them yourself," Johnson said. "But first, I need your promise."

"I promise, Jack," Dad said. "I learned my lesson."

"What about Andra?" Johnson asked.

"I can't promise anything," I said.

"I'll watch her." Dad put his hand on my arm. "Yesterday taught you that your power can be dangerous, let's move forward with caution."

I took a deep breath. "I promise."

"Ben, I hope we can get back to the way things were. You know how to reach me." Johnson opened the door and left.

* * *

Attached to this memo, please find the true results of the autopsy performed on Marion BetScrivener after her sudden death at a celebration in honor of the Supreme Prime Minister. A slightly altered and incomplete document was provided to the Scrivener, confirming that her death was caused by an aneurysm. This autopsy report shows the mixture of toxins that contributed to the cause of death, a mixture specifically designed to simulate a brain aneurysm without damaging the brain in order to preserve it for further studies. A second attachment contains the results of our examination of the subject's brain. The results of the tests suggest that Marion BetScrivener had a greater use of the totality of her brain than the average male, as is seen by the strength of the synapses connecting all areas of her brain. As has been long suspected, it appears Marion BetScrivener had developed a power or powers beyond the capabilities known to be found in human males. The evidence suggests the necessity to accelerate plans to regulate females in order to suppress the further evolution of these abilities or to keep their powers under Ministry control. The committee recommends utilizing the existing facilities designed for the Women's Training Program to isolate and study any women who might be considered a danger to New North because of the development of unexpected abilities, unless they can be controlled through marriage.

SEVENTEEN

The sky threatened snow. A few flakes began to fall as I set out toward the rendezvous point where I planned to meet Lauren and one or two other women so I could lead them to Briandra's Haven. I wasn't sure Lauren would even be there, but hoped she would. I needed her strength to help me sort through everything that collided in my brain. When writing the day before, I thought I had found a way to use my power to support others. Then I read the file on my mother and became unsure of what to do. If helping other women develop their abilities put them in more danger, was I doing the right thing?

Dad disappeared into his own room after reading the file, so I couldn't talk with him about my concerns. He barely said a word before he left that morning.

I didn't see anyone as I approached the footbridge where we'd arranged to meet. I wondered if they would even show. Perhaps the horrible events that ended the party had scared all the other women off and they wouldn't come. I wasn't sure if I was hopeful that they might not appear, or disappointed.

Andra, I'm here with the Professor. Lauren's thought reached me, and my body filled with an overwhelming sense of relief at the warm touch of my friend's mind.

Why did you bring the Professor? I stopped walking so we could have a private mental exchange before I reached them. *I'm not sure he should be involved.*

He's as upset about what happened as we are. His concern is us and our safety. Besides, he understands the possibilities behind our powers better than anyone. We need him.

I took the final steps that would bring me to the bridge. The Professor and Lauren appeared from a copse of trees on the other side.

"Professor Albert," I said.

"Andra." Professor Albert put out his arms as if to embrace me. I hesitated. He dropped his arms. "I'm so sorry about everything. I didn't know that Emily was still being guided by the need for revenge."

"Would you have warned me if you knew what she had planned?"

"Of course, and I would have done everything in my power to stop her."

"Do you plan on continuing to work with the Freedom Readers?" I asked.

"They're not all misguided people. Most of the people who work with the rebels fight for the same things as you. Johnson is a good man."

"I know he is," I said. "So are you. I'm just not sure who to trust anymore."

"Did you ask Brian to come to this meeting like you planned?" Lauren asked.

"Yes, I did."

"He's still a Freedom Reader," Lauren said. "Why can you trust him more than Professor Albert who has been so kind to us?"

"Because he's Brian, and I still haven't talked to him about Emily, and he's different, and . . ."

Trust the Professor. Lauren thought.

"I'm sorry. I'm totally crazy now. Professor, I do trust you, but . . . has Lauren explained what we planned for today?"

"We're going to meet women who may have abilities," Professor Albert said.

"I don't know how they'll react if we bring too many men along."

"True, Andra. But, you need to have me along as protection."

"We can—"

"I know, you and Lauren and these other women are quite capable of taking care of yourselves. But you're forgetting the new mandates about women gathering. What if someone from the Ministry noticed women wandering alone into the woods on a day like today?" He pulled his warm coat around him and fixed his scarf against the snow that was gaining in intensity. "At least if you have a few men with you, we can come up with some kind of excuse for the gathering, and you aren't alone breaking the law."

"That's why I asked Brian to meet us."

"Don't you think some might find it suspicious that you invited Brian Woodson and not Peter Rogerson?" Professor Albert said. "After all, word spreads fast in this small world of ours."

My face grew warm despite the snowflakes that landed on my nose. I hadn't thought of how that would look. "I'm not sure your presence will help either, then. You aren't exactly welcome at the Ministry."

"No, I'm not," the Professor said. "But I also have a long reputation for being somewhat eccentric. Nobody would put it past me to lead a group of young women out to celebrate the first snow of the season as a part of a study of the effect of cold on female behavior. Nor would they put it past me to recruit Woodson's help for the heavy lifting required if we need wood for a fire when the group of young women prove intolerant of the cold. I'm a lazy fellow, after all."

I laughed at the clever way the Professor's mind worked. I walked over, looped my arm in his, and gave him a kiss on the cheek. My instincts told me to trust him fully. Lauren smiled with relief.

"Let's go," I said. "We still need to meet up with Alice and Jenna. Heidi and Beth are supposed to be bringing another group and I want to get there before anyone else shows up."

By the time we reached Briandra's Haven, the snow had accumulated to over an inch. Brian was already there, attempting to start a fire just inside the door of the cave. "It's about time you got here, Andra," he said at the sound of footsteps swooshing through the snow. "Why you wanted to meet out here on a day like today is beyond me. I can't even get a fire started."

"I think I have someone who can help with that," I said.

Brian turned and I laughed at the surprised look on his face when he saw that I had company.

"Professor Albert! Lauren! And, I'm sorry I don't know you ladies." Brian pulled me aside and spoke in a stage whisper that everyone pretended they couldn't hear. "Why did you bring them to Briandra's Haven? It won't remain a secret location if you share it with everyone."

"It's time the Haven became a place for more than childhood dreams," I said. "Is the cave clear? There are a few others coming, and it would probably be better if we had a little shelter at least."

"How will they know how to find us?" Brian asked.

"I gave them directions."

"You gave directions to our secret hangout to a bunch of people I don't know?"

"Oh, Brian, grow up. You'll be happy once you find out why. Now let's see about getting this fire started."

"I told you, I can't. The wood's all wet."

"Alice." I turned to the small group waiting behind us. "Now might be a good time for you to show us your ability."

"With pleasure," Alice said. She walked over to the pile of wood Brian had placed just inside the opening of the cave. She picked up a piece of kindling and stared at it. In a moment the end burst into flame, and she applied it to the other kindling until the fire crackled a warm and welcoming glow.

"Incredible," said Professor Albert.

"I take it you've found some other women with powers," Brian said and pulled me into a hug. "I knew you could do it. This is great. Wait until I tell the Readers."

"The Readers are not to know about this meeting," I said.

"Why not? I know things didn't go quite as planned at the Ministry, but—"

"I'll explain later," I said. "But please, you have to promise me you won't share anything about today with the Readers, especially with Emily." I reached out to begin our secret handshake—our usual way of committing to a promise.

Brian hesitated.

"Please Brian, trust me on this," I said.

Brian completed the handshake, but his thumb twitched in the middle.

Just then we heard the approach of more people. "I think it's this way," a female voice said.

"Where are you taking us, Heidi?" This time it was a male voice that sounded familiar, although I couldn't place it.

"Why did Heidi bring a man?" Alice called from the cave. "She's such an idiot."

"Get in the cave, everyone. Lauren, can you tell who it is?"

Lauren's eyes took on the faraway look that meant she was concentrating on unfamiliar minds. She let out a surprised gasp.

"What's wrong? Who is it?" I asked.

"It's Peter Rogerson," she said.

"What's he doing here?" Brian asked.

"I don't know," I said. "But we're about to find out."

The brush parted to reveal Heidi, Beth and Peter followed by four women so bundled under colorful scarves and hats that I had no hope of identifying them.

"We finally found you," Heidi said.

"Hi, Andra," Peter said. "I hope you don't mind that Heidi invited me to your little gathering. She thought it might help to have a man along, in case you run into trouble."

"She already has me and the Professor here," Brian said. "You can head on home."

"Brian Woodson." Peter held his hand out to shake. "I haven't seen you since Andra's birthday. My father says you're doing amazing work fixing the library."

"Oh, uh, thanks," Brian said. "But, like I said, you can head back now."

"Why would I do that?" Peter said. "Some of my favorite people are here for this unexpected gathering in the woods. Why exactly are we here?"

"I told you, Peter, it's about the powers," Heidi sounded nonchalant. "Is Alice here?"

"Who do you think started the fire?" Alice came out of the cave. "Why did you bring him with you, Heidi? What does he know about the powers? I thought this was a meeting for women. For that matter, what are they doing here?" She indicated Brian and Professor Albert.

"Peter is the first person I ever told about my ability," Heidi said. "I thought he might be helpful."

Through this entire conversation hysteria built inside me. Suddenly it burst out in the form of uncontrollable laughter. Everyone turned and watched me double over and clutch my stomach. The laughter and the release of so much tension led to a joyous ache in my belly.

"Are you okay?" Lauren asked.

"I'm . . . fine . . ." I gasped for breath and wiped tears from my eyes. "Just .
. . give me . . . a minute."

"Would this help?" The Professor offered me a sip from a thermos he carried over his shoulder. "It's cider."

I took a sip of hot cider and calm returned. A group of confused faces
surrounded me; some of whom I had known for a long time, some of whom I
met at Emily's fateful party, and some who I was just meeting on this strange,
snowy day. My eyes connected with Peter's. His face reflected a mixture of
amusement and puzzlement.

"Now, let me get this straight. Peter," I said, "you know that some women
have powers?"

"Well, I know that Heidi has the ability to heal people, and Beth managed
to calm a panicked horse once."

Beth put a gloved hand over her mouth, hiding the hint of a pleased smile.

"I suspected other women might have similar powers," Peter said. "Do
you have one too, Andra?"

"That's none of your business," Brian said.

"Brian, calm down," I said. "This meeting is about sharing secrets. I trust
Peter."

"But he's Rogerson's son," Brian said.

"Yes, I am," Peter said. "But that doesn't mean I believe everything my
father tells me. Heidi showed me her power a long time ago, and I've never
told a soul. Andra and I have an agreement as well, and I've kept my side of
the bargain." He turned to Andra. "If you want me to leave, I'll go and I won't
tell anyone about this meeting. I think I'd be useful though."

"Brian, do you trust me?" I asked.

"Yes, but . . ."

"Then Peter stays."

"What about him?" Alice again indicated the Professor. "You used to work
for the Ministry, why are you here?"

"Professor Albert has helped us master our abilities," I said. "He can help you as well. He won't reveal our secrets."

"I want to help you, and learn more about the superior brains of women," the Professor said. "Might I suggest, however, that we move this discussion into the warmth of the cave?" His cap and shoulders were covered with a layer of white. "I have no desire of turning into a living snowman."

Everyone laughed as we made our way inside.

I held Lauren back for a moment. *We still have to be careful. Can you listen with your mind?*

It may be difficult once I reveal my power to everyone, Lauren thought. *Some may object, but I'll do my best.*

We entered the cave to lead the strangest meeting of our lives.

"I think we should start by introducing ourselves and sharing our abilities," I said.

"Wait," Alice said. "You've gathered us all here on blind faith, Andra. You've already seen some of our powers. I haven't seen proof of yours. Why should you be leading this meeting?"

"I have no desire to lead," I said. "But you're right. You haven't seen my power yet, and some people here have never met me. I'm happy to give you an example now."

I had come prepared with pen and paper stored in my pack. I closed my eyes to envision exactly what I wanted to happen and began to write while some of the observers mumbled in awe.

"You know how to write?" one of the unknown women asked.

"Yes, she does," Heidi answered. "Now please be quiet and let's see what happens."

After a few moments, I put my pen down. I picked up the paper and read out loud: "The snow fell quickly and accumulated just enough to keep the people of New North beside their cozy fires, enjoying their surprise snow day without having to face outdoor chores. Deep in the woods, however, over the secret clearing known as Briandra's Haven, the snow stopped and the sky cleared to a brilliant blue while the sun beamed down to create crystal glints that brightened the area."

"That's impossible," Alice said. "You can't make the snow stop above us and keep the snow falling over the villages and the capital."

"Go outside and see," I said. I had already sensed the surge that told me my writing had come to life.

Alice made her way to the entrance. "Unbelievable!" she yelled and stepped outside. The others followed.

Above us was a patch of blue sky with brilliant sun beaming down. Toward the distance, pregnant clouds heavy with snow covered the horizon.

"Will we be able to get home safely?" One of the unknown women asked. "My parents will be upset if I'm late returning. I already had to lie to get out."

"I'll make sure you all get back safely," I said. This small success boosted my confidence and hope that I could indeed find a way to use my power for good. "It's still cold, even with the sun. Shall we continue our meeting inside?"

Over the next hour the group began to recognize the possibilities that came from bringing our powers together. One woman had the ability to put any puzzle together within minutes, including machinery she had never seen before. One woman could calculate numbers well beyond the ability of the male mathematicians that worked for the Ministry. Some powers were simpler, the woman who could revive any plant life, or the one able to remember any face she had ever seen.

"All right, so we have all these abilities," Alice said. "And I'm sure there are others out there with similar powers, but what good do they do us? We can't bring down the Supreme Prime Minister and the entire Ministry. It's impossible."

"Nothing is impossible if we work together," I said. I explained how working together had strengthened Lauren's and my abilities. I told them about my connection with the Freedom Readers, but left out the more disturbing information I'd gathered over the past few days. That could wait. Then, even though it terrified me, I revealed my part in the recent accident at the Ministry. Fearful glances passed among the group as they realized that my words had killed someone. The cave became silent as they considered the information.

"You killed someone with your words?" Heidi asked, breaking the silence.

"Andra didn't kill anyone," Lauren said. She hadn't spoken much throughout the meeting so her unexpected defense filled me with gratitude.

"Someone else had a role in Minister Achan's death." I chose my words with care. "I can't reveal the details here. It's too dangerous. It's not my story to tell."

Brian gave me a questioning look but didn't push.

"Why should we trust you and the Freedom Readers?" Alice asked.

"I'm not asking you to trust the Freedom Readers," I said. "I've told you my whole story, even if I'm unwilling to incriminate others. You can choose to trust me or not."

"I trust her," Heidi said.

"I trust her," Lauren said.

"I t-trust her," Beth said.

One by one, each person in the cave voiced words of trust, including the men.

"All right, fine, we trust you," Alice said at last. "But I'm still not sure what this little group of women with powers can do to change anything."

"I'm not sure yet, either," I said, "I know the Ministry fears the power of women, so we need to find anyone who shows any sign of unusual abilities and help those powers grow. If we do that, perhaps we can make the changes we need."

"Power of Women," Heidi said. "That would be a great name for our group. POW!"

Several women laughed.

"Or P.O.W.," Alice said. "Didn't that stand for Prisoner of War or something in the old days?"

"Then it's the perfect name." Words began to form inside me, as if my ability to write reality was growing into an ability to speak and be heard. "Aren't all women, in a way, prisoners of war? We are prisoners of a silent, weaponless war intended to strip us of power, freedom and the ability to think and act for ourselves. It's time we learned to fight this war on our own grounds, and create a world where everyone, male or female, has the right to live to her, or his, full potential. I'm tired of living by rules that don't allow me to live fully, and I have no intention of obediently walking into marriage because someone says I must."

"Well, that puts me in my place, doesn't it?" Peter said.

Everyone laughed. Brian laughed the loudest.

"What's our plan?" Alice asked. "How do we gather women together and strengthen our powers?"

"With your permission I'd like to write something that will allow women to become stronger; something like the words that enabled me to hear Lauren's thoughts. We strengthen each other. I will try to help you all enhance your own abilities to some extent. What do you think? I've started something already, although I haven't envisioned it yet."

I shared the draft I'd started the day before, which led to a long discussion: about how to make it work; what changes might improve it; and whether or not it would be acceptable to manifest these connections for all women with abilities, even the ones as yet undiscovered. As I grew confident that I could write something that would help, not harm, words started forming in my head. My fingers itched to get home and start writing.

In the end, each person left with a new-found purpose to expand the ranks of P.O.W. and find some way to change the world of New North.

*　*　*

If Rom Sandovar had known about the meeting occurring in a cave tucked away in the woods, the dark shadow on his face as he sat in his office would have grown deeper and more menacing. He had just received some disturbing news from an unexpected source—news that shook him to the very roots of his belief system. He had feared this day would come long before he had manipulated the world into believing he was the voice and eye of the Lord. He believed it himself, after a series of intense dreams in his youth when it appeared the Lord spoke to him and gave him his purpose in life.

He picked up a golden paperweight in the symbol of the Eye and raised it above his head in reverence. He began a silent prayer to the god of his dreams. *Dear Lord,* he thought, *you came to me and told me that the base of all evil in this world was women. That they were the corrupting factors of all society, and that they would soon take over the world, minimizing the power of those who truly deserve it. You told me that men should maintain the gift of wealth and money and strength. Women could never use that power wisely. Women should not have any power beyond that of raising families. I watched as my own mother moved up in the ranks of society, and stripped my father of his wealth and position by caring more about the poor and the needy and the environment then about me. It angered me, and I did not know where to turn. But you, my Lord, helped me channel that anger into power. I heard your command and I solved the problem. You gave me your Voice and let me speak to the world, and I have done everything you've asked. I have become a god in my own right. So now I must ask, why are you giving these gifts to women instead of men? Why are you threatening the world that I have created in your name? Why?!*

He threw the paperweight across the room, leaving a dent in the wall. He stood and paced, before he picked it up again, checked to see if it was damaged and returned it to the place of honor on his desk. He walked to his office door, opened it and called for his guard. He had one very specific order.

*   *   *

Brian and I walked back through the gathering drifts of snow together. I filled him in on the details of Emily's past and her role in the death of Minister Achan.

"I'm going to destroy her," he said.

"You can't do that, Brian. That would just bring us down to her level. I'm not sure what's going to happen next, but I know we have to find another way to achieve our goals."

"You're right, of course." He made a snowball and pitched it at a distant tree. "How did your father handle the news from the files?"

"I don't know. He went silent. But he promised Johnson not to do anything rash, so I have to believe he'll keep that promise. He should be home by now. Even Sandovar usually sends people home early when the snow is as heavy as this."

"Let me know if you need me to talk to him. I don't know what I'd say, but I can remind him that my father wouldn't want him to do anything crazy. I better go check on Mom." He gave me a quick kiss on the cheek. "I'll see you soon. You were amazing today, Andra."

My cheek tingled where his lips had touched me. He had kissed me before, but this time my reaction surprised me. I had to stop myself from reaching up to touch the spot with my hand. My face grew warm.

"Um . . . Thanks, Brian."

I continued on to the kitchen door of my house and opened it expecting to find a cozy fire where I could melt off some of the snow. The kitchen was dark, without even a lantern to compete against the dreary grayness that poured in from outside. On the table lay a half-eaten sandwich and a cold mug of hot chocolate.

"Dad! I'm home. Where are you?" My voice echoed in the silent rooms. It was eerie. I figured my father had been called back to the Ministry for some reason. I hated the idea that Sandovar would make him go out in the snow.

I moved into the room and began to remove my wet outer gear. I tucked the precious writing from the meeting, words that I hoped would strengthen already burgeoning abilities, in a safe hideaway in our cupboards until I had time to show them to Dad. I wanted his opinion before I manifested anything. I got the fire started as quickly as possible and began to clean up the kitchen table. Someone pounded on the door.

"Open up by order of the Ministry!"

I opened the door to see two stern and unpleasant looking Ministry guards standing on my step, covered in snow. "Andra BetScrivener, your immediate presence is requested by the Supreme Prime Minister. We're here to escort you to the Ministry."

"I can't go without telling my father."

"Don't worry; the Scrivener has already been brought in. He awaits your presence as well."

My hands shook as I damped down the fire and put on my wet things. My head emptied of all thoughts, replaced instead by mind-numbing terror. I said nothing as I followed the guards to the horse-drawn sleigh that waited outside.

EIGHTEEN

I had never been in the Supreme Prime Minister's office before. The top floor of the main section of the mansion had been converted to become the most elegant office of them all. Exquisite art, painted by masters long dead, covered the walls. One wall contained an elaborately carved image of the Eye of the Lord, highlighted with gold and copper leaf. Sandovar's desk was even larger, if possible, than Minister Rogerson's but it didn't dwarf the immense space. A deep red plush carpet muffled our footsteps as the guards led me in. A large leather chair behind the desk stood empty.

Dad sat in a simple straight-backed wooden chair in front of the huge desk, his back to me.

"Dad!" I pulled away from the guard who held me and ran to throw my arms around him. "I was worried. What are we doing here?" He didn't hug me back. He didn't respond. Rough ropes held him tied to the chair and bound his arms to his side. His face was lost and confused, as if he had just woken up and didn't know where he was. He began to cough with a dry, raspy sound that made me wince with sympathy pain.

"Dad, what's going on?" I asked. "Why are you tied up? Are you all right?" I turned to the guards, anger growing inside me. "Untie him this instant. He's Head Scrivener. What's going on here?"

"You and your father have been brought here at my request." The voice that haunted my nightmares spoke from behind me. I turned as a door behind the desk clicked shut after the entrance of Supreme Prime Minister Sandovar, who lowered himself into his chair. Minister Rogerson had come in as well and moved to a seat behind me where I couldn't see him. The guards ranged themselves around the room, a silent reminder of the danger I was in.

"Your father was a little reluctant to join me for this meeting," Sandovar said. "We were forced to give him a drug to help. The cough is an unfortunate side effect. Scrivener, I see you're finally coming out of it."

"Why are you doing this?" My father's voice sounded husky and stimulated another cough. "Why is my daughter here?"

"Miss BetScrivener, please have a seat and I'll explain everything," Sandovar said.

I was tempted to ignore Sandovar and remain standing, but a look and a nod from my father made me realize that this wasn't the moment for rebellion. I sat in a cushioned chair in front of Sandovar's desk, but refused to sink back into its comfort.

"I'm sorry to have to bring you in his way," Sandovar said. "Can I offer you some refreshments?" He indicated two bottles of golden liquid that stood on a tray on his desk flanked by two empty glasses. The bottles were turned so that the labels faced the Supreme Prime Minister.

"Just tell me why you have my father tied up?" I said.

"Now, now, why so rude? Scrivener, I thought you raised your daughter to be more respectful of her superiors?"

"I raised her . . . cough . . . to treat others with respect if they deserve respect." The effort of talking set off another round of painful coughing.

"I don't think you're in any position at the moment to question my superiority, are you Scrivener? No matter, I'll ignore the rudeness for now and we can get down to business." Sandovar focused his intense stare on me. I'd always hated his eyes. I gripped my hands together and stabbed my fingernails into my palms to give myself the strength to ignore the fear those silver-gray eyes instilled in me.

"You look nervous, Andra. May I call you Andra? There's nothing to worry about, for either of you, as long as you cooperate. Allow me to offer you both refreshments again. Your father looks thirsty, Andra. His throat must be sore and dry. Are you thirsty, Scrivener?"

"I'm fine." A cough followed his words. I flinched at the dry rasp of his voice, but knew he was too proud to accept a drink at Sandovar's insistence.

"Well, perhaps you'll want something in a few moments." Sandovar turned his attention back to me. "A serious matter has been brought to our attention.

It appears that you've been hiding something about your daughter, Scrivener."

"I don't understand, sir . . ." Dad said between coughs.

"This will go much better if neither of you lie to me. I have a few questions for you, Andra. I don't want to hear a word from you, Scrivener. If you can't remain quiet, I'll have them gag you. That would make the coughing even more uncomfortable, don't you think? Do you understand?"

My father nodded. I didn't move.

"Now Andra, will you answer honestly?" Sandovar asked.

"Will you let us go home afterward?" I asked. I avoided the look of warning Dad gave me, and focused my anger at the man in front of me.

"I like her, Scrivener." The look on Sandovar's face spoke differently. "She's sassy and unafraid. That will be fixed, in time." Sandovar picked up a heavy gold paperweight in the shape of the Eye of the Lord and began to play with it. "Your release all depends on your answers. If you leave me no reason to doubt your answers, you'll have nothing to worry about."

Dad gave a subtle nod in my direction.

"What do you want to know . . . sir?" I asked.

"It's been brought to our attention that you know how to read and write. Is that correct?"

"Of course not, sir."

"What did I say about lying? You always brag about the intelligence of your daughter, Scrivener, but she seems rather stupid to me."

Dad pursed his lips and his color darkened as he held in his response. The effort forced more painful sounding coughs.

"How can you ignore your poor father's difficulty? I think you should pour him a drink. Come, pour one." I stood and reached toward a bottle of golden elixir only to be stopped by Sandovar's cold voice. "I should warn you that one of these contains poison, which will immediately kill your father, while the other will heal him. However, the cough itself will surely kill him if you don't give him the antidote. They both look exactly the same, don't they? How will you ever choose the correct one? Men, of course, are able to differentiate by simply reading the labels. I insist that you pour your father a drink from one of these bottles."

Dad's cough seemed to be getting worse every moment. A spattering of blood shot out of his mouth at his next bout of coughing. The Supreme Prime Minister's laugh gave me the courage to look into his wicked, confident eyes.

"How do I choose, sir?" I asked.

"You could just rely on luck, of course. Or, simply wait and watch your father's discomfort grow. But there's an alternative." Sandovar turned the bottles one at a time so the labels faced me. "You could show me that you do indeed know how to read, and select the bottle that will help your father. You decide."

I had no choice. Keeping my secret would mean losing Dad. I moved closer to the bottles and picked them up one at a time. One label said *Elixir to heal coughs and sore throats*. The other said, *Poison, will cause immediate death*. Neither label contained the signifying symbols women used to differentiate between medicine and poison. Dad coughed again with more blood shooting out to land in spots on his shoulder as he tried to turn his head away. I glanced once more at the Supreme Prime Minister whose eyes glinted with the knowledge of victory. I selected the elixir, poured it, and helped Dad drink.

His coughing stopped. Our eyes met. He slumped in defeat.

"You should have let me die, Andra," Dad said.

"I couldn't do that."

"How sweet," Sandovar said. "You've always been such a loving family. Now, Andra, are you going to cooperate?"

"You already have your answer. I can read. I can also write. Who told you?"

"Our source is not important," Sandovar said. "You know, of course, that you have broken the law. However, what we do with you and your father depends on how you respond to some other questions. Do you understand?"

Dad nodded.

I sat back down. "I don't have a choice, do I?"

"So sassy, no wonder your son is fascinated by her, Rogerson."

"She's definitely a handful, sir," Rogerson said.

I had forgotten he was in the room. While I tried to contain my anger at the Supreme Prime Minister, I couldn't hold back my rage at this man who had tried to manipulate every aspect of my life over the past few months. I turned to glare at him and chose my words with care. "At least you won't have to worry about me marrying Peter now. I wouldn't marry into your family if ⅄ would save the world."

My words sent the Supreme Prime Minister into a paroxysm of laughter.

"Ah, Andra." Sandovar wiped his eyes. "You're such a delight. It's a shame you've been corrupted and allowed to practice such sinful behavior. Did your parents teach you to read and write, in spite of the laws of the land?"

"No, sir. I . . . I taught myself."

"Interesting, but according to our source you came upon this ability very suddenly, is that true?"

My mind began to whirl as I realized that Sandovar knew more than I had imagined. Who would have revealed my secret? How much did he know? I blamed myself. It must have been one of the women I had just met. I barely knew them, how could I have trusted them? I should have been more cautious. Or maybe it was Peter Rogerson. Minister Rogerson's presence suggested that Peter had run home from the meeting and spilled everything. Even though Lauren hadn't heard any thoughts of betrayal coming from the group, I had no way to be sure.

"Delay won't help you." Sandovar's demanding voice interrupted my thoughts. "Is it true that you learned to read suddenly?"

"Yes, sir."

"Is it also true that you can write things into reality?"

My hands began to shake. Fear clogged my throat. My father clenched his jaw.

"Answer me," Sandovar said.

"I can write some things and they will happen. I can't make something out of nothing."

"Interesting." Sandovar put the paperweight on the desk and smiled. "Now I'm sure you're worried that I will immediately have your hands cut off, as the normal punishment for a woman who is caught writing. However, I have decided that perhaps your skill might benefit New North in some way, and at the same time you'll protect your father and perhaps even save his life, again." At a nod from him, a guard held his knife against Dad's throat.

"Don't hurt him," I said. "What do you want from me?"

you to use your ability to help me make some improvements to ..ety. First, I want you to destroy the Freedom Readers. You've heard of ..em, haven't you?"

"Of course." I tried to swallow a huge knot, my mouth dry with fear. "They're the rebels who have tried to defeat you for years."

"You know them. Good. They've been a plague on my government ever since the Lord granted me this office. For that reason, we want you to write a plague that destroys every single one of them."

"I can't do that." I flinched as the guard's knife pressed against my father's throat. A crimson bead glistened. I had never been so terrified. "Please don't hurt him. It's not that I won't; I can't."

"Why not? Not even to save your father?"

"I don't know how to cause a plague that could single out only certain people. I don't even know who belongs to the Freedom Readers." I hoped Sandovar couldn't recognize another lie. It was a partial truth at least, I only knew a few actual members. A look from Dad gave me the courage to continue. "Any plague I wrote could wipe out the entire country. And . . . if I write anything too big, or anything that goes against my beliefs, it makes me very ill."

"Killing people goes against your belief system, is that it?" Sandovar chuckled. "I appreciate your honesty. I'll make you a deal. I'll give you some time to figure out a way to rid me of the Freedom Readers that doesn't conflict with your . . . misguided moral code. If you do this, your father will return to his duties and you won't be punished for your crimes, so long as you marry and start behaving as a true woman of New North. After that, you'll only use your power at my request."

"If I don't agree to this, what happens?" I asked, although I already knew the answer.

"First you'll watch your father experience a slow and painful death. Then, you'll lose your right hand and your tongue, and be placed as a servant in a trusted household. On second thought, we'll remove both hands. I'm sure you can find a way to serve without your hands. That way you'll never be able to write again, nor will you be able to share the secret of your power."

I didn't know how to respond. I could hardly breathe.

"I see you're thinking about my offer. While you figure out how to achieve my plan, your father will remain a guest of the Ministry. I think you might benefit with some time at a Women's Training Center, don't you? That will relieve you from any household concerns while you work on this important task. Are we in agreement?"

"C-can I have a moment alone with my father? Please, sir."

"Never let it be said that I'm cruel. We'll give you a few minutes, but be aware that there are guards outside both doors. I'll even untie him so that you can talk more comfortably." Sandovar nodded at the guard holding the knife who used it to cut the bonds. My father shook out his arms.

"As a precaution, I think I'll remove any temptation you might have to write your way out of this situation." Sandovar picked up the pen set from his desk and the pile of paper next to it before exiting through the door behind him, followed by Rogerson and one guard. The other guard went out the door to the hall. I heard the key turn in the lock.

"Andra, I'm so sorry." Dad grabbed me in a bone-crushing hug. "I should have protected you better."

"This is my fault. I revealed my power to other people, one of them must have told Sandovar our secret"

"We don't know that. Do you have any reason to suspect any of them?"

"Peter Rogerson was there."

"I suppose he's the most likely suspect, but don't jump to conclusions without proof." Dad's voice sounded grave. "It doesn't matter. What matters is that you can't use your power to destroy the Readers and help the Ministry."

"If I don't, I'll lose you. I'll lose everything." I started shaking as I fought to hold in tears that I refused to shed.

"We all have to make sacrifices for the cause. I can't make this decision for you, but I know that your mother would want you to choose the path that hurts the fewest people." He caught a tear on his finger and brought it to his lips where he kissed it. "Don't worry about me. I've survived a long time and found my way out of stickier situations."

"Don't lie. I'm so sorry I got you into this."

"There's nothing to be sorry about. I love you and I'm proud of you. I know you'll think of something."

He held me in his arms and I tried to find strength from his touch.

The door behind the desk opened and we pulled apart. Sandovar and Rogerson re-entered behind the guard.

"Have you made your choice? Are we in agreement?"

I nodded, and then hugged Dad again. "I love you. I'll see you soon."

One of the guards grabbed him by the elbow and led him out of the room.

"Good decision, Andra. Minister Rogerson here will escort you to your new home at the Center. I'm sure he'll take good care of you. Be careful of our prize, Rogerson. She may still be allowed to become your daughter-in-law." With that, Sandovar swept out of the room to his private chambers.

"Don't worry, Andra," Rogerson said. "The Women's Training Center is very comfortable and I'm sure you'll enjoy your time there. You'll come out refreshed and a better fit to marry Peter."

I didn't say anything as I followed Rogerson out the door and left my shattered heart behind.

NINETEEN

I was familiar with the training center Rogerson brought me to. I'd visited Lauren there, and spent enough time to recognize the welcoming public areas—the reception rooms, the craft and game room, the smaller sitting rooms. On my first visit, I'd even gotten a tour of some of the guest bedrooms. The public areas and front guest bedrooms of the Women's Training Center exuded welcome and comfort. Warm caramel walls with bright floral accents—including arts and crafts made by the trainees—and cushioned seating invited visitors to believe that it was a place almost as good as home.

To be fair, some of the occupants enjoyed their time there, playing games with each other in the common room or welcoming visitors with smiles and hugs. These were the ones who had entered in the hopes of improving their chances to find a perfect match. These were the women who wanted to marry, but hadn't had someone to arrange it for them. Sometimes older men, looking for replacement wives, came to meet women there, to select someone who has mastered the art of being a woman. When I visited Lauren, I'd witnessed several women enter the visiting area a trainee and leave an affianced bride.

Early on, I had become aware that somehow their experience differed from Lauren's and other women forced into the center because of their refusal to marry. At each visit, Lauren had become more and more withdrawn. She became thinner while dark circles grew under her eyes. Most of the other women in the public areas glowed with the blossoming beauty of newfound confidence in stark contrast to the fading light of my old friend. "What's wrong?" I would ask, but Lauren never answered. She would simply cast a glance toward the burly attendants who hovered nearby and shake her head. On my final visit to Lauren, I had found a woman who hid behind her hair, hugged her knees and rocked but never spoke a word.

"Welcome Minister Rogerson, what brings you here today?" A large woman in a trainer's uniform greeted us as we entered. I thought her smile looked false, straining against sour lines deeply etched into her face.

"Trainer Sevrin," Rogerson said. "I assumed you had received advanced word from the Supreme Prime Minister. This is the special case he informed you about, Andra BetScrivener."

"Oh, yes." Her smile disappeared and her face matched the severe bun that pulled her black and gray hair so her forehead became taut and shiny. "I didn't expect her to come in such prestigious company. Follow me."

Trainer Sevrin led us past the welcoming entry, past the sleeping rooms filled with personal decorations and flowers, and through a steel door that clanged behind us as it shut. Behind that door I found a very different center made up of gray walls, and tiny cell-like rooms that contained a cot, a small table, a single lamp and nothing else. Through the open doors to the rooms, female figures rested in the beds or sat on the floor. A few stood to watch as I walked past, but nobody made any effort to step into the hall or say anything. Their eyes bore into me—a criminal on parade. I couldn't see any variety in those faces—they were all pale and sad, trying to hide their interest behind nonchalant looks. Some doors remained closed, but eyes peered out of the windows in each door—young eyes with vacant stares filled with fear as well as interest.

"Why are some of these doors shut and some opened?" I asked.

"The occupants in this wing have needed special training," Trainer Sevrin said. "Those who have begun to learn their lessons well are given more freedom with open doors. They're allowed to visit each other for short periods, and make their way to the facilities and classes on their own. They're also allowed daily visits to the recreation rooms, under supervision, of course. Others have not yet embraced the gentility which we endeavor to teach, so they must remain behind locked doors."

"These aren't legal women," I said. "Some of these people are young girls. They're nowhere near seventeen."

"They've been brought in under the new mandates set by the Supreme Prime Minister at the direction of the Lord," Rogerson said. "They shouldn't bother you while you work, and you are not to have any interaction with them. Is that understood?"

"Yes, Minister Rogerson," I said.

"Trainer Sevrin, have you prepared Andra's room as Supreme Prime Minister Sandovar requested?" Rogerson asked.

"Yes, Minister." Sevrin gave me a stern look and then pulled Rogerson away a short distance. "I'm a little confused, sir. We don't usually allow our special inmates drawing materials upon their arrival, especially in the difficult cases. It goes against our—"

"I thought drawing was one of the womanly arts you're meant to perfect?" Even as I spoke, I knew I shouldn't have. The painful smack across my cheek with the back of Sevrin's work-hardened hand confirmed that I should remember to think first, speak second. My impulsive retorts wouldn't be tolerated here.

"We don't eavesdrop or interrupt others." Trainer Sevrin's dark eyes glittered with malice.

A young girl, around twelve or thirteen, with dark skin, wild curls, and a wistful appearance came to her door and sent me an encouraging look. I thought I heard the sprite whisper, "We're here. You're not alone."

"Never question the methods we use here, is that understood?" Trainer Sevrin didn't seem to hear the whispered encouragement. She raised her voice as if she wanted all the observers to hear her words. "If and when our guests model acceptable behavior, we may reward them with life's little pleasures, but only those who deserve that treatment receive it. In my opinion, Andra BetScrivener, you do not deserve any pleasurable activities. Ladies, return to your rooms and close your doors." The young women and girls obeyed. I noted the inhabitants all stayed near their windows but ducked away if Trainer Sevrin glanced in their direction.

The matron turned her attention back to Minister Rogerson. "Do you understand my concern, sir? Are you sure we should supply her with writing materials?"

"Do you doubt the word of Supreme Prime Minister Sandovar?" Rogerson asked.

"Of course not, Minister Rogerson." Trainer Sevrin bowed her head.

"He's made his wishes clear," Rogerson said. "Andra is to be provided with writing materials for several hours each day, under the supervision of one of the doctors who are studying the deformities of the female brain. No female trainer may be present. Is that understood, Trainer Sevrin?"

"Yes, sir."

"Good." He turned to me and attempted to look kindly at me. "Andra, I'll be leaving you in Trainer Sevrin's expert hands. I have other things to attend to." Rogerson smiled. "I do hope you're able to resolve your difficulties, I would hate to disappoint Peter." With that, he turned and made his way back to the locked steel door, which someone opened from the other side.

Trainer Sevrin's malice poured over me as soon as he was gone.

"Nobody gets special treatment in my facility. You may have rights granted to you by the Supreme Prime Minister, but I'll be watching closely to see that you don't abuse them. I shouldn't worry, though. The orders were quite specific about where you were to be placed. Sandovar insisted you be monitored at all times. The doctors are intrigued by you. They're practically salivating over who gets to monitor you."

Sevrin led me even further into the building, past numerous uninhabited cells until we reached one set off from the others. The door did not contain a window. "This is a special room, which we call the Solitary Observation Room. This will be your home."

She opened the door to reveal a cell similar to the others with two exceptions. The first was a desk that had been crammed into the tiny space, and swallowed much of the floor. A pile of paper lay stacked on top, but there was nothing to write with. The back wall overlooking the desk contained a window made of dark glass that I couldn't see through.

"Behind that is an observation room," Sevrin said. "We can observe you at any time, not just when you're getting special privileges. You can't see us. You'll never know when we're watching, so don't try anything. Pens and pencils will be brought to you when it's time for you to work, and removed as soon as your time is up. You will be observed the entire time, so it will do you no good to attempt to hide one away so that you can entertain yourself later. I still question the wisdom of allowing you to have them, but I've been told this must be granted so that you can be studied. The wisdom of Sandovar and the Lord are beyond my comprehension." With that, Trainer Sevrin left me and slammed the heavy door behind her.

I sat on my cot and stared into space. I wouldn't let them see me cry.

*   *   *

From the second the cell door closed, my life became a series of disjointed moments. I would be left alone for what might be hours or mere minutes. Time had no meaning. I had nothing to do but stare at the walls and think and worry. At times I felt the walls closing in on me. I couldn't breathe. Claustrophobic panic set in. My worst fears came to life. The room felt smaller every minute.

My guilt over causing my father's pain grew, as did my worry for Lauren and the others. Was everyone else all right? Did I bring this on them?

At rare moments I could turn off the worry and relax toward sleep. My rest never lasted long. A voice channeled in from behind the glass wall woke me with a question or demand. They never let me sleep more than a few minutes. My mind grew confused.

I couldn't control my responses. I would often answer with a rudeness that would have shamed my father, when my anger spoke before I thought. Those moments led to immediate punishment dealt out by attendants or doctors or by Trainer Sevrin herself. They beat me with their fists. They whipped me. They tied me to my cot for hours on end.

At random intervals one of many nameless doctors walked in with writing supplies and demanded I show an example of my so-called ability but within dictated limitations. I had no choice. I wrote the words they required and tried to focus my shattered brain to manifest them. They took my work to see if my words had accomplished their goals. Sometimes I failed because exhaustion made it impossible. They relished those failures with mocking words and more abuse. Sometimes I succeeded. On rare occasions they allowed me time alone with paper and pen. "Work on Supreme Prime Minister Sandovar's request," they would say. I stared at the blank page unable to find the solution. My mind fractured. My exhaustion grew. My power faded. I was lost, alone, and hopeless.

I began to hallucinate. The people I trusted most appeared in my cell—Brian, Dad, Lauren, Professor Albert. I talked to them. The doctors watched and took notes. Inside, I knew I had to be cautious, not reveal too much. My control slipped as I spoke to my imagined friends.

Sometimes I thought I heard Lauren's voice in my head. *I'm here. You're not alone. I can help you,* the voice said.

Lauren, help me, please! I need you! I yelled with my mind, but she never answered. It couldn't be Lauren. I knew that. It couldn't be anybody. Lauren and I needed to be near each other for our silent communication to work. The voice must have come from me—from my yearning and loneliness. I wanted it to be quiet. It teased me into hope, yet, I was truly hopeless.

"Be quiet!" I yelled to the empty cell.

The doctors watched. They came in and laughed. "There's nobody here," they said. "You've played with words too long. They are destroying your brain. Women should never read or write."

Still, I kept hearing the voice in my head.

I lost track of time and any sense of day or night. Female Trainers brought me scraps of food and escorted me to the facilities. If any other occupant of these dreary cells happened to be there at the same time, I was not allowed to speak. The young women and girls made eye contact with me and gave me encouraging looks, but the silence only emphasized my loneliness and fear.

One or two of the other inmates showed up whenever I was brought to the facilities, including the dark sprite who had given me a moment of encouragement as I walked toward my doom.

The hallucinations grew. I imagined Peter Rogerson entering my cell. "How could you do this?!" I yelled. "Why would you reveal our secrets?" I attacked him, only to discover an attendant who had come to bring me food. The doctor assigned to observe from behind the glass raced in and injected me with something that made me calm but did not give me a restful sleep. It promoted nightmares instead.

My hatred of Peter grew. I couldn't believe he had turned me in. He must have turned in the others as well. I kept searching for faces I recognized from the meeting of P.O.W; nobody ever appeared. Maybe I imagined the meeting. After all, if Peter had turned us in, they would all have been punished. Why was I the only one here? Maybe I was truly losing my mind.

I was completely alone and beginning to doubt my entire reality.

After what could have been days or weeks, Trainer Sevrin came to my cell. I had only seen her on occasion, and each of those moments included either a beating or some other form of abuse. This time, however, Sevrin carried a fresh set of clothing. "You have a special visitor," she said. "We must get you cleaned up."

Sevrin led me to my first bath in a long time. She even helped scrub my back and braid my hair afterward. I closed my eyes and imagined the ministrations were those of my mother. I lost myself to memories of her fingers gently teasing tangles out of my hair, only to be smashed back into the present by the cruelty of Sevrin's touch. She ripped through knots and rubbed me raw with a towel that might as well have been made of sandpaper.

"Be on your best behavior or you'll be severely punished." Sevrin's cold voice sent chills of fear down my spine. I had already experienced the harshness of her punishment and the bite of her whip. I feared something worse.

I followed the tight bun to a private meeting room, warmed by a fire and filled with comfortable chairs.

My stomach clenched at the sight of Supreme Prime Minister Sandovar leaning on the mantel near a small sculpture of the Eye of the Lord.

"Here she is, Supreme Prime Minister." Sevrin's voice took on a tone of fawning adoration. She curtsied and put pressure on my shoulder until I followed suit. "She hasn't improved as much as we hoped with our current treatment plan. The doctors also tell me that they have been unable to discover the extent of her deformity."

"What deform—?" I began, but Trainer Sevrin's face hardened and her hand twitched with the desire to slap. I remained silent.

Sandovar chuckled. "That doesn't surprise me. I'm not concerned about the doctors' findings at the moment. Miss BetScrivener was brought here for other reasons. I thought you understood that, Trainer Sevrin?"

"Yes, sir. Of course, sir. However, the doctors have been very interested in her case."

"We will discuss that after I talk with our guest," Sandovar said. "Leave us, but don't wander too far. I won't be long."

"Are you sure you don't want an attendant in here with you, Sir? This trainee can be unpredictable."

"Do you doubt my ability to protect myself from a mere female?" Sandovar stood strong in his athletic body and cast the full intensity of his eyes on the Head Trainer.

"Of course not, Sir." She curtsied and left the room with a glare in my direction.

"Have you found a way to destroy the Freedom Readers yet, Andra?" Sandovar asked without any formalities.

It took me a moment to form words or clarify my thoughts. "How? I can't sleep. I can't think. Doctors make me write ridiculous tests. I need time to find the words."

"I see." Sandovar's voice sounded displeased. "My orders haven't been followed completely. I'll have to discuss this with Trainer Sevrin and the doctors. While I'm usually pleased with the treatment they give our special cases here, this time they must hold off until you've accomplished your assignment. The doctors here have been too anxious to understand this deformity you have and I can't blame them. They haven't had such a specimen since your mother."

The mention of Mother gave me a sharp pain of loss and love that led to anger, which burned through the fog in my brain. I found a moment of clarity. "My ability is not a deformity. Neither was my mother's, if she had one."

"Your 'abilities' go against the word of the Lord," Sandovar said. "Is that not deformity? However, I acknowledge that I need your assistance, so the doctors will have to adjust. I'll clarify my expectations so that you have time to write and are able to rest. When you've completed the task, you'll hand what you've written over to me so that I can make it happen. I presume all I have to do is read it out loud?"

"That isn't how it works. *You* can't make my words come to life."

"I can't do something a woman can do? I can make you suffer more than ever with a single word, is that understood?"

"Yes, sir, I meant no disrespect. My ability . . . it requires more than just writing and reading words out loud. I don't have to read them out loud, I have to envision what I want to happen and put some power behind it. I can't explain how it works, but I know that just reading my words out loud doesn't make them happen."

"Ah! Finally some details. Well, I still want to see your words before they are initiated. Is that clear?"

"Yes, sir."

"Do not try to write anything that betrays me, or I'll remove your father's ability to scribe one finger at a time."

"Is my father all right?"

"He's fine for now. Your behavior is the only thing that will keep him from unbearable pain. I expect to see something in writing on my next visit." With that, Sandovar opened the door. "Trainer Sevrin, please have someone else escort Andra back to her quarters. I need to clarify my desires for her care."

After that, my time became a bit more pleasant. I didn't see much of Trainer Sevrin, who sported a deep bruise on her own face after her meeting with Sandovar. I was allowed to sleep for longer periods, which enabled me to gain control over my thoughts. I spent a little time each day in the more welcoming areas in the front of the Center, as long as I didn't try to speak with any of the other women. I was even allowed to bring my writing materials with me as long as I only used them to draw, not write. A male guard or attendant prevented other women from approaching close enough to see my work, just in case. I wonder what they would have done if they knew I was creating drawings with hidden messages in my time away from the cell, as both a distraction and a reminder of who I was.

I continued to look for any familiar faces, to no avail. I observed the people who came to visit, in the hopes that someone I knew might appear. The messages in my drawing all pleaded for help for my father. I thought I could sneak a drawing to a visitor if someone I recognized would only come. I knew that I'd never be able to write words that would help me escape without destroying myself and the people I cared about. I'd never find the right words to help Dad or the other women, let alone achieve Sandovar's goal.

Time was running out.

TWENTY

I gave up all hope on the morning Trainer Sevrin informed me that Supreme Prime Minister Sandovar planned to visit again in a few days.

"He expects you to show him progress, or the first finger goes. That sounds unpleasant, doesn't it?" Sevrin's eyes glittered with malicious pleasure as she shared the message.

I sat at a desk away from the others in the welcome area, determined to come up with something to show Sandovar, but the occasional glare from the two guards who played checkers nearby as they watched over me disturbed my thought process. The cheerful jingle of bells in the door announced the arrival of some visitors, but didn't give me any sense of comfort. Feeling hopeless, I looked up to see who had entered the place of my father's doom. My heart started pounding as Professor Albert came into the lobby followed by a woman with jet-black hair and dark brown eyes whom I'd never seen before. Or at least, I couldn't recall her face even though there was something familiar about her. I gasped, which initiated a sharp look from my guards. I turned back to my drawing while attempting to watch the Professor and the unknown woman.

I strained to hear their voices when Trainer Sevrin swooped in to welcome them.

"Professor Albert, it has been a while since you visited us." Sevrin's false welcome and smile made me want to throw things at her.

"I hope I'm not intruding," Professor Albert said. "Some of the families of your current residents have asked that I check up on how they're doing." He gave a nonchalant peek around the room as if searching for specific women. His eyes met mine and his face filled with relief before he controlled his features and turned back to Trainer Sevrin. As their conversation continued, he maneuvered the Trainer toward me so that I could hear their discussion.

"You know you're always welcome here." Sevrin batted her thin eyelashes and her fake smile grew larger. "Who do you have with you? I don't recognize this young woman."

"This is a friend's daughter, Linda Fox. She thought that she might attend some training by choice and wanted to see what the different facilities were like. Linda, meet Trainer Sevrin, the best woman's trainer in all of New North."

I almost laughed out loud to see Trainer Sevrin blush at his words.

"You flatter me, Professor," she said.

"I hope it's acceptable for me to come and observe," the elegant young woman said.

As soon as I heard the woman's soft, musical tone, I realized that Lauren had entered the place of her nightmares. What was she doing there? How could she take this risk? I wanted to link with Lauren's mind, but was afraid I would cause harm. I had to be patient and wait for her to connect with me.

"I've always desired to perfect my feminine arts before I marry," Linda/Lauren said, "so that I may serve my future husband with pride."

"I'm surprised a young woman like you would select training," Sevrin said. "You seem quite elegant and accomplished already."

"I believe it's my job to come as near to perfection as possible."

I wondered how Lauren could stomach the words coming out of her mouth.

"I'm already engaged, you see." Lauren's voice took on the dreamy tone of a young woman in love, "to an important and wealthy Ministry official. I prefer not to say who so the women here don't get jealous. He has agreed to let me delay our marriage for a short time so that I can become the image of perfection, which will make him the envy of all others. He has promised to gift whichever Training Center I choose with enough money to ensure that I'm comfortable throughout my stay. Professor Albert has generously offered his services to escort me to all of the training centers, since he knows them all so well."

"Linda's father is an old friend," Professor Albert said. "Plus, this enables me to fulfill my promise to the families who have requested I check on their daughters."

"What an admirable goal, Miss Fox," Trainer Sevrin said. "I wish more women had your attitude. What would you like me to show you?"

Linda/Lauren looked around the room as if everything in it was surprising and delightful. She winked at me and then turned to Trainer Sevrin. "If it's acceptable, Ma'am, I would simply like to observe your trainees in this delightful room while dear Professor Albert meets with the women he needs to see. I find you can learn so much about a place by watching how women interact when they're relaxed. I promise not to be any bother. I can sit over there and be out of the way." Lauren pointed at a chair near my place of seclusion.

"I'm sorry Miss Fox, but nobody is allowed to sit near Miss BetScrivener." Trainer Sevrin said. "While she has been encouraged to join the community, she has taken on a vow of silence, which we do our best to honor."

I resisted the urge to yell a denial of Trainer Sevrin's blatant lie. I took several deep breathes and comforted myself with the fact that, as long as we were in the same room together, Lauren and I would be able to communicate without anyone's knowledge.

"I believe you'll be much more comfortable over here," Trainer Sevrin guided Lauren to a small armchair across the room from me. "You'll also be able to see so much more. May I have some refreshments brought over?"

"That would be lovely, if it's not too much trouble."

"I'll do that as soon as I get the Professor settled in his usual private sitting room. Professor, I assume you'll have your usual, tea and cake?"

"How can I resist when the cake here is so delicious? I don't see any of the women I've been asked to check on."

"They must be in training." Trainer Sevrin led Professor Albert toward a private sitting room just off the common room. "I'll pull them out one at a time. Who do you wish to speak with?" She closed the door behind them.

Andra, can you hear me? Are you all right? Your mind seems so confused. Lauren turned her gaze toward a group of women playing a game nearby.

Is Dad all right?

He's fine so far, although he's a prisoner at the Ministry. We've been able to get some friends in to check on him. She glanced at me and turned away. *Stop looking in my direction. Do something else while we "talk."*

I recognized the wisdom of Lauren's words, even though I desperately wanted to watch my friend—to make a connection with her eyes. Instead, I began to sketch a picture of the room.

What are you doing here? What if someone recognizes you?

Did you recognize me?

No.

You've seen me more recently than they have, and I'm sure they think I'm dead. The woman who left this place was made up of skin, bones, matted red hair, filth and rags. She clung to life by a thread.

Lauren's thoughts filled my head with pain and fear.

How could you come? You hate this place.

I had to. It was the only way to get a message to you, and hopefully, get you out.

How did you find out where I was?

Peter Rogerson.

I knocked my ink on the floor in surprise.

"Stupid woman!" One of the attendants assigned to keep an eye on me turned to the maidservant who was always on call. "Clean this mess up and get her another bottle of ink." He turned back to me. "Cover your work while she's near you."

"I'm only drawing a picture. See." I held up the sketch I'd begun. "I can't corrupt anyone with that, can I?"

The attendant just grunted and turned back to the checker game.

Peter Rogerson! I screamed in my mind.

I'm glad we're not talking out loud. That would have burst everyone's eardrums. Why are you upset that Peter Rogerson told us where you were?

He's the reason I'm here. He told his father our secret.

That's not true.

Of course it's true. He didn't waste any time once he learned of my ability.

Think about it. Lauren's internal tone was calm. *He didn't know about your power until the meeting at Briandra's Haven. He was with us at the meeting of P.O.W. when your father was taken. Peter didn't have a chance to tell his father.*

222

I wanted to smack my head at my own stupidity. Instead, I dipped my pen in the fresh bottle of ink brought by the maid and began to draw with angry strokes. *Then who? Alice or one of the other women we met at the party?*

We can't be sure, but we have a suspicion. Let me tell you what we know, and then perhaps you'll understand.

* * *

While Brian and Andra went off on their mysterious adventure to Briandra's Haven, Mama Woodson whipped up a fresh batch of chocolate muffins to bring over to the Scrivener. She placed them in a basket and bundled up for the short jaunt through the fast-falling snow when she heard the sound of a carriage pull up to her neighbor's rarely used front door.

Who would come visiting on a day like today? She thought. She peeked out her window to see if she recognized the visitor. Although the top of the carriage and horses were already covered, there was no mistaking the elaborate gold Eye of the Lord found only on the carriage of the Supreme Prime Minister.

Mama Woodson put her basket down and opened the back door to her home. The snow helped hide her movements as she made her way to the Scrivener's house, trying to remain unseen. She heard the pounding on the Scrivener's front door, a sound that didn't evoke a friendly visit. She made her way to the woodpile between the two houses, and crouched down where she could see the door but hopefully not be seen.

"What a surprise," the Scrivener said. "Is there something wrong?"

"Where's your daughter?" Sandovar's deep voice was unmistakable.

"Andra's out for the day. I'm not sure where. Off on an adventure, I suppose."

"Why would you allow your daughter out on a day like today?"

"If you knew my daughter you'd understand that she has her own mind. My apologies; it's so cold. Would you like to come in? Can I offer you some refreshments? I just got home and made some cocoa."

"There's no need for that, Scrivener. I want you to come with me."

"Where are we going, sir?"

"To the Ministry. Get your coat."

"Of course, can I just pop over to my neighbor's to leave a message for Andra so she doesn't worry?"

"There will be no need for that," Sandovar said. "I'll be sure Andra knows where you are. Now come."

Mama Woodson watched as Sandovar grabbed the Scrivener's arm with a firm grip and pulled him toward the carriage. The Scrivener glanced toward her house. She raised herself just enough so that she could be seen, and prayed that nobody else would notice. Their eyes met, and she nodded before she ducked down again until the carriage left.

Mama Woodson watched for Andra and Brian's return for hours, with the intent of running out to warn Andra as soon as she could. At the arrival of two ministry guards, who stood near the Scrivener house so they could peer through the heavy snow and watch both ends of the street, she realized that she could do nothing to warn Andra. She saw Andra and Brian come down the street together and watched through the windows as they parted ways. They looked happy about something. She watched Brian kiss Andra's cheek. For a moment her mother's heart leaped at the thought that maybe Brian had finally found his way out of the friendship zone—a secret dream she had always cherished but never discussed. She couldn't let anything stop that from happening. As soon as Brian opened the door she grabbed his arm.

"Mama, what's wrong? I told you Andra and I would be gone for several hours."

"Listen, there's no time. The Scrivener has been taken. Andra is about to be taken to the Ministry by guards. Someone must have revealed her secret. You must warn Lauren and Professor Albert. Go out the back way and be silent!"

"What about you?" Brian asked.

"I've done nothing and there's no time." She hugged him again and kissed his cheek. "Go! But be sure to come back to me."

He ran out the door without another word.

Mama Woodson started cleaning her spotless house while she awaited his return. It was the only way to prevent her fears from taking over. Hours later, she was in an unused extra bedroom at the back of the house when she heard the door open.

"Mama, I'm back," Brian said.

She rushed to him and pulled him into a desperate hug, despite the cold wet snow that covered him.

"Did anyone see you? Were you able to warn them?"

"Everything's all right, Mama. I avoided the guards and got there without any trouble. Professor Albert and Lauren have headed into hiding. They wouldn't tell me where. They promised to contact me soon."

"Did anyone see you?" Mama Woodson's heart was in her throat.

"I don't think so." He collapsed into a chair by the table. "What's going to happen?"

"I don't know, son. Get out of your wet things and I'll get you some warm soup.

"Who did this?" Brian's whole body slumped in defeat. "Why would someone betray us?"

"I don't know, but if I had to point fingers," Mama Woodson said, "I'd point them at Madame Emily DuFarge."

TWENTY-ONE

I sat at the desk in my claustrophobic room and threw down my pen overwhelmed by a sensation of elation and despair. I'd finally written something to show Sandovar, based on some suggestions Lauren had given me during our silent discussion the day before. My hope hinged on a dangerous plan concocted by Lauren, the Professor, and others; a plan I wasn't sure would work. My words also had to be clever enough to convince Sandovar that I had done what he'd asked without actually harming anyone. After all this time spent in confusion, and all the mistakes I'd already made, I doubted my words were good enough.

My future and my father's life lay in the hands and plans of people I didn't know if I could trust. I wasn't even sure I could trust my own words. I could only think about all the ways I could make mistakes or harm others. I was terrified.

I didn't want to believe that Emily had turned traitor despite my own doubts about her. I didn't like the way she used me, but turning me and Dad over to Sandovar moved beyond cruel. It destroyed any hope for the future Emily claimed to desire. It destroyed lives. How could she do that? My head buzzed with confusing thoughts and I no longer knew whom to trust.

As I expected, the door to my cell opened and a doctor entered. It never took long for someone to appear once I stopped working. "Show me what you've written," he said.

I handed him the paper without a word.

"Hm, we'll see what the Supreme Prime Minister thinks about this in a few days. I'll hold onto it until then. I assume you obeyed his instructions and haven't used your deformed power on these words yet."

"I wouldn't risk my father that way," I said.

"Good," the doctor said. "I'll send an attendant to bring you out front."

While waiting, I pondered the next part of the plan as Lauren had explained it. It asked me to revisit and rewrite the words I'd started on the day before the meeting of P.OW.—writing that had filled me with a sense of hope, but which I had never had a chance to envision. In hindsight I realized I had been foolish to wait for approval from other women. I wasted time that way, but I didn't want to change the lives of other women without their permission. If only I hadn't waited, women would already be developing stronger powers. They would already be able to help. I had intended to manifest my words after I consulted with my father, but the Ministry guards took us before I could. I am glad I had managed to hide them in a safe spot before I was taken. As far as I knew, our house hadn't been searched and Sandovar knew nothing about those words. Lauren's plan required I rewrite and improve on the words I had already written, with a few additional suggestions coming from the P.O.W. I couldn't comprehend how she expected me to do that when someone watched me at all times.

* * *

We need you to write this. The urgency of Lauren's thoughts was almost painful when we communicated the day before. *It will help with everything, I know it will.*

But how? Every time I write, I'm watched. Everything I write is checked. How am I supposed to write it?

Another woman has come forward with powers, Lauren thought. *She has the power of suggestion, the ability to make men think and do what she wishes. I'm going to request that she be allowed to visit this place with me tomorrow. She'll make the guards think you're drawing while you're actually writing. Are you always here at the same time?*

I think so. My fear and confusion consumed me for a moment. Lauren wanted me to put faith in someone new, and I barely had faith in those I was supposed to trust.

Are you all right? Lauren asked

Yes, I think. I have no sense of time here.

I remember. Lauren's thoughts darkened for a moment.

This woman's power sounds dangerous, I thought. *How do we know we can trust her? Who is she?*

"Time's up, Miss BetScrivener." One of the attendant guards loomed over my drawing. "This isn't one of your best, is it? It looks like a child's work." The scribbled mess on my paper didn't resemble any of my work and I wondered for a moment who had drawn it. The guard laughed. "Looks like your talents are waning," he said. "Doomed to become less than a maidservant, I believe. You, girl." He turned to the nearby maid. "Clean this up and have it sent back." He grabbed my elbow. "Come on, you have an appointment with the doctors."

Andra, we'll be here tomorrow, I promise. Just think about what you need to write. You can trust— Lauren's thoughts were cut off as the steel door clanged behind me.

* * *

I tried to focus on my drawing as I waited for Linda/Lauren and her mysterious guest to arrive. I didn't want to hear the guard ridiculing me again, so I set out to draw a portrait of him. I became so absorbed in my work that I didn't hear the bell announcing visitors.

"This place is ADORABLE." Cindy Rogerson's operatic voice pierced me to the bone. I turned to see Cindy walking beside Lauren's disguised figure as Trainer Sevrin led them to a special table that had been laid out for tea.

It can't be Cindy! I sent a silent shout.

I'll explain in a minute, Lauren thought as she settled into her seat with a smile for Trainer Sevrin. *You have to trust her. Trust me at least.*

"Are you sure you wouldn't prefer to be in our dining room?" Trainer Sevrin asked. "This room can get noisy sometimes."

"No, thank you, Trainer Sevrin," Lauren said. "I wanted my friend Cindy to experience this place as I did. I'm sure you've met Cindy Rogerson before, haven't you?"

"I haven't seen you since you were a young girl." Trainer Sevrin added to my shock by hugging Cindy. I had never seen the trainer's caring side. "You're not considering coming here are you? I'm sure you have suitors flocking to your door."

"That's so sweet, Trainer Sevrin," Cindy said. "My friend Linda trusts my opinion immensely. I admire her decision to perfect herself in training, but made her promise that she would get my approval before she made the final choice of Training Center. I've always known this was one of the best. Thank you for the opportunity to observe and explore." She glanced around the room. "Some of the art on the walls is exquisite. Who are the artists?"

I glanced at the art that filled the walls. While some pieces were decent, I wouldn't call any of it exquisite. I wondered what Cindy was up to.

"It's all been created by our trainees. We have some of the finest art instructors around."

"May I wander around and look more closely at them?" Cindy asked. "I always love to see how people's strokes become masterpieces."

"Of course, anything you wish. Miss Rogerson, Miss Fox I hope you both find our Center comfortable. We would love to have you here. Our maids can help you if you have any questions. I have duties to attend to." With that, Trainer Sevrin left the room.

Cindy stood and began to make a circuit of all the room's art. She started on the wall opposite my location and moved through each piece to check it from different angles. I watched her out of the corner of my eye.

Be prepared, Andra. Lauren sent. *Cindy will signal you when it's safe to write.*

How can I trust her? She's Cindy Rogerson!

Because when Peter told her what happened to you and your father, she stood up to her father. She asked him why he allowed you to be put in here. She said that she was looking forward to you becoming her sister and that she would never forgive him if you or the Scrivener were hurt. She demanded an explanation, which he wouldn't give. Later, she turned to Peter for answers. He told her the truth, that the government suspected you of having one of those dangerous abilities. That's when she confessed to having one herself. Peter brought her to us.

As Lauren explained, Cindy made her slow way around the room, moving closer and closer to me. As she came near the single attendant guard who sat with a bored expression nearby, she stumbled and fell toward him. He leaped up and caught her.

"Are you all right, Miss?" he asked.

"I'm so clumsy," Cindy said with a flirtatious smile. "I'm lucky there was a strong man nearby to catch me." She patted him on the arm. "You're my hero."

What's that all about? She's flirting with him. Is that how she plans to distract him?

Her power only works if she's had physical contact with a person. It only lasts while she remains nearby. As soon as she leaves the room, the connection breaks, and the men forget what happened. Cindy claims it only works on men, which is why we can trust her.

I stifled a laugh and watched the young vixen in action.

"Thank you so much for saving me," Cindy said. "I think I'll go back to my friend before I hurt myself." With that, she turned so I could see her face but the guard couldn't, gave a subtle nod and a wink, and headed toward Lauren.

I glanced over at the guard. His bored attitude had disappeared to be replaced by a contented smile. His focus was on Cindy instead of me.

Write, Andra! Lauren thought. *You have to finish before someone comes to take you back.*

I began to pen words I'd started long ago, with additions and changes I had thought of the night before. After the first few sentences, I checked on the guard.

He noticed my movement. "Let me see how the picture is coming." He stood to get a look at my work. "I hope it's better than yesterday."

My heart pounded and I held my breath. If he saw my words, it would prove I couldn't trust Cindy but it would also probably destroy my father.

The guard leaned over my table and touched the paper moving his finger as if tracing the lines of his face. "Hey, not bad. You're making me look almost as handsome as I really am. Keep up the good work. I'll let you stay out here a little longer today. I want to give this as a gift." He glanced toward Cindy who gave him a flirtatious wave.

She did it!

I told you she would, now write.

I wrote.

* * *

Women of power and men who believe in equality, the time for a revo-

lution has come! More and more women are stepping forward and revealing that we have secret abilities. The discovery that others share our secrets enables women to connect and help each other. P.O.W.—a group formed by and for the Power of Women—will continue to grow as women realize our power can change the world. Males as well as females will join in the hopes that P.O.W. can do what the Freedom Readers failed to do, bring about a more equal and just society.

While women's abilities range in strength and power, the growing numbers indicate that women are no longer willing to accept the laws of Supreme Prime Minister Sandovar without question. However, we also don't want to be responsible for a violent revolution. The solution lies in increasing our strength and supporting each other so we can confront those who enslave us through the power of our minds.

Lauren Freeman and I—Andra BetScrivener—increased our strength together when we learned how to read each other's minds. With these words I am making that bond even stronger. From this point on we will be able to communicate over long distances. This strengthened connection will allow us to use our abilities with more confidence as well as coordinate future plans.

With these words, I will also strengthen the abilities of other women and help them find connections and support. I am finishing words I never had a chance to manifest before I was taken into custody and thrown into the WTP. Sandovar wants something I have no intention of providing. With the support of Lauren and all of you, male and female, they cannot break me.

With these words, groups will begin to form around similar abilities. Women will find that they can help each other, and men will find ways to help as well. Sometimes two women can strengthen each other simply by holding hands. An empath can guide a healer. Two women with the ability to move small objects can join together to move larger objects. The forms of support can come in infinite varieties. Working together with supportive men, P.O.W. will gain the strength and power to change the world. Meanwhile, these words may also help free my father, who has an important role to play in this change. Go forth in power and peace.

I finished and hoped that this wouldn't be too personal or that my own doubts and fears wouldn't prevent me from manifesting the words into reality. I put the pen down. *I'm ready to try, I think. But . . .*

But what? This is the solution.

I know. I'm worried that I'll harm other women with these words.

They want this to happen. Lauren thought. *They told you so at the meeting. We've asked every new recruit for permission. Do this, it's for the best. Good luck! Cindy will continue to keep the guard distracted.*

I picked up the paper and read through my words slowly, allowing Lauren to read them from my mind as I envisioned every detail and every idea. I pictured women and girls coming forward to members of P.O.W. to share their powers. I pictured a circle of women connecting through their abilities. I pictured a group of men coming to assist them. I pictured myself, sitting in my cell, having a conversation with Lauren who sat in a house elsewhere. My heart beat faster at that, but I was strong. Finally, I pictured myself in the Supreme Prime Minister's office, hugging my father as Sandovar sat behind his desk looking pale and defeated. I took a deep breath, expecting nausea, but instead I felt empowered.

I did it. Andra thought.

I know. That was amazing. You've never let me see how you manifest words before. How will we know it worked? Lauren asked.

Make the guard take me back to my room now. If we can still hear each other when I'm there, it worked. I'll call for you when I'm in my cell. Is there any way Cindy can make the guard forget the picture altogether? I didn't finish the drawing and I wouldn't want that to cause suspicion. Will it stick once she's gone?

I glanced over at the table as Lauren whispered my request to Cindy. "I'll make it stick." Cindy didn't bother to lower her voice. She winked at me again and then focused her eyes on the guard.

I tucked my words into my dress and gathered my paper together so the guard wouldn't see the incomplete drawing.

"Time to go back to your room," the guard said. "I better not get in trouble because you're late. I must have dozed off for a second. Don't tell anyone and I'll sneak you something special from the kitchen."

"I won't say a word." I followed him out.

* * *

Lauren, I'm back in my room, can you hear me? I held my breath as I waited for a response. The seconds passed with infinite slowness.

Your thoughts are faint Andra, but I can read you. Can you read me?

I can, I can! The relief overwhelmed me and I burst into tears.

Are you all right? Why are you crying?

I've been so alone.

That's how they destroy you.

I could sense Lauren slip into dark memories. The intimate connection of our minds was almost too much. I wanted to stop Lauren's thoughts, but realized I had to help her move through this moment in order to heal. We both needed each other's strength.

They make you think nobody will ever love you or speak with you again. Lauren's thoughts weren't distracted by my reluctance. *The trainers and doctors make you hate yourself until you decide to either play their games or destroy yourself.*

It's amazing that you survived, I thought, while wondering if I would. *Your strength is incredible, Lauren.*

So is yours. . .wait a moment Andra . . . I think someone is interfering with our connection.

Lauren's thoughts disappeared from my mind. The sudden sense of emptiness, of being alone again, caused me to hyperventilate. I tried to slow my breathing as I waited for her mind to return. I didn't understand what she meant about someone interfering. Perhaps I had failed. Perhaps what I wanted was too much, and I had hurt Lauren by opening her mind to other people. I couldn't control a growing sense of panic.

I'm back. Lauren's voice sounded confident in my head. *I haven't left you. I've blocked the person, but . . . whomever it was, felt very close.*

I could breathe again.

Lauren's thoughts continued. *But, someone else is trying to reach your mind. We have to figure this out. Can you do something to distract the guards?*

They usually leave me alone if I'm meditating, as long as I don't try to sleep. Do it!

I closed my eyes and focused on my diaphragm while taking deep breaths. I slowly regained my center. *There's probably someone observing me.*

I can sense the doctor but that's not what I mean. I sensed another female sending you a message.

I had a vague memory of the voices I heard throughout my time in the Center. A voice reached out to me in my darkest moments. I always thought or wished the voice belonged to Lauren, but it never was her. A face flashed into my mind, a dark-skinned pixie with deep brown eyes.

That's the person I keep sensing, Andra. That girl you just thought about. Who is she?

She's another trainee, brought in under the new mandates. I think we've found someone else with power. Can she hear us too?

Lauren took a few moments to respond. *I don't think so. I've found her mind. It seems like she has the ability to send messages and give comfort but can't read other people's minds.*

Then I have to get a message to her. It's a good thing the doctors here still don't understand the power of the women's secret language, and I'm allowed to draw without question. I'll get a note to her somehow.

I had the sudden urge to celebrate. After all the darkness and pain, we might have found a way to succeed. And, even more important in some ways, I wasn't alone. I jumped on my cot and bounced in excitement.

"What are you doing, Miss BetScrivener?" The voice of an unknown male said through the speaker contraption that came from the hidden room.

"I just wanted some exercise, but there's no room to move."

"Oh, I see. We'll discuss the possibility of you going for a walk in the future. However, jumping on a cot is not proper behavior for a young lady. Stop immediately!"

"I'm sorry." I bent my head down in the hopes he wouldn't be able to see as

I tried to contain my laughter. I could sense Lauren's amusement in my mind as well. "Is it all right if I draw a little?" I asked the unseen voice.

"You may draw. Pen or pencil?"

"Pencil please."

In a moment, my cell door opened and a doctor handed me a set of drawing pencils. "You have thirty minutes," he said and left the room.

What happens next? I asked Lauren, who had remained connected throughout that exchange.

Cindy and I leave now and continue recruiting. Brian and Johnson will set the next phase of the plan in motion. You do what you can in there. Then, it depends on what happens with Sandovar.

My stomach fell, and all the excess energy drained out of me.

Good luck, Andra. If you need me, just focus on my name and I'll make sure we're connected.

Lauren, I'm scared.

Me too, but at least we're not alone. This connection makes me stronger. It's made me able to reach minds near you without becoming overwhelmed.

I'm stronger too, I think.

More later. Trainer Sevrin is coming.

I focused on my drawing. I wanted to make the message clear, but it had to be done on a small piece of paper that I could somehow pass to my young friend at the next "surprise" meeting in the facilities. If I stopped working, my mind wandered over all the things out of my control. What was happening to my father? How will Sandovar react to my writing? Were my words good enough? What were the Freedom Readers doing? Was Emily really responsible for my incarceration? Will my words harm the women coming forth to join P.O.W.?

Even though I had confidence in what I had written, and envisioning the words hadn't made me sick, I still knew there was a chance that my words could put a lot of people in danger. I was terrified, but it was already too late. I couldn't take the words back. All I could do was focus on this new task and get a message to my unknown ally.

I had just finished folding the drawing into a tiny square and hiding it in the waistband of my skirt when a female trainer entered.

"You're new," I said to the nervous looking young trainer. "What's your name?"

I didn't expect an answer as the trainers usually only spoke to me with orders and demands.

"I'm Trainer Alvarie," the young woman said. "I just graduated from my training program at a different center and was assigned here. Anyway, it's bath day. We need to make sure you're presentable for the Supreme Prime Minister."

"Shouldn't proper women be bathing every day?" I couldn't resist challenging the hypocrisy of my situation, even though it might earn me a beating. I could count on one hand the number of baths I'd had since entering this torture chamber.

"Well . . . you're right, of course. I'm not sure why you don't bathe every day. I'm surprised." Trainer Alvarie didn't realize that other trainers responded to insubordinate questions with violence. "Um . . . I was also told to prepare a fresh outfit, too."

"It's about time," I said. "These clothes are about to walk on their own."

"Oh . . . I'm . . . uh . . . I'm so sorry." Trainer Alvarie looked like she was about to burst into tears.

I relented. She obviously had no idea what my situation at this center was. Her experience at a WTP must have been very different from mine. "It's not your fault, of course. I apologize for my rudeness. Lead on, please."

Trainer Alvarie smiled in relief. I followed her toward the bathing facilities. My heart beat faster in anticipation. At the same time, though, I was curious as to why any woman would choose this life. Since most trainers avoided talking with me, this was my only opportunity to find out more.

"Why did you become a trainer? You seem very young to be one."

"I went into training because I was different."

"Different?" I asked. "How?"

"I can't really explain. I've always been able to remember anything I've ever seen or heard. If I was shown something one time, I could describe it right away. If someone read me a poem or a story, I could recite it word for word. I never forgot a face or a name or the words to a song or anything. My parents said I was too intelligent for my own good. People in my village thought I was strange. The girls always said no man would ever want to marry a woman who knew too much. They were right; I hadn't found a man interested in me by my seventeenth birthday, and didn't think that would change. So I entered the Women's Training Program early. At my center, they didn't criticize my ability. They actually admired how much I absorbed in such a short time. When the Head Trainer there asked if I would like to be a trainer, after I'd only spent six months with them, I knew it was the place for me. I may still be different, but at least I have a purpose now."

I bit the side of my mouth to keep the words from pouring out as I listened to Trainer Alvarie's story. Still a question burst out of me just as Alvarie put her hand out to open the door to the bathing facilities. "Do you think that perhaps your abilities are similar to the ones the Ministry is concerned about?"

The color drained from her face. "How dare you . . . I . . . um . . ." She opened the door and pushed me through. "Go get cleaned up. I'll have your clothes laundered. Your new outfit is over there." She pointed to a simple gray dress and clean undergarments folded in a neat pile on a bench. "I'll wait outside."

I was relieved that she had chosen to wait outside. I didn't mean to shock her, and at least this way I wouldn't have to deal with the confused look on her face. The more experienced trainers all stayed in and watched me with hawk eyes, even when I went to the bathroom. They watched my every move as if somehow I'd be able to destroy the entire place in the nude.

I began to undress with my back to the entrance. I heard the door open and assumed it was Trainer Alvarie checking up on me.

"I haven't even undressed yet," I said.

"The Trainer is outside. It's good to finally have a chance to speak with you." The voice sounded like it was attached to a young girl.

I turned to find my young friend with a huge smile and twinkling brown eyes. Two other girls trailed her, neither one could be much older than thirteen. I shouldn't have been surprised; somehow a few of these young girls and women managed to make an appearance every time I came to the facilities.

"It's you," I said. "I hoped you'd come. I have something to give you."

"I wish we could have talked sooner. My name is Lilah. You're Andra BetScrivener, aren't you?"

"Yes. How did you know?"

"Gossip travels quickly, even in a place like this." The three girls moved in and sat on the benches near me. "My friends and I kept coming here when we knew you would be here, hoping to have a chance to say hello. We set up a signal so we would know when to come."

"I appreciate it," I said. "It helped me deal with the loneliness."

"I'm glad." Lilah's smile lit up her face. "Did you hear my messages? I wanted you to know I was here."

"So it was you. You have a power, an ability. . . "

"I do. Do you?"

"Yes, I can't explain now, though. I . . . I have something for you."

The door opened again and Trainer Alvarie stepped through. "You haven't even finished undressing, Miss BetScrivener?" Her earlier warmth had disappeared. "Do you want me to get in trouble? Do I need to help you?"

"No, I'm sorry Trainer Alvarie. I'm sorry, for everything."

"Yes . . . well, please hurry up." She turned to the three girls who had jumped to their feet as soon as she entered. "Are you ladies finished doing your business? Perhaps you should return to your rooms."

"Yes, ma'am." Lilah and her friends curtsied. Lilah dropped a dirty handkerchief on the floor. At the same time she sent a thought into my mind. *Pick it up. Give me what you have.*

"Oh, you dropped something." The words came out of my mouth with a weird emphasis. I hoped Trainer Alvarie didn't notice my awkward phrasing. I'd never be an actress. I bent down while pulling the folded paper out of my waistband. I handed the handkerchief back to Lilah, the tiny drawing tucked safely inside.

The three girls left and I went back to undressing. Trainer Alvarie didn't leave this time.

"Miss BetScrivener," Alvarie said in a hushed voice. "You're right. I've never told anyone but . . . you're right."

"Trainer Alvarie"—I turned to the scared young woman—"You're not alone."

TWENTY-TWO

After Lauren and Cindy's visit to Andra, several members of P.O.W. met in the abandoned house on the outskirts of the capital where the Professor had taken Lauren to hide from the Ministry guards. The hovel had since become the unofficial headquarters of the group. With sparse, broken-down furniture and dirt and dust everywhere, it was a far cry from the Freedom Readers' comfortable headquarters. In the short time they'd been there, members of P.O.W. had helped clean it up and made it more comfortable. Candles and lamps filled the central room with warm light. A fire kept out the winter chill. Old cushions and handmade blankets lay scattered around so that people could at least sit on the floor in comfort.

The group had gathered to find out what Lauren had learned from visiting Andra, and make a plan for the next move. Brian searched the diverse gathering in the hopes he would find at least one supporter of the idea of storming in to save Andra. Now that planning was underway, he wanted things to move quickly, but everything took time. Everyone was preaching caution. Brian's concern for Andra and the Scrivener made caution sit uncomfortably in his body. After the Professor and Lauren returned from their visit to the Center and told him how thin, disheveled and broken Andra had looked, Brian wanted to use force to break in and get her out.

Across the room, Peter Rogerson sat tense and willing to fight, but Brian was just beginning to trust him. Next to Peter, Cindy glowed with the knowledge of the important role she had already played. Heidi, Beth and a few other P.O.W. women avoided his eyes. Most of them would want to find a less dangerous means of helping Andra, so he had no hope there.

His eyes connected with Alice's who smiled. She'd been all for setting fire to the Supreme Prime Minister's home as soon as she learned that Andra and the Scrivener were in custody. She was itching to use her ability in a dramatic way. Even in his desire to take action, however, Brian realized that fire couldn't be controlled. Finally, there was Johnson, who had only been welcomed because he was so distraught about the abduction of two people he loved. Some members of P.O.W. thought he was too entrenched in the Freedom Readers, too close to Emily to be trusted. Johnson willingly opened his mind to Lauren and hid nothing. Lauren cleared him and welcomed him. The gruff older man didn't contribute his opinion often and sat near Brian with a stoic, unreadable face.

"If we run into this blindly," the Professor said, "without a clear plan, then too many people will be hurt."

"I know," Brian said. "But they're hurting Andra in there."

"Brian." Lauren moved next to him and laid a hand on his arm. "I know exactly what she's going through. I know it sounds bad, but she's strong. She told me things had improved under Sandovar's orders. We can't do anything that will make things worse."

Lauren's disguise didn't hide the mixture of pain and courage reflected in the depths of her eyes which had always shown her emotions so clearly. Brian still hadn't gotten used to the strange brown contacts she used as part of her new look. Professor Albert had used connections with people he had on the Outside, in another country, to sneak them into New North. Contact lenses were not allowed under Sandovar's rule, as they came from a science he claimed the Lord no longer welcomed. Brian never knew how Professor Albert reached his connections, but found comfort in the idea that someone Outside knew what was going on behind the Wall. At one point someone from P.O.W. suggested they reach out beyond the walls to start an invasion that could overcome Sandovar.

"That's not the solution," Professor Albert said, always the arbiter of caution and wisdom. "We need an internal solution, not a war. We don't know what would happen to the citizens of New North under an Outsider's rule."

"We have several advantages at the moment." Professor Albert's voice brought Brian's attention back to the meeting. "First, the Ministry doesn't even know of the existence of P.O.W. They think that they have all the dangerous women under their power and don't realize the number of talented women we've found. Second, they aren't aware that the Freedom Readers have dissension in their ranks." The Professor checked with Johnson who nodded in agreement. "Third, Lauren was able to learn exactly what Sandovar wants from Andra, which is the total destruction of the Freedom Readers. Lauren made the wise suggestion to Andra to use the current dissension in the ranks of the Readers as inspiration for what she would write for Sandovar. That was brilliant, Lauren."

Lauren's cheeks turned ruby and she gave a shy smile as everyone applauded.

"Now we can plan," Professor Albert said.

* * *

The discussion that went long into the night had led to Brian's current position. He and Johnson waited in the front of Mr. Mastak's shop. Brian's hand twitched with impatience. He tried to distract himself by looking at the art. He only saw colors and shapes that his mind could make no sense of—the images took no form. They waited while Mastak finished copying leaflets marked with the emblem of the Freedom Readers, created, however, by the P.O.W. The leaflet held a message that suggested the rebel group had a big plan brewing and was looking for recruits willing to fight. P.O.W. had decided Sandovar must be led to believe the Freedom Readers were plotting an immediate overthrow of the government. They hoped it would make Andra's manifestation of dissension in the ranks of the Readers and a crumbling of their cause more believable. Johnson leaped on the idea and suggested asking Mr. Mastak for help.

"We need him on our side," Johnson had said, "since we can't afford to pay for any printing and he has ways of distributing material quickly. Mastak has worked with the Readers for a long time, but he has no fondness for Emily's tactics and usually preaches non-violence."

Mastak came from the back room with a crate filled with pamphlets. "I hope you two know what you're doing," he said. "This could be dangerous for many."

"We discussed that, Mastak," Johnson said. "This pamphlet offers a vague threat, much like the Ministry has seen before. It may set them back onto a search for Readers, but if the rest of our plan works, that won't be an issue. Besides, the government hasn't been successful in finding anyone for years, not since . . . uh . . ." He glanced at Brian, cleared his throat and continued. "The Ministry clearly suspects the Readers have been forming some sort of plan, which started with the distribution of Andra's drawings. This just reinforces their belief and adds a little fuel. They have no idea that we, um . . . the Freedom Readers had anything to do with the accident that killed Achan. This is a risk worth taking."

"What about you, Woodson?" Mr. Mastak asked. "Do you agree with Johnson?"

"We have to do something to help Andra and her father," Brian said. "I'm sure our plan will work, and nobody will get hurt. There are other elements—"

"Brian," Johnson said.

Mr. Mastak chuckled. "Johnson, you know me better than that. I don't want to know the details. I do my part and hope for the best. Be sure Emily doesn't know I printed these for free or she'll never pay for my work again." He twitched his moustache and winked. "Now off with you both, a fake revolution needs to begin."

"Let's hope it leads to something real," Brian said.

Johnson slapped him on the shoulder and headed out the door, box in hand.

* * *

Time yawned forward for me. Since I had completed the writing for Sandovar, pending his approval, I wasn't allowed writing materials after my return from the bath, not even to draw. Nobody observed me either, as if my danger had dissipated. I almost missed the distractions and questions from unseen faces. They'd disturbed my sleep but at least it had been a sign I wasn't alone.

Completely alone.

I lay on my cot and stared at the ceiling. I reflected back on the whispered conversation I'd had with Trainer Alvarie while taking my bath. I took a chance, trusting the power of the words I had written earlier. I told Alvarie that other women outside the training centers, women who had unique abilities, had begun to join together and form a group called P.O.W. in order to fight against the injustices laid upon us by the government of New North. I also told her that I suspected many of the women trapped behind the steel door had abilities as well.

"But they're so young," Trainer Alvarie said.

"Weren't you young when you realized you were different?" I asked.

"I was." Trainer Alvarie giggled for a moment. "I guess I wasn't really different after all."

"Your ability is unique," I said. "Every woman's ability seems unique to that woman, even though there is some overlap. I believe that we all can strengthen and change our abilities with practice. Your knowledge, your intelligence, your ability to remember everything is incredible and could help so much."

Trainer Alvarie didn't say anything. She swallowed and picked up a towel. "We better get you dried off, dressed and back to your room. I have other duties to attend to."

"You won't tell anyone what I've told you, will you?" I asked. I tried to sound confident but, inside, I was worried I had made another mistake. "Our secret protects you as well. We need your help to make change."

Alvarie avoided my eyes. "I won't say anything," she said, "but I don't know if I can help. I need time to think."

Trainer Alvarie helped me finish getting ready, led me back to my cramped quarters, and left without another word.

I hadn't heard or seen another soul for hours, except for one flash of a message sent to me by Lilah with the cryptic thought *the trainees are gathering.*

I had contacted Lauren a few times, but the distance made sustained discussion difficult unless Lauren could focus her whole attention toward me. *I want to talk with you, Andra.* Lauren sent. *But I have to focus here. We're making plans and there are a lot of minds around. I'll tell you more as soon as I can.*

But I'm alone again. I almost hated myself for the desperation in my mind.

You're not alone. Lauren sent thoughts of love and support. *We're all here for you, but that's why I need to focus.*

So I was left staring at a blank gray ceiling. I couldn't rest as my mind whirled with thoughts, hopes, and fears. When I finally managed to fall asleep, I dreamed of intense silver-gray eyes condemning my father and me to death before leading an army of training center attendees out to destroy all the people I cared about. I woke with clammy skin, heart racing. Nothing had changed. I was still alone and could do nothing but wait until Sandovar came to see me.

* * *

"These have appeared everywhere over the past few days." Sandovar threw a pile of pamphlets on the table in front of me; his eyes squinted in anger. "Do you know anything about them?"

"How could I, sir? I've been here all that time," I said.

"This is why the menace of the Freedom Readers must be destroyed. Even if they don't follow through with the threat, as they always fail to do anything big, they cause dissension within the populace. They make people think there might be a reason to overthrow MY rule. My rule is the will of the Lord. I will not let this country crumble into the decay that would occur under the Freedom Readers. Freedom is a fallacy. If you haven't found a way to destroy them yet, I'll order two fingers removed from your father's hands as soon as I return to the Ministry. Is that understood, Miss BetScrivener?"

"I . . . I think I've done what you've asked without bringing a plague onto the whole community," I said. "One of the doctor's has what I've written. I thought he would give it to you when you arrived."

"Trainer Sevrin!" Sandovar's bellow prompted an immediate response as the trainer stumbled through the door with a look of terror on her face. "Who has the last thing Miss BetScrivener worked on? I demand to see it at once."

"I was just bringing it, Supreme Prime Minister." The doctor appeared in the doorway. "I wanted to be sure it got to you without alterations, sir, as it seems to be just what you wished."

"I'll be the judge of that." Sandovar grabbed the paper and began to read. Trainer Sevrin and the doctor stood nearby with nervous looks. Sandovar noticed them. "Get out! This is between me and our guest." The trainer and the doctor scurried away without a word and closed the door to the meeting room behind them.

Sandovar went back to reading. I closed my eyes and focused on my breathing to control the knot of fear that formed in my stomach. A deep chuckle caused me to look at the Supreme Prime Minister.

"This is very clever, Andra," he said. "Very clever indeed, using the Freedom Readers to destroy themselves because of dissension in the group. Of course, nobody dies, and I'm not sure keeping my enemies alive is a wise move. I can have you remedy that for me in the future once you've become more comfortable with the idea that sometimes death is the only solution for those who challenge the word of the Lord. Now, all I have to do is read this out loud, correct?

"I told you, Supreme Prime Minister, that doesn't work," I said. "This will only happen if I manifest it, if I make it into reality."

"Then do it." Sandovar slid the paper across to me and tapped on it with a beefy finger.

I took a deep breath, preparing myself for the scariest part of the plan. "I won't do anything else until I've seen that my father is alive and well."

Sandovar's eyes bored into me. I could see the calculating look on his face. The seconds ticked by on a clock that hung on the wall, an ominous sound in the silence.

"Very well," Sandovar said. "I'm not accustomed to having my orders ignored, but perhaps this time I will make allowances. I'll arrange to have you brought to the Ministry later today." He grabbed the paper, stood and walked out the door, leaving me alone.

I leaned back in my chair and started to shake as a combination of tears and laughter burst out of my body. *Lauren*, I thought, *I think it worked.*

* * *

A few hours later, I found myself back in the huge office where my nightmare had started. My father was again seated in the hard wooden chair, but this time, ropes did not bind him. He was groggy and frail, as if he didn't have the energy to even stand on his own. Dark shadows emphasized the gauntness of his face.

"Dad, Dad!" I ran to him and put my arms around him. He raised his arms to return the hug. His arms shook with weakness.

"What have you done to him?" I turned to Sandovar, who sat at his desk with an amused look as he watched the reunion of father and daughter. "You call this good condition? He looks like you've been starving him."

"Your father has received rations every day, but you can't expect us to serve him food from the head chef. Your father is a picky eater, I'm told. His current grogginess comes from a drug to ensure his compliance for this visit."

"Another poison that will kill him? Another test for me?"

"No, simply a muscle relaxant," Sandovar said. "He should come out of it soon. However, now that you mention it, I do have a test I'd like to conduct. Have a seat and we'll discuss it."

I hadn't expected another test. What if I failed? Would my father die? I moved my chair closer to Dad so I could hold his hand both to give and receive strength.

I wished Lauren was linked in, but we had decided it would be safer if my attention was on Sandovar alone.

"I've done what you asked," I said. "What further test do you want?"

"The doctors at the Center have told me that you can, indeed, manifest your words on most occasions. Yet, I refuse to believe that a mere female can do something I'm unable to do."

"I told you—"

Sandovar raised his hand to cut me off. "You told me I can't read your words to life. I would like to test that theory."

"The words I wrote about the Freedom Readers may take time to happen, you won't know right away if they work."

"That's why I've come up with an alternative. Scrivener, the walls in this old building are not particularly thick. I'm sure you're aware that you've had a neighbor over the past few weeks?"

"Yes, sir, I was aware." Dad's voice sounded sluggish. I squeezed his hand.

"The man in the room next to you has been our guest for many years," Sandovar said. "We originally brought him here because he had some important information. He proved stubborn and didn't respond to our questioning techniques."

I shuddered at the thought of what techniques they used on this poor unknown man.

"Eventually he cracked and led us to an important discovery. As a reward, and because of his talent, we spared his life. Of course, he couldn't be allowed to spread any information about us, so we offered him accommodations here at the Ministry and ensured his permanent silence."

"What do you mean?" I asked without thinking.

"We removed his tongue, but that's not important. Scrivener, could you describe the sounds that come from your neighbor?"

"I . . . I've heard the sounds of sawing and sanding and . . ." His eyes grew big, and his face crumbled into horror.

"What is it?" I asked.

"Your father has simply realized who we are discussing. This man was known as a skilled artisan throughout New North, so I granted him life in exchange for his woodworking skills. His presence at the Ministry has been kept from your father to avoid providing temptation and distraction, as they had always been good friends. His artistry is featured throughout the ministry building. He carved this desk, for example."

The edges and legs of the massive mahogany desk were carved with a decorative design of intertwining flowers, animals, and the symbol of the Eye of the Lord. One flower stood out—a special rose.

"Brian's father. Mr. Woodson," I said.

"I knew you could figure it out," Sandovar said. "Woodson has made attempts to leave us over the years, but he has never succeeded. I would like you to write something that will allow him a successful escape. I'll read it, and prove that I'm indeed able to bring your words to life. If I succeed, we both win; I'll have more power and you will have reunited the Woodson family."

"You'll just capture him again," I said.

"No, if he escapes through my voice, I'll allow him to remain free. If the escape doesn't happen, no harm will come to him. He'll simply remain in my employ." Sandovar slid a paper and pen toward Andra. "I suggest you schedule his escape to happen soon."

I searched for advice from my father, who merely nodded his head. I wished I could read his mind. I reached out a shaking hand and picked up the pen.

* * *

It didn't take me long to write an escape for a man I remembered like a second father. Of course, for the action to actually happen, it required a little time. I had to resist the temptation to make the words manifest themselves as I wrote them. I yearned to free Mr. Woodson, but at this moment, I realized, it was more important to make Sandovar recognize his inability to use words without me. If we succeeded, the Woodsons would be reunited soon enough.

I wrote. Sandovar read. We waited.

Sandovar ordered food brought up. The elegance of the dishes showed they were from the Minister's Lounge, which offered soups and meats cooked in unusual ways. I hadn't seen such abundance and richness of food in weeks. From the ravenous look in my father's eyes, I knew he hadn't either.

"Don't eat too much," I said. "You might get sick."

"You'll waste delicious food." Sandovar grabbed a bowl full of meat and vegetables dripping in juices. "You might as well enjoy yourself while we wait for word of the escape."

I took a small bite of a potpie. The food tasted like wood in my mouth—flavored by fear.

After he had his fill, Sandovar settled down on a leather couch near the fireplace. "You may as well make yourself comfortable while you wait. Scrivener, I'm sure you have work to do. You may use the small desk by the window. There should be plenty of supplies. Andra, I want a drawing of myself to commemorate the moment. I had some charcoal pencils and drawing paper brought in. They're on the small desk as well. There's a drawing board leaning against the desk. I shouldn't need to remind you not to write anything." He posed with a regal look on his face, exuding power and confidence.

"Why would my father have work to do?" I asked. "He's been a prisoner since you brought us here."

"Andra . . ." Dad placed his hand on my arm in the familiar warning gesture before he made his way to the appointed spot and began to examine pen nibs.

"Being a guest of the ministry didn't excuse him from his duties," Sandovar said. "Our guests must earn their keep. Now, about that drawing . . ."

I grabbed the supplies and sat on a chair opposite the Supreme Prime Minister. I attacked the paper. If I had the courage, I would have drawn him with malignant, festering wounds and devil's horns, but I knew that would only bring punishment to us both.

Two hours passed. Sandovar called a guard in. "Please go up and check on our special craftsman. I've received word that he might try to escape today."

"Should I arrange a search party just in case, sir?" The guard asked.

"No need, just see if he's gone and tell no one." He turned to me. "Now we shall see that you're not special, Miss BetScrivener."

Ten minutes later, the guard returned.

"Craftsman Woodson is in his room, working on the wall hanging you requested, sir. He showed no signs of trying to escape."

Sandovar's eyes gleamed with anger. He walked over and slammed his hand down on his desk, making the guard jump. "Dismissed," Sandovar said. "Tell no one."

The guard scurried out of the office. I moved to grab my father's hand.

Sandovar turned toward us, his face darkened in anger. "So it appears you told the truth. No matter, your words are now mine to command." He picked up the words written to destroy the Freedom Readers from within. "Manifest this, and then you'll both remain as my 'guests' until we see that it has worked."

"You promised you'd release us once I did as you asked," I said.

"Yes, but I won't know if you've done as I asked until I receive evidence that the Freedom Readers are no longer a concern. However, I'll do you one favor. You may stay here with your father instead of returning to the Training Center. I warn you, if I find you're using his materials to write anything, both you and your father will regret it. I'll have paint and canvas sent to you, I'd like you to paint my portrait—that will keep you busy and earn your room and board. Now," he shook the paper in my direction, "make this happen."

"Go ahead, Andra," Dad said. "You've already written the words. You made your decision. At least we'll be together."

My heart broke at the sound of disappointment in my father's voice. He hadn't read my words, so he had no way of knowing that I'd planned something that would appear to be destructive, but would do no more harm than had already occurred. I crossed to the glaring older man, took the paper from him followed by a deep cleansing breath, and focused on my words.

TWENTY-THREE

*The end of the group known as the Freedom Readers started within.
After years and years of failed attempts to achieve their goals, as well
as years of sitting and waiting for opportunities that never appeared,
the members were growing restless. An attempt to spread information
about the strength of women's brains was soon foiled by Supreme Prime
Minister Sandovar's government, who laid down a series of mandates
in the hopes of stopping the rumors from spreading; although without
knowing the method of spreading the message they could not be sure of
total success. Members of the Readers from all over New North began
to suspect traitors in their midst, which led to deepening distrust. Fac-
tions formed. Those who wished violent rebellion stood against those
who wanted to find a more peaceful way of overturning the government. Rumors began of an imminent rebellion, but nobody was sure
who started them. Men and women who believed in the power of female
brains gathered in strength against those who sought power for power's
sake. As the distrust among the Readers grew, its ability to function less-
ened until the group eventually disintegrated altogether. Traitors to the
group brought this information to Sandovar in the hopes of finding support and positions within the Ministry itself.*

I had no guilt about the words I had written and manifested for Sandovar,
because I knew that much of this had already happened. I'd written the dissolution of a group that was already falling apart. I hadn't mentioned any names,
so Sandovar would have no way of retaliating against individual members. I'd
also included a line that allowed for P.O.W. to grow stronger, as more men and
women, even some Freedom Readers, joined them. I'd done what I needed to

do to save my father and protect the members of P.O.W. and others. The only flaw, I now realized, was that Sandovar wouldn't know for sure until some-one came forward and told him of the end of the Freedom Readers. I didn't know when that would happen, or who would bring the news. Dad and I were trapped unless a traitor came forward.

The room that held us in confinement was much more pleasant than my cell at the Women's Training Center. It was like a simple private room at an inn, up in the attic. Angled ceilings indicated we were under the eaves. A small window let in light and air, with a view of the world below. It had its own bath-room, a bed, a desk, a comfortable chair and room to walk, at least until ser-vants brought in an additional cot for my use. I could hear the sound of a hand saw coming from the room next door. I walked to the wall and touched it.

"Did you know it was Mr. Woodson?" I asked.

"Not until Sandovar spoke today. I never imagined they would keep Pat-rick alive this long."

"I need to tell Lauren what happened," I said.

"How do you expect to do that?" Dad sat on his bed, removed his glasses and ran a weary hand over his eyes. "You can't get a message out, not even in the women's language."

I sat next to him and kissed his cheek. "We found a way to strengthen the connection between us. I can talk to her in my head."

Dad surprised me with a laugh. "I should have known not to underesti-mate you, Andra. Tell her everything, but be sure she doesn't let Brian rush in here with fire in his eyes to save his father and the two of us. I can't have his death on my conscience."

"I know, Dad. I know."

I called for Lauren in my mind. She'd been waiting. I shared all the details of recent events, including what I'd written regarding the Freedom Readers. At the end of our conversation, Lauren sent one final thought: *We don't need the Readers, but we'll get you all out. Have faith.*

* * *

After several days of being cooped up in the small room with my father—interrupted only by servants bringing tasteless food and random checks by guards to ensure I did nothing but paint—I was almost relieved when a guard came to lead me up to Sandovar's office.

"I'm coming too," Dad said.

"You're to stay here and work," the guard said. "Supreme Prime Minister Sandovar's orders."

"I'll be fine," I said. "If anything happens, someone will know." I hoped he realized I was already contacting Lauren to listen in on the meeting.

Nothing had changed since the last visit to this office, except that Minister Rogerson was also present and pacing back and forth across the carpeted floor.

"Rogerson, stop pacing and sit down!" Sandovar's voice sounded different to me. He looked menacing, angry, and a little unsure in a way I never expected to see in his ever-confident, pompous demeanor. He strode toward me, took me by the elbow, dismissed the guard and led me with force to the seat by the sofa.

"You're hurting me," I said.

"That's nothing compared to what I'll do if you don't explain yourself immediately," Sandovar said. His silver-gray eyes bore into me with their hateful glare.

"I don't know what you mean, sir," I said. "What have I done wrong?"

"You helped them escape," Rogerson said.

"What do you mean? Helped who escape? The Freedom Readers?" I asked. I had no idea what he was talking about. The intimidating glare of these two men made it impossible for me to focus and send a quick mental question to Lauren. I only hoped she was listening and had an idea what was going on.

"This has nothing to do with those rebel pests," Sandovar said. "Explain to me, Miss BetScrivener, why . . . only a few days after you left the top Women's Training Center in New North! A group of young girls and women who were receiving special attention from the doctors there, in accordance with mandates I established . . . how did those women simply disappear from the facilities?"

"I swear, Supreme Prime Minister, I have no idea."

Lauren, what's going on?

They escaped, led by Alvarie. They're with us now.

"You didn't write something that helped them leave the center?" Sandovar asked.

"Of course not," I said. "When would I have done that? The only thing I've done over the past few days is work on your painting. You've had guards checking."

"You understand that I'm having guards search your room at the moment. They're checking everywhere, including your father. I've considered allowing them to search you as well, but will reserve that pending their findings in your room. They'll tell me if they find anything out of the ordinary, and your father will know my anger."

"You mean you'll have them strip search me?"

"I could ask Minister Rogerson to do it."

"It would be my pleasure, sir." Rogerson leered at me and moved to stand behind my chair.

"I swear, sir. I know nothing about this."

"You can't explain how a group of girls and women got through a locked steel door and past a center full of trainees and their guests without a single person knowing it?" Sandovar asked.

"I wouldn't even know what to write to make that happen," I said. "That sounds impossible."

"You've proved some things are possible," Sandovar said. "However, I believe you're telling me the truth. Rogerson sit down again; it disturbs me how willing you are to step into your son's territory. Andra, if the guards find nothing, you'll be returned to your father's room. However, all writing materials will be removed. I'll find other ways for you and your father to earn your keep."

I took a deep breath to control my response. "I understand, Supreme Prime Minister. Thank you."

Rogerson and a guard escorted me back to our room a short time later. All the writing materials and my painting supplies had been removed. Dad looked disheveled and unhappy, evidence that the search of his body had been less than pleasant.

"Did they hurt you, Andra?" He asked as soon as it was safe to talk. "Did they touch you? If they did, I'll kill them myself. What happened?"

"I'm fine. I'm not sure what happened, but I'll find out."

* * *

Trainer Alvarie tossed and turned all night after her discussion with Andra in the bathing facilities. When she went on duty, early the next morning, she knew she had to learn more, to understand more. She decided to approach trainees whenever she found the opportunity in order to discover if they did, indeed, have hidden abilities. She managed to do this often, as many of the more experienced trainers dumped extra work on the newcomer so they could spend time with the women in the more pleasant areas of the center. Andra was the only trainee who had been under constant observation through an observation room. Even those who remained behind locked doors most of the time had a modicum of privacy allotted to them.

In hurried conversations she learned about Lilah's ability to send messages to other people's minds. Once Lilah realized that Trainer Alvarie was one of them, she reached the minds of girls and women who Alvarie needed to meet. Lilah encouraged them to share their secrets. After receiving Andra's drawn message, Lilah had begun searching for more girls and women who had powers tucked away behind cell doors. The search moved quickly in a place where rumor thrived. It didn't take long for Lilah to learn the truth about all the trainees, even without the ability to visit each one. She passed that information along to Trainer Alvarie, who could move freely between the cells.

In addition to Lilah's ability, Alvarie found: a girl who could sing anybody to sleep with her beautiful voice; a young woman who had a degree of telekinesis, which enabled her to move small objects; a girl who could send daydreams into the minds of others; a young woman who could read the emotions of any living creature; and many other varieties of abilities. As she began to talk to each of the trainees, Alvarie came to understand something she'd hidden away in her own mind before, that the government and religious mandates against women were intended to keep women down. She grew angry and decided she had to do something about it.

She waited for Andra, who didn't come back.

It wasn't until a few days after Sandovar had allowed Andra to visit her father at the Ministry that Trainer Alvarie got any news.

"Excuse me, Trainer Sevrin." Alvarie knocked on the open door to the head trainer's office. "I was scheduled to work with trainee BetScrivener today, but she doesn't seem to have returned to her room."

"Andra BetScrivener has been removed from our care. No loss. She was a hopeless case."

"Has she been moved to another center?"

"Not that it's any concern of yours, but I'm told she will be remaining as a guest of the Ministry for a while. I don't understand why that wicked young woman is being granted such an honor, but it's not my place to question the will of Supreme Prime Minister Sandovar. He speaks for the Lord. Nor is it your place, Trainer Alvarie, to be concerned about trainees no longer under your care." Sevrin picked up the list of symbols that indicated which trainer was doing which duty, and tapped it with a pencil. "Now, if I'm not mistaken, you have other duties to attend to. You're dismissed."

Alvarie scurried away, her mind filled with questions. How would she proceed without Andra? She made her way to Lilah's room, where a small group had gathered. She watched them unnoticed for a moment. Their whispered conversation was filled with an excited energy she'd never observed before. She could only define it as hope.

"Ladies . . ." she began.

The women jumped up at her voice. "We'll return to our rooms at once," one of them said.

"No, don't." Alvarie checked up and down the hall to be sure they were alone. "Ladies, it's come to my attention that perhaps none of you . . . none of us . . . belongs in this training facility. I believe our skills might be needed elsewhere, don't you think?"

The trainees all nodded silently with wide, unsure eyes.

"Then, ladies," Alvarie said. "I believe I have the beginnings of a plan."

It took several days, whispered moments, and secret meetings in the bathing facilities—the only space large enough to hold a number of people and accessible to the trainees without too much supervision—for them to develop the details of the plan, preparing them for all contingencies. Part of the problem came from the desire of each woman to use her power to contribute in some way, if possible. In the end, they used as many abilities as they could.

In the middle of the night, when Trainer Alvarie was the only one on duty—which she had volunteered for—they began. Lilah helped coordinate by passing messages to all involved. The one with telekinesis unlocked the door that kept them separate from the world. The girl who could sing walked out first while the others remained behind the steel door where they couldn't hear. She sang like she'd never sung before, to ensure that anyone around remained asleep or fell asleep, including guards. She then opened the door to let her friends come through in safety. Once they were all out, they locked the steel door behind them and simply walked out of the Training Center. From that point on, those who had abilities to distract others, used them on anyone they met until they were far enough away to be safe. After that, it was simply a matter of finding P.O.W. headquarters. Someone recalled the drawings that had resulted in many of them being put into the training center. One of them remembered seeing a framed version in an art store so they headed there, where a cheerful Mr. Mastak helped them get in touch with the people they most wanted to meet.

*   *   *

Andra, Lauren sent after she finished sharing Alvarie's story and I repeated it to my father. *Our numbers have grown. Women are learning how to join together in strength. More men have joined as well; brothers, fathers, and friends. We're working on a plan to get you out. I need to focus on the people here. They have me scanning anyone who wants to join us, to make sure they aren't spies for the Ministry or for Emily. I may be out of touch for a while.*

"Dad and I will be patient." I sat next to my father on his bed and squeezed his hand. I said the words out loud, not just in my mind, so he could hear at least part of the conversation. "I just wish we could do something on our end. We have no writing materials anymore."

Professor Albert wants you to be prepared anyway. He thinks your part isn't over. Think of words that can help us all, and we'll get the materials to you somehow.

"What words? I don't know what Professor Albert wants."

He doesn't know either. Talk to the Scrivener, you'll think of something. I'll be in touch once I know more.

With that, we were alone in our room, with nothing to do but listen to our long lost friend woodworking next door while we debated the words I needed to write to change our world.

TWENTY-FOUR

Without the ability to paint or write, time in the small room passed with everlasting slowness. One good thing was that I made sure my father began to rebuild his strength even with the tasteless food. We sustained each other. I didn't fall into despair and loneliness like I did in my room at the training center. Dad didn't starve himself. We spent the days in endless drudgery and complex projects provided by the Ministry. We had been assigned the task to mend and clean artifacts damaged when the library collapsed. The collection reflected times long past, when people traveled freely around the world and brought home souvenirs. At first, I liked working with the beautiful creations made of wood, stone, metal or jewels. I made up stories in my mind about the history of each object. The project appealed to my artistic side. Each item had to be cleaned, checked for damage and repaired.

Soon, however, the chemicals used to clean the objects ate my hands, making them dry and uncomfortable. The fumes gave us both headaches. The only positive side was that sometimes Librarian Bookman would drop off a load himself and keep us company for as long as he could before a guard or other duties forced him out. He passed on information about the outside world, including news of a violent uprising headed by some frustrated Freedom Readers that was crushed by the Ministry and led to the imprisonment and the suspected death of several people.

"Did I cause that?" I asked when we were alone again.

"We can't be sure, Andra." Dad put an arm around my shoulders and squeezed. "The truth is that many people in the Readers have wanted to attack the Ministry for a long time. I'm sure that Emily's behavior in the matter of Achan influenced them. If she could kill, why can't others? That has nothing to do with your words."

I had told him exactly what I'd written, but even his encouragement couldn't erase the doubt in my mind. We spent endless hours in whispered discussions about the most powerful words I could write to help P.O.W. without bringing about dangerous, unexpected surprises. We both thought we'd come up with an idea, but I still feared causing something horrible with my words. I was almost relieved I didn't have access to writing materials, as it gave me an excuse not to try.

Messages from Lauren came at infrequent intervals. *We have a plan to get you out,* she explained. *We'll be moving on the Ministry as soon as possible.*

But you'll be killed or imprisoned. I thought with concern. *The Readers already tried and failed.*

Not if you can write us words that keep us safe. Let us know when you've done it. Do it soon. Someone inside is finding a way to bring you supplies.

Who? How?

I don't know the details. Johnson wanted to protect his contact.

It was comforting to know there was someone inside the Ministry willing to help. I only hoped my words were the right ones.

The next day, Librarian Bookman came in with a guard, both carrying heavy loads. The librarian had some books with him that he needed to consult Dad about.

"Stay away from the books," the guard warned me. "We've brought you this to work on." He placed a large object covered in cloth on the desk, while Dad and the librarian set up on the bed. "I'll be watching," the guard said. "Don't do anything funny. Librarian Bookman, Miss BetScrivener is not to approach the books; Supreme Prime Minister's orders."

"Don't worry," Bookman said. "I know better than to expose young female brains to the dangers of words. I'm sure Andra will be much more interested in what I've brought her to work on. She's an artist at heart. Go on girl, look at it."

I uncovered a carved wooden horse's head that had cracked down the middle, revealing elaborate layers of wood held together with wooden nails and glue. The signature of the artist lay etched into one of the layers. Carvings of garland and jewels adorned the outside of the head, with remnants of paint sticking to them, including gold on the mane. It reminded me of Johnson's rocking horse that took me on so many wonderful, imaginary adventures.

"This is beautiful," I said. "What was it for?"

"According to my research," the librarian said, "this was once attached to some sort of ride for children. I've borrowed some tools from your neighbor to help you fix these. These tools could be useful for many things." Bookman placed some wood glue, a brush, and a sharp carving chisel on the desk next to the horse's head, and winked at me. "Your neighbor would fix this himself, but he's in the middle of an elaborate wall-hanging for the Supreme Prime Minister's office."

I began to examine the head more closely while Dad and Bookman talked. The guard watched at first, but soon wandered over to the men who were having an interesting debate. The wood dented under my fingernail. I picked up the chisel and etched a line on the inside of the crack. I glanced over at the old librarian who smiled, nodded, and put a finger to his mouth

"Are you all right working on that alone?" Dad asked.

"Of course," I said. I adjusted the horse so that my back faced the bed, the guard, and the door to cover my movements. I took the tool and etched words inside where they would be hidden once I glued it all back together.

The women and men of P.O.W. used their abilities to stage a peaceful protest that overturned the Ministry and destroyed Sandovar.

I focused on envisioning exactly what I hoped would happen, adding detail after detail in my mind while I worked to hide my words underneath wood and elaborate decorations. The old librarian had left with the guard long before I finished my work

I turned to my father and called for Lauren's attention at the same time. "It's done," I said to them both. *It's done.*

* * *

More than a week later, on the day P.O.W. intended to act, I paced around the limited space of our room.

"Please settle down, Andra." Dad picked up the mask he was working on. "You've done what you can. You might as well take your mind off of it and do something else."

"How can you focus on this grunt work when our friends are heading toward danger? You know that, given the chance, Brian will fight his way in to save us."

"They've managed to control him so far. Although they must have locked him up to do that, or at least stuffed him so full of muffins he couldn't move."

I laughed despite my fears.

"Seriously, I have faith in you, Andra. Faith in the words you've written. If the other women involved in P.O.W. have half the talent, intelligence, and bravery that you've shown over the past few weeks, the Ministry will never be able to stop them."

"I'm so scared."

"I know." He opened his arms to hug me. I burrowed into his shoulder and let the tears flow.

A knock on the door followed by the sound of the key in the lock made us both jump. Minister Rogerson, with a smile on his face, followed a guard into our room. "You're both to come with me to see Supreme Prime Minister Sandovar," he said. "It appears that your words have succeeded, Andra, praise the Lord."

Dad placed his hand on my arm to prevent my reply. "Lead on, Minister Rogerson," he said.

When we arrived at Sandovar's office, he sat at his desk talking to a woman whose back was to us, dark hair held up with an elegant comb.

"Ah, welcome! My other guests have arrived." Sandovar stood and gestured for us to come in. His silver eyes twinkled with malevolent joy. The woman rose as well, and turned toward us.

Emily's face drained of all color as soon as her eyes met mine. "I don't understand, Supreme Prime Minister," she said. "I . . . I thought you had placed Andra into a Women's Training Center?"

"Of course you did," Sandovar said. "After all, it was your information that led me to the discovery of this young lady's deformity. However, we decided that we should reunite the Scrivener with his daughter, for reasons of our own. Do you question the decision?"

"No, of course not . . . Sir."

"I see by the look on Andra's face," Sandovar said, "that she was, perhaps, unaware of the role you played in the change of her circumstances. Is that correct, young lady?" He turned to me with a wicked smile.

I started shaking the moment I heard the words that confirmed Emily's duplicity. Dad gave me another cautionary touch, but I couldn't hold back. I pulled away and moved to confront Emily, who cowered back until she fell into the chair behind her.

"You did this! You turned me in? Why would you tell him? I don't understand."

"Andra, please don't attack my guest," Sandovar said. "Have a seat and everything will be made clear."

I moved back and sat down with a thump. Dad sat next to me.

"Madame DuFarge has been a valuable asset to my government ever since the loss of her husband," Sandovar said. "She has been a gracious hostess who knows everyone worthy of knowing in our community, even some of the undesirable elements."

"So you've been working for the Ministry all along, not the Freedom Readers?" I asked.

"Not exactly," Emily said. "After my husband . . . I truly believe in the cause of the Freedom Readers, and have from the beginning, but . . ."

"Madame DuFarge has a major character flaw, one that I both admire and despise in a woman," Sandovar said. "She craves power, and she'll do whatever is necessary to hold onto her position in our society."

I never removed my eyes from Emily's face, which went from the pale of shock to a shade of red I didn't think possible. Emily pursed her lips and lowered her eyes as the Supreme Prime Minister continued.

"As is typical of women, her desire for power led to unwise decisions," Sandovar said. "She became involved with some people who gave her money and prestige in return for certain favors. Several years ago some of those favors became difficult for her to pay—she began to recognize her folly in doing things for these men and found some of the demands disturbing. She wisely came to me for help, because without my support she would have lost everything. We negotiated a deal. I had long suspected that she had imprudently become involved with a different dangerous group, the irritants known as the Freedom Readers. In exchange for my protection and the assurance that she would continue to live the life of power and privilege to which she'd become accustomed, Madame DuFarge agreed to give me some vital information that would help me combat their pestilence. Through her we learned about an attempt to break into important files in the Ministry, which led to the capture of your neighbor. She also provided us information about a woman determined to spread false information to other women, by creating a language only women could read."

I sensed a shift in my father. He removed his hand from my arm and his leg began to shake. His face had turned to stone.

"Madame DuFarge's information enabled us to prevent that woman from doing any further or permanent damage."

With an animalistic cry, my father jumped out of his chair toward Emily. Minister Rogerson and a guard moved in to hold him back. Sandovar stood and walked around the desk until he was inches from my father's face.

"Do you really want to attack this woman? All she did was provide information. She didn't pour the poison. Have a seat or I'll tie you down. I think you need to hear Madame DuFarge's news."

Rogerson and the guard forced my father into his seat.

I fought the urge to grab Sandovar's precious gold Eye of the Lord paperweight and smash it into his smug smile and evil eyes. My own eyes filled with tears of rage and pain but I didn't let them flow. I focused on my anger. "You killed my mother," I said to Emily. "Then you tried to destroy me. Why?"

"It was either her or me." Emily's voice lacked emotion. "I envied her, you know. She carried power within her. By giving the Ministry a tip about her, I was able to accomplish two goals; save myself from complete destruction and gain power within the Freedom Readers. I won either way."

"Why did you reveal my secret?"

"You haven't figured that out yet?" Emily asked.

"Obviously not. I don't seem capable of following your twisted thought process."

Emily winced at my words.

"I think I understand." Dad's voice was thick with unshed tears. "When you realized Andra had her mother's talents—with drawing and painting, with words—you feared the Readers would begin to look up to her as they did Marion. You set out to destroy Andra from the start, out of spite and jealousy."

"Yes." Emily tilted forward, hands folded together as if in supplication. "You have to understand, I don't have any special abilities beyond my skills with talking, entertaining, and organizing. If women keep coming forward claiming to have extra-normal abilities that surpass my normal ones, then I'll become powerless again. I can't be powerless. I won't be powerless."

"It appears that you lied to me about the rebels, Miss BetScrivener," Sandovar said as he returned to his seat. "You knew who some of them were all along. I'd be very upset with you, if your plan hadn't worked so well."

"What do you mean?" I asked.

"That's the news Madame DuFarge has brought to me. I'll let her explain."

"The Freedom Readers are no more," Emily said. "After you walked out on the day of the accident that killed Minister Achan, people began to take sides. Some simply walked away. Others decided to attempt an insane plan of attacking the Ministry with weapons in hand. They were killed or imprisoned. The remainder can't seem to make any decisions. The Readers are no more." She turned her head to glare at me. "It seems you played a role in their destruction. How dare you sit there and judge me if you've used your words to destroy the Freedom Readers."

"Your choices began the doubt and mistrust, that's what destroyed the Freedom Readers." I said. "It was never my intent to have people killed or imprisoned."

"You'll never understand, will you Andra?" Emily said. "You can't control the entire story, no matter how many words you write, or how good your intention is. You can't make others move to the words of your plan without affecting someone's life. You sit here and act so innocent, but really you thrive on power as much as I do. The only difference is that your power comes from something inside of you."

I hugged myself as her words sank in and avoided Emily's eyes. "I . . . I tried to write words that wouldn't harm anyone. I had to save the people I love, and prevent something worse." I met Emily's stony glare again. I gestured toward Sandovar who sat watching us with the look of a cat waiting to attack its prey. "He wanted me to destroy you all with a plague, which could have killed everyone, even people not involved. What choice did I have?"

Emily turned to the Supreme Prime Minister, "Sir, you told me that as long as I continued to feed you information, you wouldn't move to destroy the Freedom Readers. You said that keeping their presence alive but under control would make your strength seem all the greater if you decided to put them down. Why would you change your mind?"

Sandovar's laugh sent a chill down my spine. "I enjoyed the game for a while, Madame DuFarge, but the rebels have now simply become a thorn in my side. While I appreciate all you've done for my Ministry, I believe you've reached the end of your usefulness. Rogerson, please take Emily to her new accommodations. Scrivener, it looks like you and your daughter will have another neighbor."

"You're putting me in custody?" Emily asked.

"For the time being. We'll discuss your options after I'm done with the BetScriveners."

"This is your fault." Emily leaped toward me, fingers curled into claws.

Dad jumped up and grabbed her wrist in a hold that brought tears to Emily's eyes fueled by anger that flamed into his face. I worried that he would break her with the slightest flick of an arm. "You've done this to yourself, Emily." I had never heard his voice filled with so much hate. "You killed my wife, even if you didn't pour the poison yourself. Stay away from my daughter." He released her wrist and she fell into a sobbing pile on the floor. Rogerson helped her up and guided her toward the door.

I gasped for breath. Emily's attack had terrified me, but my father's violent reaction affected me even more. As I focused on calming my breath and my heartbeat, something Sandovar said became clearer.

"Supreme Prime Minister Sandovar . . ." I lost control of my voice, which squeaked out of my mouth. I cleared my throat before continuing. "Sir, you just said that we're gaining another neighbor. You told us that once I got rid of the Freedom Readers for you, you would let us go."

"I said that, didn't I?" Sandovar picked up his paperweight and twirled it in his hands. "I believe that I will need the benefit of your power to create a world that will truly please the Lord. I think that perhaps the Lord's message needs to move beyond the Wall. I cannot tolerate the corruption outside our walls and worry that women out there may overstep their bounds as you have tried to do. I fear that it's in my best interest to have you and your father remain as guests to the Ministry. I will, however, return your writing supplies to you—"

At that moment, someone pounded on the door and didn't wait for a response before bounding into the room. Two guards bowed their heads with terrified looks on their faces.

"What's this disruption?" Sandovar said. "How dare you barge into my office?"

"We're sorry, Supreme Prime Minister," the older guard said. "We seem to have a situation developing. There are women, sir, lots and lots of women."

"What do you mean by that?" Sandovar asked.

"There are women in the Ministry. They're everywhere."

"What are you blathering about?" Sandovar walked to the door and opened it. I heard the distant sound of female voices calling to each other from below. "Take our guests back to their room. Be sure their door is locked and remain on guard. You," he pointed at the two remaining guards, "come with me. We'll put an end to this nonsense."

The older guard gestured for us to move toward a back stairway that would take us up to our rooms in the attic of another wing.

Lauren, be careful, I thought as hard as I could, but didn't receive any response.

TWENTY-FIVE

"Ladies, are you ready for the first wave?" Alvarie stood with a group of P.O.W. women on the street in front of the Ministry. Most of the women in the group had some form of power to distract and ensnare minds. Lauren, whose strengthening ability to read minds from long distances would help anyone who panicked if they ran into trouble, stood by Alvarie's left. Lilah stood to the other side ready to send messages and keep the entire operation running.

"Let me at those men." Cindy bounced with excitement. "I bet I could take this whole ministry down by myself."

"Cindy, even though you can distract the ministry workers, we still need to move with caution," Alvarie said. "This isn't going to be easy, and everyone plays a part."

"You're too cautious, Alvarie. Why did they put you in charge?"

"She's in charge," Lauren said, "because her brilliance came up with this plan. Now be quiet so we can get any further instructions."

Alvarie found it difficult to speak after Lauren's compliment. She was unfamiliar with the sense of pleasure gained by someone acknowledging her abilities. Once she had accepted her reality and led the women out of the Training Center, she realized that her abilities extended beyond a perfect memory. She could plan and think and manage any situation. Given a problem, she could quickly sort through all the possible solutions and narrow it down to the best. In the discussions with P.O.W., when they were trying to figure out what the next move was and how to get Andra and the Scrivener out, Alvarie found the solution. They planned to use the powers of anyone who was willing to participate in a way that, she hoped, would keep everyone safe. As she stood in front of the brave group of women with buoyant faces, she swallowed the lump of fear and doubt that blocked her words.

"We all know our duties," Alvarie said. "Cindy, you enter first to distract the guards in front. As soon as she accomplishes that, those of you who can sing people to sleep or send visions into minds, spread out quickly and work your magic on anyone who might get in the way. At any sign of danger, retreat and let Lauren know. Empaths, telepaths, and those who have telekinetic ability, move further into the Ministry. You are searching for people who might be sympathetic to our cause or any prisoners you can find. Stay with your teams. Healers, stay close by in case you are needed. Telekinetics, use force only when necessary to protect us all. Everyone, be on the alert for any messages Lilah sends, she is the only way we can communicate with you."

The group nodded or mumbled their acknowledgment and shifted closer to their assigned teams.

"Lilah," Alvarie said, "please tell the men we're going in."

* * *

"What's taking so long? We need to get in there," Brian blew on his hands and bounced up and down in an attempt to get warm as he waited in the woods toward the back of the Ministry, the remnants of winter's chill made the wait uncomfortable.

"Be patient, Woodson," Johnson said. "I'm as anxious as you are to get to your father and the BetScriveners, but we've waited this long out of caution. If we move too quickly now, people might get hurt."

"I know, I know. I've heard it all before. You stopped me from storming into the Ministry when we found out my father was alive. Excuse me for wanting the wait to be over."

"At least you're going in." Mama Woodson stood near her son, with a mixture of anxiety and frustration in her face. "Why wouldn't you let me go in with the first wave of women?"

"You know why, Ruth," Johnson answered. "You don't have a power. I promise, when it's safe we will get you to Patrick."

"So why did you keep me out?" Alice asked. "I have one of the strongest abilities of all the women. I still don't know what's wrong with starting a fire as a distraction."

"Alice, you know you have no control over the fires you start," Jenna said.

"I'm learning control. That's a ridiculous excuse. Why didn't you go with the first wave? You're the strongest telekinetic we have. You've become stronger every day."

"We all decided that it was best for Jenna and you to move with us, because Sandovar may be with the prisoners," Johnson said. "Alice, could you please stop complaining. We're all worried and you aren't helping any."

"Have faith, everyone." Professor Albert smoked a pipe while sitting on a log nearby. "You heard what happened to the Freedom Readers when they went in well-armed. We have to believe that Andra's words and Alvarie's plan, combined with the power of these amazing women can accomplish what nobody expects."

A hand fell onto Brian's shoulder. "Brian, you know I'm as impatient as you are," Peter Rogerson said. "I want to save Andra. I want to reach my father and somehow knock some sense into him. But, let's look at it this way, we've sent our secret weapons in first. Alvarie's plan is good, and if my sister's ability can't take out the entire Ministry with a flutter of lashes, nobody can."

Brian laughed. Since they'd started planning the Ministry takeover, he'd learned to admire and respect the young man caught between his father's beliefs and his own desire for a more equitable world. "It feels so bizarre to have the men hanging back while the women go into battle," he said.

"Not all the women. I want to fight for your father," Brian's mother said. He put his arm around her. She patted his hand and sighed.

"Let's hope it isn't a battle," Johnson said. "It is a little unusual. But with a plan and an army like ours, I think we'll make history."

* * *

"Let's head in," Professor Albert said. "Lilah just sent word."

The group of P.O.W. men and a few women picked up their belongings, including a limited amount of weapons, and prepared to move. Mama Woodson grabbed her satchel as well.

"Mom, you promised you would stay outside until we told you it was okay," Brian said. "I'll bring Dad to you."

"Brian, there is no way I'm letting you go in there without me. I'm tired of sitting and letting everyone else fight for me. Now, either be quiet and let's get going, or I'm going in without you."

Mama Woodson headed with a determined pace toward the back entrance they intended to use.

Brian checked with Johnson for advice. Johnson shrugged. "She's a strong-minded woman, who are we to stop her? Let's go."

* * *

The sight inside the building had the whole group looking around in awe. A few ministry workers stared off into space, distracted by whatever visions or compulsions had been placed in their minds. As they walked by offices, they saw government workers snoring with their heads on their desks, as a result of being sung to sleep. Sometimes they heard the whispered voice of one of the women, but other than that, everything was eerily quiet.

"We're heading up to Sandovar's office," Johnson said. He checked the gun he had strapped to his back. "You need to get to the other wing and up to the attic rooms."

"We're on it," Brian said. "Mom, if you're coming, stay close."

"Good luck, everyone," Johnson said. "Use powers only if necessary."

"The same goes for you and your gun," Jenna said.

"Good luck," Professor Albert said. "Be safe."

Brian and Peter led the way to the right, which would take them to the other wing and the stairs. As they left the busier areas of the Ministry, the place fell into a deep, waiting silence.

* * *

I paced. I walked between the tiny bathroom and the door. If I walked long enough I'm sure the carpet would have turned into dust under my feet. Dad sat on the chair by the bed, tossing the mask he'd been working on earlier from hand to hand. We couldn't hear what was happening in the floors below.

When we first returned to the room, we banged on the wall to the adjoining room that housed Brian's father, shouting at the top of our lungs "Help is coming!"

That didn't last long. The guard stuck his head through the door. "Stop that or I'll tie you up and gag you!" he said.

He left, relocking the door behind him.

A few minutes later, we'd heard a knock through the wall. I knocked back, but there was no other response.

Time passed and we couldn't hear anything from below. I tried to contact Lauren.

"Why doesn't Lauren answer me?" I asked.

"She's probably dealing with a lot of minds at the moment, Andra. That's got to be difficult."

He lapsed into silence. His face echoed the darkness of his thoughts. I saw it in his eyes.

"Dad . . . back there. Were you really going to kill Emily? Did you mean to hurt her like that?"

He threw the mask onto the bed. His eyes glinted with unreadable emotion. "I don't know. My anger overcame me once before, right after your mother died—was murdered. I wanted to destroy everyone, but Johnson stopped me. I never thought I could kill someone, but . . ."

I moved over, sat on his lap, and gave him a hug.

"You haven't sat in my lap for a very long time, Andra." He put his arms around me and hugged back.

We sat in silence. A soft click that sounded like the lock turning, but without the jangling of keys, made me jump out of the comforting embrace. We both turned toward the door, expecting the guard to enter. Nobody came in.

"I swear I heard the door unlock. Did you hear it too?"

"I thought I did."

"Should I try it?" I asked.

"If the guard sees you, he'll tie us both up."

"I have to try." I laid a hand on the doorknob and found no resistance. With infinite slowness I opened the door a crack. No guard appeared. I opened it wider to peer out. The guard leaned against the wall near the stairs. He had a silly grin on his face and waved at me, with a giggle that I would never have expected from the gruff man.

"Dad, something's happening," I said. "The guard's there, but . . ."

"Let me see." He moved me to the side and peeked out into the hall.

"Hello," the guard said with a smile. "Isn't it an incredible day?"

"What could have happened to him?" I asked.

"I can't be sure, but it seems that this is the handiwork of some of your new friends. I wonder if they unlocked all the doors." He moved to the room that held our long-lost neighbor. I swallowed my nerves and followed. Would Mr. Woodson be okay? Would he be damaged beyond redemption? Dad gave a soft knock before he opened the door.

Brian's father stood by a large worktable, with a carving tool in one hand. He looked up upon our entrance and dropped the tool with a clatter before he ran to my father and enveloped him in a bear hug. All the while guttural sounds came from Mr. Woodson as if he wanted to talk with a mouth no longer able to form words. Tears welled up in my eyes. I tried to stop them, until I noted the tracks of tears pouring down their faces. Mr. Woodson turned to me and gave me a hug and a kiss on both cheeks. He ran over to his table, grabbed a small pad and pencil, and wrote a message, which he handed to Dad to read.

What are you doing here? What's happening?

"That requires a long explanation," my father said. "We need to get out of here first."

Mr. Woodson grabbed the pad again.

"'How's Brian? Ruth?'" Dad read. "There's a possibility that Brian's nearby, Patrick. Let's go search for him, shall we?"

He opened the door and looked out cautiously before gesturing to us to follow. The guard made no move to stop us, content to watch us leave.

"Despite the addled look to our guard, I suggest we move with caution," Dad said.

Mr. Woodson grunted in agreement and we tried to move silently. As we passed the room just beyond ours, I realized I had something to do. I stopped.

"Emily," I said.

"What?" Dad asked.

"Sandovar ordered Rogerson to put her in the room beside ours. Do you think her door is unlocked as well? Do we let her know?"

"Andra." He hesitated as if selecting his words with caution. "I don't know. Sandovar was right. She gave him the information; she didn't pour the poison. She's hurt you and Patrick more than she's hurt me. She took away his freedom and his voice. She took away your mother and tried to destroy you. The decision has to be yours."

Brian's father's eyes glittered with emotion. He took his pad and scribbled a response. He handed it to Dad, who had trouble reading the angry words. "Lock her in!"

"We don't have the key," I said. "The guard does."

We turned toward the guard, who now sat slumped on the floor, staring at the ceiling as if watching an incredible dream.

"I'm sure we can get it from him," my father said. "Do you want to lock her in?"

I stared at both thin and malnourished men; one damaged from his years in custody and cruel punishment. I then looked at the door that hid Emily.

"I want to talk to her first."

Emily sat in a chair staring out the small window in her room. At the sound of the door opening she stood up with hope on her face; although that look soon turned into one of surprise and disappointment. "How did you get in here?" Emily asked.

"Somehow the doors have been unlocked. I believe someone's come to rescue us."

"Who? The Readers are no more. I told you that."

"Emily," I said. "You started something. You inspired me to create messages that would reach out to women all over New North. You showed me the possibilities that came from women having strength and power that men could not conceive. You made me see the potential of bringing people together to fight against the inequities and cruelty of Sandovar's rule. It worked. Women have been coming forward and joining together to strengthen each other. Men have been joining them as well. You could have been a part of that, but you chose to fight for only one person. You chose power for power's sake."

Dad approached with the key. I could hear the sound of footsteps and muffled talking coming from the back stairs.

"I'm going to lock you in here again," I said. "It's probably the safest place for you at the moment. Later, I'll let the women and men of P.O.W. decide what to do with you."

"P.O.W.? What are you talking about, Andra?" Emily's face had drained of color once more.

"I'm talking about the Power of Women."

With that, I closed the door and locked it behind me.

"Don't leave me here!" The cry came with the sound of fists pounding against the door.

"What do we do? Someone's coming."

"We've got it under control," Dad said. He had taken the gun out of the guard's belt, while Mr. Woodson ran into his room and grabbed a heavy hammer. They stood at the top of the stairs and waited.

"Please don't hurt anyone," I said.

"We'll try not to. Getting out of here and finding out what's going on downstairs is our biggest priority."

The voices began to get closer.

"Thank goodness." Dad lowered his weapon and placed it on the floor. "It's Brian."

The group with Brian stumbled up the stairs. I was pummeled by hugs and greetings from Alice and Jenna. Peter came up and swung me into a hug that made me squeal.

"Put me down," I said. "I have to see Brian and his dad." When I turned, I realized that Brian wasn't alone. The reunion between the three Woodsons was almost too painful to watch. Mama Woodson clung to her husband gasping for breath as tears poured down her face. Mr. Woodson put one hand on the face of the woman he loved, and one on the face of the man next to her. He stared as if searching for something. I thought he might be looking for the boy he'd left four years earlier. At that moment, I noticed for the first time that my best friend had become a very handsome man.

The chatter and noise of the reunion might have continued forever if Alice's snide voice hadn't interrupted. "This is all wonderful and lovey-dovey and stuff," she said, "but we still have to get out of the Ministry. Who knows if Johnson and the others were successful in detaining Sandovar? We haven't heard anything from Lilah. How about we set a little fire up here as a distraction, and get out of here?"

"No!" everyone yelled simultaneously.

"It's too dangerous," Brian said.

"We can't do that," I said. "Emily is in that room."

"Shouldn't we get her out?" Peter asked.

"No," I said. "I'll explain later. Let's just go."

Brian gave me a questioning look but then nodded in agreement. On the way downstairs, Peter whispered a hurried explanation of how they'd gotten into the Ministry.

"Lauren's here? Why hasn't she responded to me?" I asked.

"We thought it was best if she focused her energy on the people leading the different groups," Brian said. "She's staying connected to our minds. She knows we've found you. Lilah sent me a message that Lauren burst into tears at the news. Most of the P.O.W. members have already made their way out of the Ministry. Lilah has called everyone left to meet at the rendezvous point in the Atrium."

"Are Johnson and Professor Albert okay?" I asked. "Did they get Sandovar?"

"Oh no!" Brian grabbed his head as if someone had just screamed into his brain. "Lilah sent another message. They're in trouble. We have to get to the Atrium fast."

"Follow me." Dad took the lead. "I know this place better than anyone else here."

We ran without further discussion.

* * *

When we arrived at the Atrium, we discovered a haven exploded into chaos. Several ministry guards held guns on Lauren, Lilah, Heidi, Alvarie and a few women and men whom I didn't recognize. Minister Rogerson had Professor Albert in a tight hold on the other side of the large space. In the center, Johnson and Sandovar were in a vicious fight over a large, sharp knife. Johnson's usual gun was nowhere to be seen, and he had a bloodstain growing on his arm. Sandovar had always maintained an athletic physique. Despite the differences in height and age, Sandovar somehow overpowered Johnson.

"This isn't supposed to happen. Why is Johnson hurt?" I said.

"Perhaps his intentions weren't peaceful enough," Dad said.

"We need to do something to help him," Brian turned to Jenna. "Can you do it?"

"STOP!!" Jenna threw her arms out in separate directions with her yell. I was amazed at how much stronger she had become as she managed to tear the two fighting men apart. Sandovar crashed into the far wall and then fell with a surprised grunt and a stunned look. Jenna pulled the knife out of Sandovar's hand and flung it in another direction. Johnson didn't travel as far but still landed in a moaning heap. Before they could react, Jenna turned to the guards and disarmed all of them so that their weapons landed near their captives. The men in the group grabbed the guns and pointed them at the guards. As soon as the guards were weaponless, one of the women I didn't recognize ran to Johnson and began to look at his wound.

"She has healing powers," Alice said.

Meanwhile, Peter raced across the room and wrestled his father away from Professor Albert.

"Father, stop this!" Peter said. His father released his grip on the professor. Professor Albert ran toward us.

"What are you doing, Peter?" Rogerson said. "These people are traitors and abominations against the will of the Lord."

"No, they aren't, Father," Peter said. "The abomination is the abuse of power and inequitable rules this man has been laying on our community for years. These are merely people. They're women who have more intelligence and ability than most men I know, and brave men who support them."

"Father, I'm one of them." Cindy appeared in another entrance to the Atrium.

"Where did she come from?" I asked nobody in particular.

I had Lilah call her because of Minister Rogerson's presence. Lauren sent a message into my mind.

I've missed you— my thoughts were interrupted by the drama unfolding in front of me.

"What do you mean, you're one of them?" Rogerson asked.

"Father, haven't you ever wondered why I can charm the attention of almost any man in the room, but they never seem to remember me once I'm out of their way? They've never asked for my hand. I used to think I was just unlucky, but I have a power. I can control men's minds for a while, at least until I'm not with them anymore."

"But, that's . . . you're my daughter . . . and Peter . . ."

"Father," Peter said. "I can't be who you want me to be."

"I love you, Father," Cindy said. "However, if you continue to support the Supreme Prime Minister's attack on women, I won't return home."

Rogerson fell to his knees, shaken and speechless.

"Dad, no!" Brian's cry along with a scream from Mama Woodson brought my attention away from the Rogerson drama toward Sandovar. Mr. Woodson had somehow gotten hold of the knife and with guttural cries from his tongue-less mouth leaped toward Sandovar, who had regained his feet. Dad stood nearby, gun pointed in a shaking hand trying to find a shot that wouldn't kill his friend.

"Don't shoot!" I cried. He lowered the gun.

Sandovar threw Mr. Woodson's attack off with ease; the man who had wasted away in prison for four years was no match for the strength of someone who had only grown in power and control. Sandovar didn't bother to wait for another attack; he swung a vicious punch that sent Brian's father to the floor, unconscious. Brian ran into the fray, causing another agonized scream from his mother. I moved to embrace the woman who shook in terror. Brian grabbed the knife from his father's open hand and turned to face Sandovar.

"Brian Woodson," Sandovar said with a confident smile. "I should have known you would follow in your father's misguided footsteps. Do you think you can defeat me? Just try." He turned his powerful glare toward Jenna. "Don't even think of interfering with your obscene ability. As a matter of fact," he nodded at a guard who had moved near Jenna, "disarm her and the Scrivener."

The guard gave Jenna a punch that sent her sprawling, while another grabbed the gun from my father's unsuspecting hand and pointed it at Jenna's still body.

Brian lunged at Sandovar, who somehow managed to grab the knife wielding hand. The wrestle for control moved across the Atrium floor, knocked over plants and sculptures, and disappeared in and out of trees.

"I have to stop this," I said.

"There's nothing you can do." Dad grabbed my arm to stop me. "I'll help him." He turned and moved into the fray.

"No, don't!"

He kept moving.

I ran toward Mr. Woodson's crumpled frame and began to search his pockets for the pad and pencil he used to communicate. I had my back to the fight, until an agonized cry came from the women observing. When I turned, Brian had crumpled to the ground, blood pouring from a wound in his stomach. Mama Woodson ran toward him, but one of the P.O.W. men held her back. Sandovar turned to engage my father.

"No!" Tears poured down my face as I continued my frantic search. I couldn't let this happen.

"Scrivener." Sandovar's deep booming voice carried across the room. "I always knew you'd challenge my authority one day. I should have had you killed along with your wife."

Dad yelled a wordless war cry and leaped into battle.

I finally found the pad and wrote a few hasty words: *Nobody who supports women dies from the fight with Sandovar.* I closed my eyes to concentrate on manifesting them clearly, picturing wounds healing and everyone smiling in celebration. Another cry forced my eyes open. Somehow my father had wrestled the knife away from Sandovar. I held my breath as the scene unfolded.

"This is for my wife and daughter," Dad plunged the knife into Supreme Prime Minister Sandovar's neck. Blood spurted as the most powerful man in New North fell to the ground. The silver light in his terrifying eyes darkened into the unseeing eyes of death.

I ran to my father. "Are you okay?"

"I'm fine. Brian needs help."

I raced to my friend, but one of the women with healing powers had reached him first. "Don't worry," the woman said. "I've staunched the wound and begun the healing process. It will take time but he'll be all right."

"What about the others?" I asked. I looked around the Atrium to see that healers had already moved in to help those who had been knocked uncon-scious or hurt. Johnson, pale but stronger, pulled himself to his feet and made his way over to Peter. Minister Rogerson still kneeled on the ground as if in prayer. Two P.O.W. men I didn't recognize managed to regain control of the gun, and the guard who had grabbed it stood with his hands up. Mr. Wood-son and Jenna, both groggy, sat upright and awake. Mama Woodson ran a soothing hand over her husband's forehead. He smiled, grabbed her hand, and kissed her palm. The guards all held their hands up in surrender.

"Alice, what are you doing?" Lauren's cry made me turn again. The smell of smoke filled the air, provoking a cough. Alice had carried some plants over toward Sandovar's body and started a small fire near him. She coaxed it to grow.

I ran over to Alice. "What are you doing? Put it out."

"I thought we should get rid of the evidence. You don't want your father to be accused of murder, do you?"

"Put it out." Minister Rogerson's hoarse voice, thickened by emotion, star-tled me. He walked toward us with sad eyes that glittered in the flame. "The Scrivener won't be imprisoned for murder. I'll testify that his actions were in self-defense."

A guard ran to the controls for the sprinkler system that kept the plants healthy. Water poured down on everyone. The flames sizzled out.

"What use is this power of mine if I can never have any fun?" Alice said.

"Thank you, Minister Rogerson," I said.

"Andra, I'm not sure what happened today," Rogerson said. "I don't un-derstand why it happened, but I believe the Lord has his reasons. My son has always spoken highly of you and I see why. You would be welcome as part of my family."

All eyes watched me. I glanced over at Peter who stared at his father with confusion and then blushed when he met my eyes.

"Minister Rogerson," I said. "Your son is a wonderful person, whom I'm proud to know. However, this all happened," I waved my hand to indicate the soaking people and the destruction around us, "because we believe women and men are equals and shouldn't be required to do anything they're not ready to do. I don't know whom I'll marry or if I'll marry. I know that I'd like to be able to make that decision myself."

Rogerson nodded and turned to his children. "Cindy, what are your thoughts on this?"

"Father, I'm too young to get married. I want to have parties and have fun, but I don't want a husband . . . yet."

Rogerson sighed. "Peter, let me guess. You don't want to marry either."

Peter glanced over at me and then back at his father. "Father, I don't want to marry someone who isn't in love with me. I think Andra BetScrivener is an amazing woman, but I'm willing to wait and see what she decides."

A weak voice called from behind and distracted me from having to respond, unsure what I would even say.

"Andra," Brian had pulled himself up and leaned against the woman who helped him. "Andra, we did it," he said. He put his hand out for our secret handshake.

I returned the handshake and then gave him a hug.

Professor Albert, who had been quiet the whole time, moved to stand near Lauren and the others. "A job well done, everyone," he said. "But we're all forgetting one big question. New North no longer has a ruler. What happens next?"

I looked around at the people dripping as a pool of water tinted by blood spread across the floor. I smiled, suddenly filled with a new feeling . . . possibility and hope.

EPILOGUE

Several months had passed on the day four friends converged on Briandra's Haven to hold a celebratory picnic before our lives became even more hectic. The warm sun glittered off the flowing river, birds sang, and the scents of early summer filled the air. I took a deep breath and smiled.

"Do you remember the last time we came here?" I asked. "It was the beginning of P.O.W. in the middle of a snowstorm."

"I thought we were crazy that day." Lauren sat by the river, throwing leaves and sticks in and watching them disappear downstream. "We were gathering women together who had these unknown abilities in the hopes of changing the world. I didn't want to tell you that I thought it was impossible."

"You didn't know Andra as well as I do," Brian said between bites of a sandwich from a basket we'd brought with us.

"Brian, leave some for the rest of us," I said.

"There's plenty here. Stop interrupting. As I was saying, when Andra BetScrivener sets her mind to do something, she gets it done."

I turned away to hide my pleased smile.

"Did you write our election as representatives into reality?" Peter asked.

I turned to Peter. "You got elected because of who you are. Alvarie got elected because of her incredible mind. I don't know why I got elected. I haven't written anything big into reality since that day at the Ministry."

"So you had nothing to do with ministers resigning or with Emily's release to house arrest?" Peter said. "You had nothing to do with the meeting of people from all over New North, which led to a new elected government? You had nothing to do with the opening of the Wall and the beginning of diplomacy with Outside?

"Nothing except the role we all played. I won't write anything into reality again unless I know that my words won't cause people harm."

"You've stopped writing altogether?" Lauren asked.

"Not altogether. I helped my father, Professor Albert and the others create the revised constitution of New North including protections and guidelines for women who use their abilities to help, not to hurt. I just didn't try to manifest the words. I want to see what we can do as a team, women and men working together to create the world of our dreams."

"That sounds like a great idea," Brian said. "I think we should celebrate with muffins, don't you?" He pulled a plate of chocolate decadence out of the basket.

"Sounds good to me," I said. We laughed and grabbed the food.

THE POWER OF THANKS; THE POWER OF WORDS

Although the image of a writer sitting alone in a room and pouring her heart onto the page is a prevalent one in our society, we all know that nowadays the world works differently. Andra BetScrivener needs the support of a group of friends and collaborators to get her words out in the world. In the same way I—the writer behind her words—need the help of so many people to share these words with my readers.

It all started with the seed of an idea as I took a course with the Long Ridge Writer's Group, under the fine tutelage of Kris Franklin. He guided me into the beginnings of this manuscript, and helped me discover the true audience for this work. However, before the story began to come to life, I met my characters, which leads me to a very special thank you to the original Andra . . . Andra Watkins. We met through the powerful world of blogging and I became intrigued by her name, which means many things depending on the language. Andra told me that in Swedish it means "Other", but she also heard that it is the Celtic word for "seeing the way for others." For the Greeks it means strong or brave. All of these seemed to apply to this character who was coming to life, so I asked permission to use her name, and a friendship was born. The original Andra has also become, in some ways, a mentor into the world of publishing and for that I will be forever grateful.

The support that I have received from the blogging community has been immense. While I can't name everyone here, as the list would simply be too long, I will ever be grateful for the kind words and encouragement from so many I've met in this virtual world. They got me through the times of doubt, and helped me believe in the possibility of pursuing my dreams. I especially have to thank my dear friends Sue Kraus and Sharon Sears, the people who started me blogging (even though they don't blog themselves). They led me to a world of words that has given me the courage to share my own.

I also need to thank my early readers: Anna Jany Nesbitt whose editorial feedback was priceless; Dorienne Hoven whose young eyes gave me hope; and Laurence King whose insight and close reading helped me strengthen every moment of the manuscript. I also want to thank the young editor who gave me a critique at a Society of Children's Book Writers and Illustrators conference. Her somewhat perplexing comments led to an overhaul and strengthening of the manuscript that I might not have reached without it.

Endless thanks go to my talented cover artist and friend Jackie Haltom, who has inspired me on so many levels. She helped me find my visual voice— a means of expressing myself through art and images not just words. I believe her influence helped inspire the secret language of women, and I am so hon- ored she agreed to create with me. I look forward to many future projects together.

Thank you to Word Hermit Press for their enthusiastic support and guid- ance through every step of the process.

Finally, of course, I need to thank my family. Barbara and Bennett Kramer gave me life and the power of words. My only regret is that my father is no longer around to see me achieve this dream, but I think he would be proud. My sister, Deb and my brother Steve have given me pep talks when I needed it most. And finally much love to my husband Nathan and my daughter Sarah. They are my home. They are my inspiration. They give me the courage to find my words. I can only hope my words will also serve as inspiration for Sarah to create the world of her dreams.

AUTHOR BIOGRAPHY

Lisa A. Kramer has spent her life learning, creating, and exploring the world through theatre, writing, travelling and collaborating as an educator. She has lived in nine states and two countries (including Japan). She holds a PhD in Theatre for Youth, an MFA in Theatre Directing, and a BA in English Language & Literature and Theatre. She has published non-fiction articles in journals specializing on Theatre for Young Audiences, as well articles aimed at young people for *Listen Magazine*. In addition to young adult novels, she has ventured into the world of short stories, and has stories for adults in several of the *Theme-Thology* series published by HDWPBooks.com and available on Kindle, Nook, and Kobo. When not writing, Lisa shares her love of the arts and the power of story as co-founder of heArtful Theatre Company and as adjunct faculty at various colleges and universities. She also spends time enjoying New England with her husband, daughter, and two dogs from her home base in central Massachusetts. To learn more visit her at Lisa A. Kramer: Woman Wielding Words (www.lisaakramer.com) or email her at lisaakramer@lisaakramer.com.

CPSIA information can be obtained at www.ICGtesting.com
Printed in the USA
BVOW02s1809230615

405801BV00004B/193/P

9 780990 859390